*Entangled in a
quest for justice...*

*Can the truth
be discerned?*

Web of Intrigue

Portraits

Web of Intrigue

SUSAN TAGGART

BETHANY HOUSE PUBLISHERS
MINNEAPOLIS, MINNESOTA 55438

8755332

Web of Intrigue
Copyright © 1998
Susan Taggart

Cover illustration by William Graf
Cover design by The Lookout Design Group

Published by Bethany House Publishers
A Ministry of Bethany Fellowship International
11300 Hampshire Avenue South
Minneapolis, Minnesota 55438
www.bethanyhouse.com

Printed in the United States of America by
Bethany Press International, Minneapolis, Minnesota 55438

Library of Congress Cataloging-in-Publication Data

CIP data applied for

ISBN 0–7642–2069–1   CIP

For my Joe

My hero and God's

gift of love and support.

SUSAN TAGGART brings to BHP her prolific talent as both a novelist and a screenwriter. Susan's penchant for drama, mystery, and intrigue has been seen in countless animated and live-action television episodes, as well as in plays and novels. A mother of three and grandmother of six, Susan and her husband reside in Arizona.

Prologue

*A*n unexpected tornado warning had just been issued for the Dallas-Fort Worth area. Dark clouds churned and tumbled, rolling rapidly toward North Dallas and the Galleria Mall as a heavy sense of foreboding hung in the Texas air. Angry, relentless winds whipped at the young woman's long denim skirt. Catching her breath, she frantically scanned the deserted parking lot for her tan Bronco.

The intensity of the storm pushed against the small woman, holding her back from safety. Rain began pelting her tanned skin, and long wisps of blond hair, blown loose from her usually immaculate French braid, struck her blue eyes with great force. She winced from the sting, tears welling up from the biting wind.

She had waited at the appointed time and place, praying that her message reached the only person she was certain could help her stop the mayhem surrounding her. The appointment had not been kept. She could wait no longer.

As she hurried through the parking lot, she nervously fumbled in her purse, the tips of her fingers urgently searching for the keys. She should return to the mall and wait out the storm. But Michael was waiting for her. He would be terrified. She had to get to him.

Adrenaline caused her heart to race as fear flooded her soul and her palms grew sweaty. The feeling had become familiar in the past few weeks. Was she being followed? Watched? Stalked. . . ?

It wasn't just the storm. She had been through countless sudden Texas storms. Something far more sinister, far more deadly was threatening her. Instinctively, she glanced over her shoulder. She saw no one. She was alone.

The wind grew stronger, swirling the dirt and debris as the dark clouds closed in like a suffocating blanket. Just a few more feet to the safety of her car. . . .

⁂ ⁂ ⁂ ⁂

Sirens wailed in the damp Dallas night. A motorist slowed while passing a shocked crowd standing on the edge of Castlewood Road. He strained to look into the nearby ditch. A police officer, wearing a yellow slicker, used his flashlight to notify the intrigued motorist to move on.

An ambulance and two more Dallas police cars raced up to the site and pulled to a stop. The officers jumped out. "Over this way," called an excited bystander, pointing into the depths of the muddy ditch.

Occasional lightning flashed and thunder rolled, rain still lightly falling. Broken tree limbs and twisted street signs gave evidence of the heavy storm that had passed through only hours before.

From street level, the wheels of the shattered late model Bronco were all that could be seen as the vehicle rested upside down in the mud. Several splintered warning barriers were lying in pieces on the road.

Rotating red lights and strobing camera flashes cast a surreal glow on a group of police officers holding back the curious onlookers as paramedics emerged from the ditch carrying a filled body bag.

One

*A*s Morgan pulled her sky blue Cadillac Catera into the parking garage of the tall, glass office building, she could hardly recall the twenty-minute drive from Golden Valley to downtown Minneapolis. In fact, everything she had done that morning, from getting out of bed to adding the sterling silver barrette to her brown curls, seemed lost in a murky fog.

Tommy, the garage attendant, cheerfully said, "Morning, Ms. Carruthers," just as he did every morning. "Have a great day."

A great day? Not for her. Morgan absentmindedly managed a smile as she grabbed her leather briefcase and laptop computer from the front seat of her car.

Hurrying to catch the elevator, she glanced at her watch. She was shocked to see that it was 10:47. Without fail, Morgan was at her desk checking interoffice email by eight o'clock every morning. Clearly, today wasn't like every other morning.

The elevator doors silently slid open on the eleventh floor. Striking gold lettering on costly, light brown linen wallpaper spelled out: *The Heritage Design Firm.*

Stepping off the elevator, Morgan stopped short, nearly colliding with two secretaries hurrying back from their coffee break. "Sorry," Morgan said softly, realizing she was not paying attention. Without even so much as a "good morning," the two women disappeared around the corner.

They know. Just as Morgan had feared, the office grapevine must have shifted into high gear very early that day. *By now, they all know!* Morgan's first instinct was to get right back onto the elevator, but the doors had closed. There was no escape.

If only I can just get to my office! Morgan thought. Hurrying down the long hallway, it looked as if she just might make it. But then, en route to safety, her greatest fear was realized.

"Morgan." The deep, resonant voice was unmistakably Kevin's. Though she attempted to convince herself otherwise, Morgan had an unexplainable need to see his face. She turned to face the striking figure of Kevin Whitney.

Words failed her, and her mouth felt cotton-dry. She was sure he could see right to her core—exposing her failing effort to hold herself together. Unable to think of any intelligent words, Morgan breathed a sign of relief when Kevin finally broke the torturous silence.

"Morgan, I've been worried. I didn't know if you were . . . all right." She knew his concern was sincere. Last night's pain lingered in the shadows of his chiseled face. "Are you? Are you okay?"

Morgan, aware of their precarious position in the hallway, felt all eyes turning their way. In a soft voice, she said, "Please, Kevin." Swallowing hard in a poor attempt to feign composure, Morgan continued, "There's really no need to worry. I'm fine. Really. Just . . . fine." Her words were clipped and hurried.

Liar! She wasn't fine and he knew it. She was devastated. Her heart broken.

"I tried to call you at home, but . . ." Kevin stopped.

Morgan looked up at him, wanting to say how much she needed him, how much she wanted them to be together the way they used to be. Instead, keeping her voice low, she said, "Please don't. Please, Kevin, you made everything perfectly clear last night." Caught in his gaze, the moment was unbearable. "Kevin, I'm late. They're waiting for me to go over the . . . the Landsberg plans."

Morgan turned and rushed into her office. Quickly she closed the door and leaned back against it, feeling as if her knees would give out. Her laptop and briefcase dropped to the light beige carpeted floor.

Tears she had held back in the hallway came freely now that

she was hidden from sight. "Oh, Kevin . . . why?" She was angry and hurt and . . . alone.

She tried to work, but it proved impossible as thoughts of last night played over and over in her mind. *"I never wanted to hurt you, Morgan."* The compassionate tone of Kevin's voice hadn't stopped his every word from piercing her heart.

Three and a half years ago, Heritage Design transferred Morgan from Chicago to Minneapolis to head-up a new corporate design division. It was a dream promotion, both in status and salary. The entire Minneapolis office gave her a welcome party, and suddenly, there he was, all six feet of him, looking as if he'd just stepped from the pages of *GQ*.

Morgan remembered staring at him—she couldn't help herself. The sleeves of his white, starched shirt were rolled up to reveal strong, tanned arms. The top button was undone and the Gucci tie loosened. Kevin was confident, gorgeous, and single—a combination difficult to dismiss.

When their eyes met, Morgan's breath caught in her throat. He was definitely going to be trouble. Not even a year later, Kevin and Morgan were deeply in love. The success of an office romance was slim at best, but Morgan knew they would be the exception.

The firm had its share of gossip, and they made sure Morgan heard all the stories about this incorrigible ladies' man. But Morgan loved a challenge, and the rumors made Kevin even more appealing. Soon even the skeptics had to admit that the brown-eyed gal from Piney Bend, Texas, had achieved the impossible: She had tamed Kevin Whitney.

"Marry me, Morgan." But no matter how many times he asked her, Morgan always found a reason to put it off . . . for a while longer. It wasn't that she didn't love him, because she did, very much. They were perfect together.

"Then at least move in with me, honey," he urged, with that drop-dead smile of his. Many times his reasons seemed so sound and she thought she was just being a prude. There was no reason to carry the expense of two homes when they were spending all of their free time together. But the act of physically moving in with Kevin and giving up her own townhouse was something Morgan just couldn't do.

Was it because good daughters of East Texas Baptist preachers didn't have live-in relationships? Or was there something even deeper keeping her from making any kind of real commitment to Kevin?

"Don't you think it's about time for a wedding?" Beth, Morgan's older sister and closest confidant, asked this familiar question almost every time they spoke.

"We're working on it," was her standard answer. But the truth was she rarely wanted to talk about it. How long had she expected Kevin to wait around?

Beth lived in Dallas, and the sisters hated that they couldn't get together over long lunches or enjoy shopping sprees at the mall. Instead, they spent hours on the phone. At Morgan's urging, Beth finally learned to use her teenage daughter's computer. Email zipped back and forth between them, but the phone bills told the real story: They loved to talk.

Beth liked Kevin, often telling Morgan, *"Don't you dare let this one get away, Morgie."*

Until last night, Morgan had made herself believe that someday she and Kevin would get married. Then her entire family, especially her mother, would breathe a collective sigh of relief.

In the past six months or so, Morgan had taken on several prestigious design projects that had absorbed her energy completely. She adored her work. Lost in the excitement and creativity of her assignments, Morgan had not taken notice of the strain and distance steadily developing in their relationship. She and Kevin were spending less and less time together, he traveling and she working late. Weekends were spent in the office. Phone calls and email became infrequent.

She had no reason to question the extended trips Kevin was making to Cincinnati. The firm had put him in charge of an important project there. Finally, when Morgan's wake-up call came, it was too late. Kevin had an important project in Cincinnati all right—and its name was Cynthia.

Apparently, for Kevin there wasn't a lot to say. *"Morgan, I'm sorry . . . but it just happened."*

No, it didn't just happen! Morgan thought to herself as she lowered her body onto the large curved arm of her couch, trying to take it all in. Her pain gave way to anger. *"Things like this don't 'just happen,' Kevin. You let it happen!"*

Morgan wanted so much to hate him. But she couldn't. She had lost track of just when they started drifting apart. Morgan realized she had told him, in a thousand ways, that he was not the first priority in her heart. Was it his fault? Or her fault? Regardless, placing fault wouldn't change the fact that Kevin was in love with another woman.

How many other things in her life was she taking for granted?

Though Kevin had tried to soften the blow, it was impossible to do. She could see how painful it was for him. Her hands gripped the edge of the couch as his words pronounced a truth she had long known. *"Morgan, I want a wife who's there for me . . . and I want children."*

There, he'd finally said it.

Morgan would never be able to give Kevin, or any other man, children. Eight years ago, at age twenty-six, her life had been both saved and irrevocably changed by an emergency hysterectomy.

How could she have agreed to marry him? She knew Kevin would one day realize he wanted and needed a family. Morgan could never have been enough. And she knew that for Kevin, adoption wasn't a consideration.

The tragedy of her situation haunted Morgan. *Why is God punishing me?* she wondered. Every time Beth talked about her own two children, Morgan felt incomplete. She'd never know the joy of holding her own child.

She recalled her mother trying to console her. *"All things work together for good to those who love God."* Sure! Where was the good in this? It had left a hole in her heart that Morgan was desperately trying to fill. If only she worked hard enough, made enough money . . . But success, recognition, and possessions hadn't helped.

Two

*T*rying to work proved useless for Morgan. Though surrounded by the evidence of her success, she felt alone and lost, faced with a harsh reality. Truth had left her no place to run.

Last night after Kevin left, Morgan was in no mood to talk to anyone, not even Beth. But suddenly she wanted nothing more than to hear her sister's reassuring voice. With her, Morgan didn't have to pretend. Pushing the automatic dial button next to Beth's name, she listened to the familiar, rhythmic tones.

Morgan paced anxiously as Beth's phone rang and rang. "Please be there, Beth. Please!"

"Hello." Her sister's voice sounded strained and tired.

"Beth!" Relieved, Morgan grabbed the receiver and sunk into her chair. "Thank goodness you're there. I just had to talk to you." Without waiting for her sister to say another word, she began to pour out her broken heart. "Kevin and I . . . Beth, the relationship's over."

"Morgan, not now, please. This isn't a good time. Maybe later. I've got to take a shower and get dressed."

The fact that it was after two in the afternoon and Beth still wasn't dressed would have alarmed Morgan under normal circumstances. "Beth . . . please. Just a few minutes . . . I have to talk to you, sis. Don't you understand? Kevin's left me."

Beth sighed, sounding exasperated. "Left? What do you mean?"

"He's in love with someone else. What am I going to do, Beth? It . . . it just doesn't seem possible. But it's really over."

Morgan desperately needed her sister's support, but she received nothing but silence. Confused by the awkward pause, she rushed on, needing her best friend to know how deeply she was hurt. "Remember all those trips to Cincinnati? Well, apparently it wasn't for work. There's another woman. Some corporate attorney he met there. I wanted to die when I saw him this morning. How can things change so suddenly, Beth? I should have seen it coming. Why didn't I know?"

Beth, who for all of Morgan's thirty-four years could be counted on to jump in and help Morgan through everything—from losing a tooth to burying their father—said nothing.

"Beth? Say something! Don't you care?" Morgan began to feel her anger at Kevin spilling over to Beth. "Kevin's in love with someone else. He's going to marry her!"

Beth finally responded. "Why are you so surprised, Morgan?"

"What?" Beth's words felt like a slap in the face to Morgan. "You're acting as though you think this was my fault!"

"Wasn't he a bit of an inconvenience? Your career has always come first." There was a cutting passion in Beth's voice that had nothing to do with Morgan and Kevin. "How often were you there for Kevin—really there?" Her question had an icy edge that cut across the miles.

Morgan was suddenly defending herself, without knowing why. "I was with him as much as I could be. . . . He wasn't always there for me, either, you know." Morgan stopped abruptly. "Wait a minute. What's going on here? Why am I the bad guy?" Morgan squirmed in her high-backed leather chair as she nervously ran well-manicured fingers through the brown curls that tumbled along her shoulders. "Beth? I need you. Why are you acting this way?"

Beth's voice had an unfamiliar coldness, "I'm sorry it happened, Morgan. But . . . you'll get over it."

Stunned, Morgan felt betrayed and angry. "I'll get over it?" She repeated the incredulous words. "My entire life just fell apart and . . . I'll get over it? Thanks a lot!"

"Believe it or not, Morgan, but there are more important things than your love life. You're not the center of *everything*."

Morgan's first instinct was to hang up, but her concern for

Beth's bizarre behavior kept her on the line. Where was the caring and understanding Beth? Over the past few weeks, Morgan had noticed a subtle and disturbing personality change. She was never sure what kind of mood her sister would be in when they talked. Morgan questioned her about it, but Beth offered vague excuses for her behavior—stress, a hormone imbalance, not enough sleep.

Morgan was worried and didn't want to push the situation. "You're right, hon. I can be pretty self-centered. And it's not fair of me to expect you to always be there for me. I'll get over this thing with Kevin."

"I wasn't trying to hurt you, Morgie. I've got so much on my mind. It's just that—" Beth paused, hesitant to continue. When she spoke again, her voice was barely audible. "Scary, evil things are happening, and I've got to do something about it."

"What are you talking about?" Morgan was frightened by her sister's words. "Beth, honey . . . are you all right? Is there anything I can do?"

"No. I wish there were." Her words became disjointed and unfocused. "I'm not sleeping. Most nights only two or three hours. I'm tired, Morgie—so very tired!"

"What about the sleeping pills? Are you still taking them?"

"Pills don't help. It's the nightmares. . . ." Panic wrapped around every word. "They never stop. But they're real."

Now Morgan felt like the big sister. It was Beth who needed her. "Honey, where's Troy? I think I should call him."

Beth turned on her with a vengeance. She adamantly screamed into the phone, "No! Don't do that, Morgan!"

"But does he know what's going on? Does he? He should be there, taking care of you."

"If you call him, I'll never forgive you." There was a long pause, and the next time Morgan heard Beth's voice it was more composed and familiar. "It will all be over soon. Honest."

But Morgan had heard a terror in Beth's voice she had not heard before. "I think I should call him, but I'll wait a day or two." It was the only way Morgan could calm Beth. However, Morgan wasn't sure she could keep her promise. "Honey, let Troy help you. Promise me you'll talk to him."

There was a long silence. Then Beth spoke. "Don't worry,

Morgan. I'm taking care of things. I just need a little time. It'll be over soon."

Morgan wanted to ask what would be over soon, but she knew this was not the time. "I'll call you in a day or two. We'll talk then. But if you're not sounding better, I'm going to talk to Troy. I have to, Beth."

"Things will be better then . . . I promise."

Realizing how fragile Beth was, Morgan wished she had not dumped her woes on her older sister. "Beth, I hope one of these days your little sister will grow up."

"You won't. But that's okay."

Morgan felt encouraged by the small smile she heard in Beth's words.

Beth continued in a more serious tone, "Morgie . . . do you ever miss the way things used to be? You know, when we were at home together and . . ." Morgan could hear Beth's voice catch as she fought back tears. "It was so safe. So perfectly innocent."

Morgan wanted to throw her arms around her sister and tell her everything would be all right. Whatever was causing her so much pain, Morgan wanted to fight it, defeat it—for Beth.

"Thanks, Beth," Morgan whispered, suddenly realizing that her sister had unwittingly given her the direction she yearned for—the answer to the tormenting question, *What do I do now?*

"I've made a decision, Beth. I'm coming to Texas! I need to spend some time with Mom in Piney Bend. Why don't you meet me there? Take some time away. It'll do us both so much good."

"I can't. Not now. Not until I've finished what I have to do here." But there was a longing in her voice that let Morgan know how very much Beth wanted to rush to meet her in Piney Bend. "I'll come later. I promise."

"Okay."

"I love you, Morgie."

"Love you, too."

The extraordinary conversation between the two best friends in the world ended, leaving Morgan strangely frightened. Was there something she could have said or done?

She stared at the phone, wanting to call Troy but remembering her promise. Morgan laid her head back into her tall, brown leather chair and closed her eyes. Once she returned home, she could spend time with Beth. Help her. Discover what was causing such anguish.

Yes, Beth, I do miss the way things used to be.

In the executive washroom, Morgan reapplied what little makeup she wore. Her mother's flawless complexion had been passed on to both of her daughters. Removing the barrette from her hair, Morgan ran her fingers through her curls, then replaced it neatly. She was pleased with her reflection in the full-length mirror—pleased, that on the outside, the devastation she was feeling was not evident. Her corporate training was paying off.

Morgan walked quickly toward Carl Mercer's office, avoiding eye contact with co-workers in the hallway. She approached Carl's private secretary, Harriet. She looked up from her computer keys. "Good afternoon, Morgan."

"Hi, Harriet. Could I please see Carl?" Her Texan accent had been softened by time spent in Chicago and now Minneapolis, but it was certainly still apparent and thicker when she was tired or upset.

"Of course, you can go right in."

Her relationship with the vice president of Heritage Design, one of the most distinguished corporate interior design firms in the country, was an extremely good one. Carl had been the one who requested Morgan's transfer to the Minneapolis office.

Morgan knocked softly, then entered. The attractive, graying executive of about sixty immediately rose from behind his large walnut desk. Carl's strained smile made it apparent to Morgan that the news of Kevin's new love had made its way to the top. "Morgan, come on in. Glad to see you."

Morgan wasn't in a chatty mood, and she got right to the point. "Carl, I've decided to take an indefinite leave of absence. I hope this won't be a problem."

He looked shocked. "But, Morgan, you can't. Not right now. What about the new West Plains Bank and Trust Building? I promised them the best—and that's you."

Morgan had given this prestigious account her all. Her devotion to that assignment was the thief who stole her time and energy away from her relationship with Kevin. It had been the final straw.

"It's wrapped up, Carl. The client has signed off on the drawings and specs. I'll see to it there are no loose ends. You can let Bill Castle take it from here."

Carl walked closer to her, compassion in his eyes. "It's not just the account, Morgan, I'm worried about you."

Carl was well acquainted with Morgan's tenacity, and she could see that he clearly understood her decision was not open for discussion. "I know, Carl. But trust me on this one. I'm . . . well, burned out. I have to get away." Morgan knew she could be honest with him. "This breakup with Kevin and the stress of the past few months here at Heritage . . . I just need to put some distance between myself and Minneapolis." She didn't want to disappoint him. "Carl, please don't ask me not to go."

"I won't. Take the time, Morgan."

Carl's understanding support meant so much to her. "Thanks. I wish I could've given you more notice, but . . . sometimes things happen too fast."

"Listen, Morgan, I think you should know the board's been making some big decisions regarding your future with Heritage Design. Whenever you get back, we're ready to talk about that vice presidency."

Under any other circumstances these words would have thrilled her. Morgan was good at what she did, one of the best. She had paid her dues and dreamed of this opportunity. "Carl, that's wonderful. Thank you." Timing was everything. It took only one shattering evening to completely change her priorities. "When I get back, let's have that talk."

"Stay in touch," he said warmly. "If there's anything I can do for you, let me know. We'll miss you around here. I'll miss you."

Morgan knew Carl was afraid she might not return. At the moment, she could say nothing to reassure him. He was a good friend. Morgan forgot office decorum and gave him a warm hug. "I'll call. And thank you for your friendship."

Morgan quickly left, closing the door behind her.

Three

*T*he phone still in her lap, Beth caught a glimpse of herself in the mirror on the small dresser across the room. What she saw unnerved her: a gaunt, weary woman tangled in the sheets of her unmade bed in a wrinkled cotton nightgown, her long, blond hair, usually so neat, tangled and falling loosely down her back, the room dark and depressing with curtains drawn against the sunlight. She was thankful Morgan hadn't seen her.

2:15 P.M.! The glowing red numbers on the clock radio next to the bed were another reminder that Beth's life was totally out of control. This wasn't like her at all. Before this all started, she adored early mornings. They gave her the marvelous gift of time—time to work with her beloved roses or to quietly read with a cup of wild cherry tea. Desperate tears emerged uncontrollably, and she made no attempt to wipe them away.

Beth was suddenly struck by the thought that the children would be coming home from school soon. She had to get up and pull herself together. But she couldn't. The fear and depression paralyzed her. They weighed her down, making it more and more impossible for Beth to face each new day. Her life had been stolen from her! Anger welled up in her throat. Her fists pounded the pillow and she screamed, "Go away! Leave me alone!" Her tears became sobs. As her anger gave way to terror, Beth pulled the pillow close and hugged it tightly, murmuring, "God, help me. I'm so . . . scared."

The Woodsen's beautiful, red-brick two-story house, with its rolling green lawn and picturesque gardens, was a showpiece on Jasmine Court. Beth adored her home but could have been very happy with something less pretentious. It was Troy who wanted the big house in one of North Dallas's most exclusive neighborhoods. But the gracefulness and beauty of the surroundings belied the terror that had found its way inside—totally unexpected and uninvited.

Very early that morning, as usual, Troy had quietly showered and dressed. All the while, Beth pretended to be asleep. But her mind searched for some way to tell him of the horror she had let into their lives. *Would he believe her or think she was going mad?*

As she lay there, the scent of his soap and favorite cologne brought vivid memories of the handsome young man she'd fallen in love with sixteen years ago. Troy had made no excuses for the kind of man he was, and his strength and tenacity excited her. For Troy Woodsen, being a success meant having financial security, as well as position in his profession and in the community.

She knew exactly what kind of driven man she had married. How could she complain now? He had held her in his strong arms and shared his dream with her. But over the years, Beth began to feel that he needed her less and less. She watched as the dream gobbled up more and more of his time—his precious time. Beth knew she could ask Troy for anything . . . but more of his time.

When they made love, he was tender and passionate. But many times Beth felt he wasn't really there. Troy's body and hers were one, but his thoughts drifted to places she could not follow. She could have competed with another woman but was powerless to compete with his dream, Woodsen Development.

Troy started his career by planning and building successful strip malls throughout the Dallas-Fort Worth area, and now he was expanding throughout Texas. His talent for buying up the right property within days of it becoming "hot" had landed her husband in the good graces of financiers and prominent businessmen throughout the state.

Before he left that morning, Troy lovingly stroked Beth's hair. He bent down, softly kissing her cheek. The warm breath of his whispered words danced over her ear, "Bye, sweetheart. I love you."

If Beth had opened her eyes and looked at the man she loved so deeply, she would have begged him not to leave. So instead, she gripped the pillow until her knuckles ached. *Don't go! Don't leave me here alone . . . with him!*

Beth listened to Troy's footsteps descend the carpeted stairs and the beep of the alarm as he reset it. Moments later, she heard the dreaded sound of the garage door opening, then closing. His white Lexus was spiriting him away from her and into his own world.

Beth was barely able to get herself together long enough to see that the children got off to school. Nine-year-old Michael was visibly worried about his mother. It broke Beth's heart to see the concern in his young eyes.

Jenny, fourteen and busy with her own life, was growing distant from Beth. *"I miss you, Jen,"* Beth would sometimes whisper, as she watched her little girl changing before her eyes. She had always been worried about her children growing up and going out into the world, but now, with what she had discovered, she was terrified.

After talking with Morgan, Beth found herself thinking of her life in Piney Bend. The lost simplicity and innocence overwhelmed her. Looking for something to give her solace, Beth opened a drawer in the bedside table. Putting her hand inside the small, dark space, she touched the well-worn, white pocket-size New Testament she'd had since she was a child. A baptism gift from her parents, its embossed gold letters, almost worn away, still read: *Beth Ann Carruthers.*

Before she could pull it out, she felt something crawl across her hand. Beth screamed, jerking her hand back. The drawer fell to the floor, flinging its contents onto the plush, white carpet. Horrified, she saw a large spider scurrying for the safety of the darkness between the nearby dresser and the wall.

"No!" In terror, Beth grabbed a newspaper lying near the bed and brought it down again and again on the eight-legged intruder. Her rage escaped in deafening bursts. "Stop it! Stop it! I can't stand it anymore!"

Drained, Beth collapsed to the floor and leaned back against the bed. The spider was clearly dead. Her small Bible lay on the floor next to her, where it had fallen in the melee. She picked it up, and, using the worn golden ribbon bookmark, opened it to 1 Peter, chapter five. In a soft, trembling voice Beth again read the words she had read so many times in the past weeks. " 'Be vigilant; because your adversary the devil walks about like a roaring lion, seeking whom he may devour.' "

In prayerful despair, she said, "You know my tormentor, Father. My God, I can't do this alone. You promised that with you we could do anything. Help me to end this. Please."

Her hands trembled as she took a three-and-a-half inch computer disk from its hiding place in the back of the Bible. She slowly pulled herself to her feet, then ran into the hallway.

Beth knew she had to hurry. Soon Jenny and Michael would be home. She couldn't let them find her still in her nightgown. But something else demanded her attention. This torment had to end.

The door to Jenny's bedroom was closed. A cartoon-lettered sign shouted *Stop! Do Not Enter.* A not-too-subtle reminder to her little brother that he wasn't welcome inside.

Beth opened the door and rushed into the lovely, comfortable room. Looking past the ruffled bed piled high with stuffed animals and teenage memorabilia, her eyes focused on Jenny's computer. It sat on a small, white wicker hutch in the corner.

Cute pink, green, and purple cartoon hippopotamuses, lounging on bubbles, floated aimlessly around the screen—Jenny's favorite screensaver. So innocent. So childlike.

Beth stared at the screen for a long moment, and then she inserted the disk into the A: drive. As her hand touched the mouse, the hippopotamuses magically vanished, and the computer program icons surfaced on the screen. She hesitated only a moment, then her hand unsteadily pointed the mouse to the Internet icon. Double-clicking, she opened the program.

In an instant, the computer dialed the Internet server. Beth's bleary eyes were riveted on the bright blue screen. She heard the

computer dialing the number. After the high-pitched connecting tone, a disembodied male voice said, "Welcome." She had
to do nothing more. Her tormentor would come to her.

Her wait was brief. When the bell sounded, her tense body
jerked. She watched as an Immediate Message window popped
open. He had arrived.

ARA: WB ... i've missed you beth. you know how
i enjoy our little chats :) we've become such
good friends ... wouldn't you say...
GDWORD: The spider!!! You put it there! You did
it, didn't you?
ARA: just a little reminder my dear ... he was
harmless—this time. you must understand beth ...
you can't turn away from me that easily...
GDWORD: How did you get into my house? My room?
ARA: LOL ... i can go wherever i choose...
GDWORD: Stop it! Stop following me!! I feel you
everywhere. I can't sleep. I feel sick all the
time. What do you want??????
ARA: it is you who must stop beth.... your
attempts to expose me will only make things more
deadly for you :-(
GDWORD: But they didn't know ... how could they
have known??? They thought it was a game. We all
thought it was a game!!
ARA: i don't play games ... poor lonely beth
... it's too bad you did not find comfort here
... i'm really very accommodating...
GDWORD: I can't let you go on poisoning their
minds. It's over! I'm not afraid of you anymore.
I know what you're doing! They're innocents.
ARA: the easiest prey. <Grin>
GDWORD: I know what you are. Who you are! But
it's over. I've found out how to stop you.
ARA: I can't allow you to interfere.
GDWORD: I'm not signing on again.
ARA: IMO that is very unwise ... and poor old
troy ... what will he do with you? look how i

```
have already changed you ... and i haven't even
started yet...
GDWORD:  I'll tell him the truth.
ARA:  he'll think you've lost your mind :))
remember, I'm watching you ... and jennifer ...
and precious little michael.
GDWORD:  Don't you dare touch my family. It's
over!!!! I'll find a way to stop you! God will
stop you!
```

Beth's fingers flew across the keyboard, typing words she knew would pierce the heart of her enemy.

```
GDWORD:  The Lord is my Shepherd I shall not
want.
ARA:  you cannot stop me ... i will do whatever
i please to you and to your cherished family ...
just watch me ... TTYL
GDWORD:  He makes me to lie down in green
pastures, He leads me beside the still waters.
He restores my soul. He leads me in the paths of
righteousness
```

Suddenly, the Instant Message window said *Ara is no longer online.*

Beth's hands ached from the force of her typing, and her nightgown was wet with perspiration. She had to hurry. Quickly, she went to the A: drive and opened a file named Heretics on the floppy disk.

She began typing: *March 4. It is almost over. I know what I have to do. There is no time to waste. I am going to the one person who can help me stop this madness. Troy, I love you. I'm so sorry. So very sorry, but I had no choice.*

Four

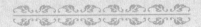

Groups of teens were scattered throughout the Cybersurf Café, loudly laughing and talking. The menu at this North Dallas version of the sixties' diner offered coffee, soft drinks, food, and tantalizing computers with uncensored Internet connections.

When it opened several months ago, news of its presence in the community spread, and the high school crowd made it the "in" place to "get connected." Here, with their hamburgers and fries, they could surf the Web by renting time on the computers. They eagerly ventured from chat room to chat room, looking for excitement and titillation, searching out faceless cyberfriends, and sampling the tempting and often forbidden subject matter on the hottest Websites.

Cybersurf's sterile millenium decor was resplendent with shiny stainless steel and multicolored, twisting neon. Besides the usual tables, this special café had high, circular cyberbooths, each equipped with a computer. Large viewing screens, at every corner, showed the latest music videos. As with every generation, this one had found its hangout as they searched out new ways to push the envelope—to walk on the edge.

An animated party of teenage girls giggled as they crowded together in a cyberbooth. The center of attention was Pam Ruston, a perky, cute fifteen-year-old, and a very busy computer screen. Her long auburn hair fell around her shoulders, a striking contrast to her creamy complexion, speckled here and there with freckles.

"Sure he's going to tell you he's cute. Who's going to know?" giggled one of the girls.

"What if I tell him I'm eighteen and . . . available? Let's see if he runs scared or takes the bait," said Pam with a sly grin.

The girls were enthralled. They watched as Pam deftly typed her enticing messages with long, well-manicured, hot pink porcelain nails. On her right index fingernail was a small, perfectly painted black spider. She'd been painting it there for months now.

Les, the somewhat overweight, twenty-something manager of the Cybersurf, leaned into the booth. "How's the surfing today?" he asked the girls.

"Les, you were right about the Rage Room! This chat's really out there."

"Yeah, and she's carrying on with this guy who calls himself Menace," added one of the girls.

"Sounds tough," Les replied.

"Yeah . . . like I'm scared. He's probably a big sweetie," Pam replied, continuing to type in responses to her new computer admirer.

"Look! Menace is from Dallas. And he wants to meet you, Pam! Wow. What're you gonna do?" asked another girl.

"Yeah! Are you gonna run . . . or take the bait?" They all laughed.

Les raised an eyebrow and added, "Watch it out there, girls. There are some real screwballs running around the Web."

"I've never actually dated one of them, but there's always a first time." Pam looked fascinated. "It's tempting. Maybe this is the time."

The girls vicariously enjoyed Pam's flirting game, each assuming anonymity was their protection.

Les warned, "It's no kiddie playground out there, Pam."

"You jealous, Les?" she replied, returning her attention to the computer screen. Les laughed as he moved on to greet other surfers.

In a far corner cyberbooth, a soul occupant sipped a soft drink. Fingers expertly entered a memorized Web address, then nervously tapped on the stainless steel tabletop. The message—

Please wait while that site is contacted—appeared on the bottom of the Internet screen. After a moment, the screen began to slowly reveal an eerie graphic, pixel by pixel.

When the graphic was completely downloaded, it was a dark and foreboding comic book-type illustration of an ominous alleyway. The cyberspace visitor, obviously familiar with this site, immediately clicked on the animated icon of a hand seductively tempting the guest into the alley. The next graphic took the visitor deeper into the corridor. Then, as in an animated cartoon, the screen zoomed in and revealed red, fiery smoke escaping from a menacing, jiggling sewer cover.

"Welcome to the Catacomb," purred a slithery, computerized female voice. "Enter your password."

The visitor knew exactly how to access the depths of this site. He quickly typed in *Cyclosa* and hit the Enter key. The grim cartoon continued as the sewer cover dissolved into a swirling red vortex that drew the visitor down into the animated underbelly of the Catacomb.

The following words crawled ominously across the screen:

> *Warning: This site and the chamber chat areas are not monitored or censored in any way. Here, I am the only authority. I am the only censor. So if you do not want to be violated by what you may see or experience on this site, leave now and do not return!!!*

A Private Chamber Chat window popped open. Words, typed by unseen hands, communicated with the visitor.

```
ARA:  WB cyclosa ... did it arrive?
CYCLOSA:  Yes. I got the package today.
ARA:  good.... everything was undisturbed?
CYCLOSA:  Yes.
ARA:  handle it carefully ... do you fully
understand your assignment?
CYCLOSA:  Yes. But, I'm worried. What if
something goes wrong?
ARA:  you will see to it that nothing goes wrong
. . . if you follow my instructions to the
letter everything will go as planned . . . i'm
```

```
disappointed . . . i thought you trusted me :-(
CYCLOSA:  I do, Ara. I do trust you.
ARA:  remember who takes care of you ... don't
forget, my spiderling, you must do this for the
common good.
CYCLOSA:  I know. I will do it. Soon.
ARA:  do not contact me until it is finished.
```

The visitor's connection with the Catacomb was abruptly severed, and contact with the entire Internet was lost. The cursor blinked on a blank screen, and the cyberbooth was now empty.

Five

The pay phone was in the back hallway of The Black-eyed Pea Restaurant in Addison. "Dedra Koehler, please." Beth waited while the operator transferred her.

"You've reached the office of Dedra Koehler. I'm not here now. Please leave a message after the tone and I'll get back to you when I can."

"Oh no." Beth sighed with disappointment. This wasn't what she had expected.

After the tone, Beth hesitated, then spoke nervously, "Ms. Koehler, you don't know me, but . . . I've just got to talk to you, immediately! There's no time to lose. It's very, very important. It's urgent!" Suddenly, feeling as though she was being watched, Beth reached for the button to hang up. Then, refusing to give up, she continued, her voice betraying the panic she was feeling in her very soul. "You can help. I know you can. I can't leave a number. But . . . tomorrow at two P.M., please meet me . . . on the first level of the Galleria Mall . . . the circular marble bench outside Saks Fifth Avenue. I'll recognize you. Oh, please come! I'll be waiting."

Morgan rushed toward the baggage area. The Dallas-Fort Worth Airport was crowded. But simply being back in her beloved Texas made the heaviness of the last few days lift. This would be a good trip. She could feel it. If only Beth could come to Piney Bend with her—that would make it perfect.

Usually, Morgan went right from DFW to her sister's house, but she had already decided that today would be different. After talking with Beth the day before yesterday, she knew a weepy, heartbroken sibling wasn't what Beth needed. *I'll call her instead*, Morgan reasoned to herself.

Morgan spotted a bank of pay phones in the American Airlines baggage area. She pulled her stacked luggage carrier, loaded with her laptop computer, briefcase, and carry-on bag, to a vacant phone. Remembering it was a toll call, she searched for her calling card, slid it through the groove, then dialed the familiar number.

Please be there. One ring and a familiar voice answered. "Hello!"

Morgan tried to hide her disappointment. "Hi, Jen. It's your aunt. I'm at DFW."

Her fourteen-year-old niece, Jenny, looked so much like her mother had at that age. But she was certainly not going to be petite like Beth. Troy's height, over six feet, almost guaranteed Jenny would be tall and a knockout.

"Hi, Aunt Morgie. Mom's not here. Just a sec . . ."

Morgan could hear the alarm system beeping in the background. Jenny had obviously just gotten in. A moment later, she said, "Sorry—I got it just before it went off! Hey, Mom said you might be coming down to visit Mamaw."

"You know Texans, we just can't stay away very long. I think it's something God put in this red dirt."

Jenny sounded rushed. "Don't know when Mom'll be back. I just got home from school and she was gone."

Morgan was relieved to hear that Beth was getting out of the house. "How's she feeling these days?"

"I don't know. But she's been more than a little weird lately. You stopping by or what?"

"I've rented a car, but I think I'll drive straight to Piney Bend. Your old aunt needs a little rest. Tell your mom I called and . . . well, just tell her where I am and that I'll call her in a day or two."

"Okay." Jenny was obviously in a hurry to end the conversation. "Bye, Aunt Morgie."

"Bye, honey."

Jenny hit the Off button on the portable phone and tossed it onto the green-and-white checked seat pad of a kitchen chair. Out of habit, before she headed upstairs to her room, she hung her house keys in the usual spot, a peg sticking out from a colorful, wooden plaque hanging just inside the laundry room. Shaped like a pot full of flowers, it had five wooden pegs at the centers of five blossoms. One for Jenny's keys, her mom's, Troy's, Michael's, and the extra "just in case" set.

On Jenny's chain with her keys were a favorite Precious Moments angel her grandmother had given to her and a gold *J*. Her keys and the extra set were the only ones on the plaque.

Starved, Jenny checked the refrigerator. Nothing filled the bill, so she pulled out a can of Dr Pepper. As she popped it open, she noticed a message written in yellow chalk on the small kitchen blackboard: *Jen—Please wait for me. Put on the alarm and don't let anyone in. Love you, Mom.*

"Get real, Mom." She took a drink of Dr Pepper as she erased the message with a paper towel. Using the same chalk, she wrote: *Aunt Morgie at DFW. Will call later.*

Jenny grabbed her books and ran up the stairs and down the hall to her room. It was her favorite place in the house. Beth had decorated it with ruffles and frills, but as Jenny got older, she was allowed to add her own touches.

She kicked off her shoes and ran to the computer. The floating hippos on the screen made her giggle. It took less than a minute to log onto the Internet and enter her favorite cyberspace chat room: the Talkie.

Her chat room nickname hid her real identity. It was Tinker, from her very favorite story, *Peter Pan*. Here in the chat rooms, Jenny could be anybody she wanted, even a fairytale character.

The idea of being able to talk with kids from anywhere, about anything, was a real turn on to her. She saw from the "Who's on Line" list that some of the regulars were already there. Jenny jumped right into the chat with total abandon.

TINKER: Hi, everybody.
MARKIE: Hey! Hi there, Tinker.
KIP: Hi, cutie. :-)) What's up?
TINKER: Not much. Just a lonely afternoon.
Wanted to chat.
SIZZLE: You don't have to be lonely. You've
always got us.
DESIREME: You came to the right place. Markie
was just asking me out. <snicker>
MARKIE: ROTFL ... sorry, babe, that was before
Tinker got here. I bet you're a real doll. What
do you look like?
DESIREME: Hey, I thought you and I were
cooking, sweet thing. ;-)
KIP: Back off, Markie. Tinker's my cybergirl.
Aren't you?
TINKER: LOL ... you're so funny. Hey, Sizzle,
have you ever really dated a guy you met in the
chat room?
MARKIE: She's just a big talker, if you ask me.
SIZZLE: Yeah, Tinker, I really did. Just one,
so far. But I'd do it again. What've I got to
lose? <grin>
TINKER: What was it like? Was it exciting?
KIP: Yeah, give us the juicy details. <pant,
pant>
SIZZLE: He was a looker. But my folks don't
know about it.
TINKER: Are you going to tell them?
SIZZLE: Probably not. The guy told me he was
sixteen. But he was really twenty!! I'm fifteen—
where else would I meet a guy like that?
MARKIE: Jail Bait! Hey, you could put the guy
away for life!
KIP: If I tell you I'm tall, dark, and handsome
and I'm seventeen, you're gonna believe me? What
a dork. Why am I gonna give you all the gory

```
details when I don't know what you look like?
Aren't we all playing games here? Maybe you're
250 pounds of ugly ... mmmm!
TINKER:  You're mean, Kip.
```

Jenny, lost in this new and exciting world, was startled when suddenly a computerized male voice said, "You've got mail." Overcome with curiosity, Jenny moved her mouse pointer to the small mailbox in the upper left hand corner and clicked. A New Mail window popped open. It listed one email from Jeeper.

She recognized Cade's screen name. Although Cade was two years older and lived a couple of houses down, they had been friends for years. The name *Jeeper* referred to Cade's pride and joy, his blue '96 Jeep Wrangler, a gift from his mom on his sixteenth birthday.

```
To: Tinker
From: Jeeper
Subject: What's Up?

   Greetings, Jen. I noticed you were online. Thought I'd
let you know I'm running over to your school to pick up
Rebecca. We'll stop by. Maybe we'll go for a ride, grab a
bite or something. See ya later. CADE
```

Glad to know that she'd probably get out of the house, hopefully before her mom got home, Jenny rejoined the Talkie chat.

```
TINKER:  I'm back.
```

Six

*B*efore leaving DFW, Morgan made one more call, knowing her mother would be waiting to hear from her. Gloria Carruthers' bubbly voice was a welcome sound. "I'm so excited to see you, honey. You come on down and stay as long as you want."

"Thanks, Mom. See you in about two and a half hours."

"Drive carefully. And don't bother to stop, unless you're starving. I'll have supper waitin' on the stove."

It felt good to be so far from the dirty slush of a late snowfall in Minneapolis. The small towns she passed through were so familiar, contrasting distinctly from the city, where things changed so fast—one day a building was there, the next it wasn't. But out here, some of these old places had stood their ground, changed only by the ravages of time, for as long as she could remember. Here, Morgan could sense a slowing of life's pace, which was welcome solace for an uneasy heart.

The odometer on her rental car showed only 573 miles. It was a brand-new, cool green Infinity. Morgan ran her right hand over the soft leather seat. Taking a deep breath, she thought, *There's nothing like the smell of a brand-new car*. She smiled. "The most expensive perfume in the world."

Her cell phone was lying on the other seat. Unable to stop thinking about Beth, she picked it up and began to punch in the number. But she stopped, cleared the readout, and tossed the phone onto the seat. *I'll call her tomorrow*, Morgan decided.

Truthfully, Morgan wasn't in the mood to talk with anyone,

not even Beth. Though the drive through the East Texas countryside was restful, she had to admit it was far from pretty this time of year. The trees were bare, and much of the grass had only spots of green. But it was home, and Morgan hadn't come here for the view.

It wasn't much trouble for her to locate a country music station—this was Texas, after all. At home in Minneapolis, Morgan listened to "easy listening" stations, but she wasn't surprised to find herself yearning for old Patsy Cline, Loretta Lynn, and Waylon Jennings tunes.

Her mind wandered to thoughts of Kevin. They had been so good together. Her love for him wasn't going to simply vanish because she'd left. Love was more stubborn than that.

She missed him. Missed hearing his voice. *Just reach for the phone.* Her hands twisted on the steering wheel. She longed to talk to him. Remembering his smile, she was tempted, but this time her head won out over her heart. Kevin had made his choice and it wasn't her. She needed to accept the truth.

Turning up the radio, she joined voices with Patsy Cline. The familiar words brought tears. It was definitely crying music . . . and there was no one around to see.

Seven

J enny was still surfing the Internet when a chime sounded and an Immediate Message window popped open. It surprised and intrigued her.

```
ARA:  hello jenny.... how nice to find you
online.
TINKER:  Hi. Who are you?
ARA:  we have mutual friends ... i thought it
was time you and i got to know each other...
TINKER:  But I still don't know who you are.
ARA:  you'll get to know me better ... very
soon. right now i just wanted you to know i'm
here ... i want to be your friend ... a secret
friend :)
TINKER:  What's your real name? Who are you?
ARA:  you'll find out soon, jenny ... TTYL
TINKER:  But who are you?
```

Her question met with the words: *Ara is no longer on line.* "Wow, that's creepy," she said out loud.

"What's creepy?"

The question startled her, and she whirled around, looking terrified. "Who—"

"Hey, you look like a deer caught in the headlights, kiddo," Cade laughed.

"That wasn't funny, Cade. Don't sneak up on me like that!"

"Sorry, Jen, but nobody's downstairs." Cade and Jenny's

best pal, Rebecca Hunt, had let themselves in and come upstairs looking for her. Rebecca, a pretty girl with long brown hair pulled back in a ponytail, was also fourteen. Her short-skirted, navy-and-white cheerleader outfit bore the raised navy letters *RHS*—Roosevelt High School.

"We just came on up. Cade thought you'd still be on the Web," replied Rebecca.

"Guess my mom's not home yet."

"No car in the drive," Rebecca answered. Her cheeks were still flushed from cheerleading practice.

"Got your email, Jeeper," Jenny told Cade.

"You're really hooked on that chatting stuff, aren't you?" he replied.

"No more than you. Personally, I think you're a closet computer nerd." Both girls laughed.

"Hey, what was it that was so creepy?" he inquired again.

"Oh, nothing, I guess. Just got into a private chat with someone called Ara." She made a quizzical face and shrugged. "It was just kinda creepy—he came out of nowhere. The guy said we had mutual friends. Probably some jerky friend of yours, Cade."

Jenny signed off the Internet and changed the subject. "Hey, Rebecca, how was practice?" she asked. "As if I'll ever find out again."

Rebecca sat down on the bed and grabbed a big white teddy. "Everybody misses you." She snuggled the bear. "No cheerleading for a month? That's such a bummer."

Jenny sighed. "Guess I'm lucky they didn't drop me from the squad."

"Heavy duty punishment for a few low grades," Cade added. His dark, almost black hair was much longer than would have been allowed in the Woodsen household. At sixteen, he was almost six feet tall and very slender. "My mom never looks at my grades."

"Good thing, huh?" Jenny giggled.

"I'm squeezin' by and . . . no problem, babe."

"Yeah, but things were different when your dad was still around," she added without thinking as she plopped down on the bed next to her best friend.

Jenny's remark clearly disturbed Cade. "Yeah . . ." He paused a moment, running his fingers nervously though strands of long, straight hair that invariably fell right back over his right eye.

"Jenny!" Rebecca punched Jenny in the arm, shooting her a how-could-you-be-so-stupid look.

"Sorry, Cade. You know me. I have this mouth . . . and . . . well, I'm sorry."

His retort was cool and unsuccessfully covered his true feelings. "Hey, so he hit the road. Big deal. I didn't need the grief." Cade's demeanor quickly changed, and a mischievous grin came across his face as he jiggled his car keys in his blue jean pocket. "Let's split!"

"Guess who's at the Cybersurf? We drove past and I saw *her* going in." Rebecca's scorn was clear.

"Has got to be your favorite person, little Miss Pam Ruston." Jenny was all too familiar with the feud that flared last quarter when Pam dated a guy Rebecca had a huge crush on. Even though Rebecca really didn't care for the guy anymore, she had refused to let it go.

"She'll just be green when she sees these two lowly freshmen riding around with a junior!"

Jenny hopped off the bed, pulling Rebecca to her feet. Running past Cade, who was standing in the doorway, she grabbed his arm. "Let's get out of here before my mom gets home, or she'll probably lock me in my room until I'm thirty-five!"

Three houses down, Lynn Stiles, a very attractive redhead in her early forties, leaned seductively on the fender of a new red Ford truck. Her attire, as usual, would have been more appropriate on Jenny.

Lynn stared at the handsome, well-built man in his late twenties as he unloaded several heavy sacks of cement from the bed of the truck. "Thank you so much. Just carry 'em on back through that gate."

"Yes, ma'am," he said, flashing a toothy smile at her. Lynn had more than a passing interest in the young man. His sandy hair was curly and cut very short. Beads of sweat ran from his temples, dropping onto a tight yellow T-shirt. The sleeves were rolled up to reveal powerful, tan arms.

Noticing the threesome coming across the yard, Mrs. Stiles called, "Hi, girls."

Jenny and Rebecca waved. Cade, obviously wanting to avoid any contact with his mother, rushed ahead and quickly swung his body up into the driver's seat of the Wrangler, which was parked in their circular brick drive. "Come on. Get in!" he called impatiently. "Let's get outta here."

"Okay, we're coming!" Rebecca called. The two girls glanced over their shoulders to watch the young man disappear behind the house. Rebecca rolled her eyes and leaned close to Jenny. "Wow! Did you see *that*!"

"Hush." Jenny replied, noticing that Lynn was approaching. The girls grabbed the roll bar and climbed into the Jeep, Jenny in the front and Rebecca in the back. "Afternoon, Mrs. Stiles," Jenny greeted.

"Cade! You be careful now!" his mother said sweetly. "See you later."

Cade refused to acknowledge her and instead started the engine and pulled the Jeep out of the drive. By the time Cade turned out of the cul-de-sac and onto the main street, the Wrangler was going much too fast.

Jenny, absorbed in a conversation with Rebecca, didn't notice her mother's tan Bronco as it passed them. But Beth saw her. "Jenny!" she gasped, both angry and worried. Once again, Jenny had defied her.

Trying to keep track of her fourteen-year-old was all but impossible. While mother and daughter had once been very close, now their relationship was crumbling before her eyes. Frustrated and not knowing what to do, Beth had turned to Troy, asking him to talk with Jenny in hopes that he could break through the wall she was building. But in her heart, Beth knew he didn't have the time. Their schedules were so different that father and daughter rarely saw each other. Another casualty of her husband's success.

Seated beside her, Michael eagerly devoured a rapidly melting Dairy Queen cone. "Space Racer! Wow, Mom, this is super!"

"Now, remember your promise. Don't go on the Internet. Just play with the game. Okay?" Beth reached up to the visor and pushed the garage door opener as she pulled into the drive.

"Sure!" He struggled to open the tight cellophane wrapping on the new CD game package.

As the garage door raised, Michael's excitement overcame his good sense, and he was out of his seatbelt and almost out the door before Beth could stop the car.

"Michael!" Beth's irritation with her daughter was spilling over, and her patience was short. "I could use some help with the . . ." She could see there was no use finishing her statement. The youngster had rushed in through the garage and was already using his key to open the door into the house.

"Don't forget to turn off the alarm!" Beth called.

He stuck his head back out. "It's not on!"

Beth took a deep breath, trying to control her anger. Not only had Jenny left without permission, she hadn't even turned on the alarm.

Lost in her thoughts, Beth was tense and edgy when she leaned into the back of the Bronco to gather her grocery bags.

An unfamiliar male voice startled her. "Like some help, ma'am?"

"What?" She whirled around, color draining from her face. Beth was relieved to see one familiar face. "Lynn!"

"Sorry, honey. We didn't mean to frighten you," Lynn said.

"Well, you did." Beth didn't bother to hide her displeasure.

Sensing the powerful presence of the young man standing beside her neighbor, Beth felt uneasy. His emerald green eyes were so exquisite they electrified her. She wanted to look away but couldn't. It took Beth a moment to regain her composure.

Lynn and her now ex-husband had been neighbors for years, but only casual acquaintances. Cade's friendship with Jenny was the only reason Beth knew much about the family at all, though

Lynn always acted as if she and Beth were the best of friends. "I saw all those bags in your car. So I said, 'Justin, you get on over there and help Beth.'"

The smiling stranger accidentally brushed against Beth as he reached inside her car to grab the bags. She quickly moved to the side.

"Justin, this is Beth Woodsen. Beth, Justin Maguire."

"Hello, Mr. Maguire." Beth's response was anything but cordial. She didn't want this man inside her car or her house. "I really wish you wouldn't, Mr. . . ."

"Mister always makes me feel uncomfortable. Just Justin . . . at your service, ma'am." He smiled easily as he carried all four bags effortlessly in his arms. Beth's anxiety increased as she watched the stranger disappear inside the house.

"Isn't he just the sweetest thing? He's doing some work around my place. What with Bruce gone now, there's a passel of things that need fixin'." Lynn followed close behind as Beth hurried toward the door. "One day, there he was on my doorstep. He looked like he could do the work. So I thought, why not? And I hired him."

Beth was paying no attention to Lynn's words. Her hope that she would meet this Justin person exiting through the laundry room was dashed. Instead, she was horrified to hear his laughter coming from her kitchen.

"Michael!" Beth's voice was frenzied as she ran into the room. She stopped short as she saw Justin use his pocketknife to slit the cellophane packaging of Michael's CD game box.

"There you go, young man."

The boy ripped the cellophane away excitedly. "Thanks!" Enthusiastically, Michael lauded his new acquaintance. "Mom, Justin knows all about computers. He said he could help me. . . ."

Beth quickly moved behind Michael. Putting her hands on his shoulders, she pulled him close to her—away from the stranger.

"I'm sorry if I said something wrong." Justin snapped his knife closed and returned it to the pocket of his khaki shorts.

"Go upstairs, Michael. Now!" The boy was surprised and

hurt at the tone of his mother's remark. Embarrassed, he pulled away and ran from the kitchen.

Lynn looked startled. Forcing a nervous smile, she said, "I'm sure Justin was just trying to help."

"Yes, I'm sure he was. I guess . . . I'm a little unnerved." Beth felt awkward and shaky in her own kitchen. Her words were clipped and decidedly cool. "You'll both have to excuse me. I've got to start dinner." It was clear she wanted them to leave.

"We have to go anyway. Justin's taking me to look at bay windows. I think I'm going to let him put one in my kitchen. I think that'd be real nice."

The man nodded, giving Beth a friendly smile. "So long. Sorry I frightened you," he said, following Lynn out through the laundry room door.

"Good-bye." The minute they were out the door, Beth hurried to close it. Before she could, Justin turned and looked directly at her with those mesmerizing emerald eyes. "If you or your boy have any trouble with that computer, Mrs. Woodsen," he smiled roguishly, "just give a holler."

His eyes were the last things she saw as she closed the door and nervously fumbled for the deadlock.

Eight

Morgan turned down the familiar street in Piney Bend almost exactly two and a half hours after leaving the airport. She wasn't surprised to find her mother sitting on the porch watching for her. When the unfamiliar Infinity turned into the red dirt-and-brick driveway, Gloria's face filled with a warm and excited grin. She got up and began waving. "Hi, honey!"

It didn't take long for Morgan to settle into the familiar surroundings. After a delicious supper, the two talked and talked over coffee and homemade peach cobbler. Morgan centered her gaze on her mother, stating, "It's so good to be home."

Gloria lovingly touched her daughter's hand. "Are you doing all right, Morgan? I know you didn't come here just to sample my cobbler."

Morgan took a deep breath and sat back in the old kitchen chair. She knew she couldn't keep something this traumatic from her mother. Gloria had always been able to look into her daughters' eyes and somehow see their heartache.

Gloria's question broke the dam, and Morgan found herself telling her mother all about what had happened only two days ago. It seemed unbelievable how drastically a life could change in mere moments.

Gloria listened with patience, love, and compassion. Morgan was grateful. "Mom, I needed to be here with you."

"You're a strong woman, Morgan. I'm so proud of you. I thank God every day for you and your sister." Morgan knew it was true. "God's got a plan for your life, honey. And His own timing for things."

How many times had she heard that? Gloria's faith against all odds was an amazing thing to Morgan, but it was something she had not been able to manifest in her own life.

"You've always been so in touch with God. How have you done it all these years, Mom?" Morgan sincerely wanted guidance. She was seeking something solid to hold on to—something besides her own strength, which was letting her down.

Gloria laughed. "Oh, if you think that, then I'm a pretty good actress. We all wander away, but He never lets go. Never."

Her mother's reassurance calmed Morgan's questioning faith. *Is God truly like that? I hope so*, Morgan thought to herself before acknowledging how exhausted she really was. "I'm getting tired, Mom. I think I'll take a hot bath, then head for bed."

After her bath in the large, iron-footed tub, Morgan climbed into her familiar bed. The springs made soothing squeaks she knew intimately. She smiled and, without warning, felt years younger. No matter how old she was, she always felt like a child in her mother's house. The window by the bed was cracked just enough for her to hear the crickets and an occasional passing car.

"Father, thank you for this wonderful place. And take care of Mom." Upon finishing the simple words, Morgan realized she hadn't prayed in a long time. Her exhaustion allowed only brief thoughts of Kevin, and the fear she might end up crying herself to sleep never materialized. Morgan slept peacefully.

☙ ☙ ☙ ☙

When she finally woke, it was after ten A.M. Snuggling under the yellow-and-white wedding-ring quilt her grandmother had made, Morgan stretched, and a satisfied smile found its way to her lips. She could hear her mother moving about in the kitchen. The sounds, the smells—everything said home. Yes, this was exactly where she needed to be.

The spring morning was almost gone by the time Morgan dressed and joined her mother in the kitchen. Wearing well-worn blue jeans and a coral T-shirt, her brown, shoulder-length hair pulled straight back in a ponytail, Morgan looked almost like a teenager. The jeans were a far cry from the Channel suits still hanging in the closet of her Minnesota townhouse.

"Morning, Mom!" Morgan gave her a big hug.

"Well, sleepyhead, I didn't bother fixin' you any breakfast. You were so tired, I knew you'd sleep late. Why, it's about time for lunch."

"Don't you try to wait on me. I can take care of myself. You go on with your life. Mmm . . . that coffee smells good." Morgan moved to the coffeemaker. There beside it was "her cup," painted with silly smiley faces and colorful, childish letters that spelled Morgan. She had made it in Girl Scouts. "Mom, how great! I didn't know you still had this!" She filled it with coffee and added two Sweet'n Low packets.

Gloria seemed pleased that the cup delighted her daughter so. "I just never see enough of you, sugar, or your sister. My goodness, you'd think Dallas was a million miles from here. And you, way up there in that cold country."

"Sorry I don't get home more often, Mom. I'll try to do better." Morgan sipped her coffee as she leaned against the cupboard.

Her mother wiped her hands on her hand-embroidered apron, then fiddled with the tuning dial on a small Motorola radio from the '50s. "My lands, listen to that static. I just use the old thing to get the morning and noon news."

That little radio still sat on the same shelf it had occupied as long as Morgan could remember. Once a bright cherry red, the years had turned it an ugly reddish-brown, but it still worked— an amazing testimony to Motorola.

"Why don't you buy a new one? Let's go downtown this afternoon and I'll get you a new radio. A gift. How about that?"

"No need to spend good money on a new one," Gloria replied, determined to tune in the local station. Her stubbornness was rewarded. "There, you see. It works well enough."

Morgan couldn't help but smile. "Good for you, Mom. Maybe you'll get another forty years out of it," she said, sinking into a kitchen chair and thumbing through a *House and Garden* magazine.

"Now, you hush. They don't make things as good as they used to." The enjoyment of seeing her daughter sitting at the kitchen table was written all over her face.

Gloria put a pot of black-eyed peas on the stove for supper. "I made some chicken salad, and we've got a dollop or two of that peach cobbler left. Would you like a sandwich?"

"I'll get something later, Mom."

"It's nice to have someone to cook for besides myself."

Morgan noticed the small town radio announcer's voice droning in the background, his Texas accent so thick she could barely understand him at times.

". . . and those are the beef and hog prices. Now for the local news and weather. Increasing cloudiness. Today's high is seventy-five degrees, with a light northerly breeze. And here in Piney Bend, Mrs. Edna Potter's funeral will be held at Foster's Funeral Home tomorrow at two P.M. with a viewing tonight beginning at six. Will Youngblood's still laid up at Memorial Hospital, and Nancy Willams will . . ."

Morgan tuned the voice out. What a different world it was here in Piney Bend. Simple. Calm. Many times she'd wished she could be happy staying right here. But Morgan knew each time she visited that after a few days, she'd become restless. She'd begin to long for the hustle and bustle of the city and the satisfaction of her career.

Glancing through the morning's mail that was stacked on the edge of the kitchen table, Morgan noticed a letter and several photos lying open. She recognized her sister's handwriting. Picking up the photos, she looked at each of them. Morgan hated the tinge of jealousy she felt when she saw Beth's family.

It was amazing how much Beth looked like their mother. Gloria was a lovely woman—short, only about five foot three—with a slim figure and a sweet, caring temperament. Morgan had always marveled at how differently she had turned out. At age thirteen, Morgan had already passed up her older sister and her mother in height. At five feet eight inches, she was the family beanpole.

Beth never caught up. To this very day she was still a cute, petite blonde, with cornflower blue eyes just like their mother. But she always seemed to be fighting extra weight, something Morgan knew little about. *I just hate you,* she recalled Beth saying the last time they were together. *You never stop eating . . . and look at you.*

They may have been different heights, and certainly different temperaments, but Morgan and Beth had very similar facial
features. It was abundantly clear that they were sisters.

Morgan knew Gloria was proud of both her daughters. But
she also knew that her mother and father, Cleve, had had a special dream for Beth Ann. Their secret prayer as they sent their
first daughter off to Baylor University had been that she would
meet an eligible, spiritual seminary student. That would have
suited them just fine.

Instead, Beth fell for a handsome, strapping young man
from Austin—Troy Woodsen. And he was certainly no seminary
student. The first time she brought him home to meet the family, Cleve had barely finished the last bit of pecan pie when he
asked, "You a godly man, Troy?"

"I'm doin' my best, sir," Troy had answered, giving Beth a
wink.

Cleve was not about to let him off that easily. "Either you
are or you're not. There isn't any 'in between' territory. I don't
cotton to no wishy-washy believin', son."

Morgan had jumped in, seeing that the young man needed
a different kind of saving at that moment. She announced,
"Daddy, Troy goes to church with Beth every Sunday. I don't
think you're going to have to worry about him."

"Thanks," Beth had mouthed with a relieved smile.

"My daughter's not marryin' a non-believer, Mr. Woodsen.
Unequal yokes—that's big trouble. You want to marry my girl,
you get yourself down that aisle and into that baptismal. You
hear me?" Their daddy was nothing if not plainspoken. Beth and
Morgan both thought they would die of embarrassment.

Any other man would have run for his life. Instead, Troy
stood right up to his full six foot two inches and told their daddy
he intended to marry Beth. If it took getting saved to do it, then
he'd walk the aisle that very Sunday in Cleve's church. The two
men spent the afternoon talking until Cleve was convinced Troy
was making this decision for the right reasons.

Morgan had to admit that she was pretty impressed, and, to
her dismay, she was also attracted to this big ranch-hand kind of
guy with the rugged, attractive face. She also liked his determi-

nation and gutsy fortitude, very like her own. Morgan knew he was a young man on his way to the top with a vengeance—full of Texas-sized dreams. If only he'd had a brother, perhaps a twin.

Morgan knew the first time she ever saw them together that Beth loved Troy more than life itself. He was the one, and that's all there was to it. If her sister hadn't already fallen for him, Morgan just might've made a bid herself. But to Troy, she was just the little sister. He had given his heart to Beth.

They appeared to be the perfect couple and Morgan was happy for Beth. She deserved the best. And it looked like she had found it.

Her mother's voice brought Morgan back to the present. "What you thinking about, honey? I hope you're not pining over Kevin."

"No . . . actually, I was remembering old times. Being home brings back a lot of memories. I love it here."

"I'm so sorry your daddy didn't live to see the big success you've made of yourself. He'd pop his buttons, you can be sure of that."

"I hope so."

She missed her father. Over six years ago, on a wintry Sunday in early January, Reverend Cleve Carruthers delivered one of his very best sermons on "the Lord's grace and unending forgiveness." And afterward, while taking his regular Sunday afternoon nap, he peacefully went to "join the saints"—a favorite quote he used at every funeral.

Morgan gazed out the kitchen window. Sunshine danced through the branches of the pecan tree that stood tall in the middle of the backyard. She and Beth had spent so much time playing, giggling, and fighting under its spreading branches. Daddy's flower gardens were slowly waking up after an unusually cold winter. The thick Bermuda grass was still a bit brown, but it was, as always, beautifully manicured.

"Is the church gardener still coming by?"

"My lands, I don't know what I'd do if he didn't. But Mr. Brewster's gettin' a mite old for this kinda work."

"I think he keeps coming so you'll fill him up with your honey-sweetened iced tea," she teased her mother. "Beth and

I always thought he had a little crush on you."

Gloria looked as embarrassed as a schoolgirl. "Go on, now. You stop that kind of talk, Morgan Carruthers."

Morgan was suddenly overflowing with love for this wonderful woman. She couldn't stop herself from jumping up and throwing her arms around her. It surprised Gloria. It was very un-Morganlike behavior.

The hug lasted a long time. "Thanks, Mom. Thanks for everything."

Gloria's effort to hide the tiny tears of joy failed as she dabbed at her blue eyes with the corner of her apron. The last thing Morgan wanted to do was cry, for if she started she might not stop. She quickly changed the subject. "Maybe tomorrow we can drive up to Dallas. Spend a day or two with Beth and the children. Would you like that?"

"Now, don't you go rushing things. You came here to rest. Give yourself a few days. Your sister will understand."

Gloria reached for a large, straw sun hat. Taking it from its wrought iron hook near the back door, she tied the floppy hat over the twisted knot of thick white hair. Morgan watched approvingly. At sixty-seven, her skin was still lovely. Every bit the quintessential southern lady, Gloria wouldn't think of allowing the Texas sun to touch her face or shine directly into her clear blue eyes.

"I saw some pesky weeds sticking their heads up in Daddy's flower garden. Think I'll just nip 'em in the bud right now." Gloria seemed to have innately sensed Morgan's need to be alone. "I'll be right out back, honey."

"Love you," Morgan said softly, not needing the words to be heard. The back screen door shut with a familiar and comforting thud.

Morgan walked to the stove. As she opened the lid of the pot and stirred the black-eyed peas, her attention was suddenly drawn to the extraordinary urgency of the voice coming from the little red radio.

"The Dallas-Fort Worth area remains under an extensive tornado warning. There have been two touchdowns. One in far north Dallas and the other just east of Hurst. The extent of injuries and damages is not known at this time."

Nine

*T*he evening now cool, mother and daughter sat restfully in the old front porch swing as they often had years before. Gloria put her arms into the sleeves of her cardigan sweater. For Morgan, relieved to be out of the Minnesota cold, it felt invigorating.

So many happy as well as sad moments in their lives had played out in this swing. It was here that Beth told Gloria she was going to marry Troy. And Morgan sat in this very spot during one excruciating evening, waiting for her Freshman Frolic date—who never showed up.

Tonight, the two women giggled as Gloria retold stories about a young, feisty Morgan. Morgan adored listening and the laughter felt good. "Mom, I didn't fight with Bobby Jackson to see who would lick the ice cream maker paddle. You made that one up, didn't you?"

"You certainly did, Morgan. He was a year older and a head taller, and you just took him right to the ground."

When Morgan finally got her breath, she sputtered, "Ice cream always has been *very* important to me."

Gloria went on with the hilarious story. "Arms and legs were flyin' in all directions. Why, it took your daddy and Uncle Ed to pull you two apart. You were such a bully."

"Were? I still am." Morgan gave the swing a big push and swung them way out over the edge of the porch.

"Oooohhh!" Gloria laughed. She held her stomach with one hand and the chain supporting the swing with the other.

They were having such a good time. Morgan couldn't remember the last time she felt this relaxed.

Morgan and her mother sat in the swing for what seemed like hours, talking, reminiscing, and watching the lightning bugs play hide and seek in the hedge that surrounded the large porch.

"Daddy loved watching your eyes sparkle when he'd put a lightnin' bug on your finger."

Morgan felt the warm, loving memory as though it had happened only yesterday. "He told me one day I'd meet a—" Morgan stopped in mid-sentence. The laughter vanished. "Well, it doesn't matter. Things are what they are." Trying to regain the lightness of the early moments, she wiggled her bare ring finger in the air. "Sometimes I wonder if I'll ever wear anything on that finger except a lightning bug."

Gloria slid forward on the seat and dragged her foot to slow the swing. "Honey, don't let this thing with Kevin make you bitter. There's someone out there just waitin' to give you a ring much bigger than a lightnin' bug. And he'll give you all the love you deserve. I'm sure of it."

Morgan realized one reason she had come to this peaceful place. "I thought Kevin was the one, Mom." She paused, searching deeply into her mother's blue eyes. "I need for you to understand my relationship with him. I *really* loved Kevin. It wasn't just some kind of . . . fling."

Gloria hesitated, appearing to carefully weigh her words. With great love and understanding, she said, "I know it wasn't a fling, honey. You . . . you don't have anything to explain to me."

This was the best her mother could do, and Morgan knew it. There was no way Gloria's beliefs could allow her to approve of that kind of intimacy without the sanctity of marriage.

After a long silence, Morgan continued, "I always felt you and Daddy thought Beth was . . . well, better at following the rules than I was. She's always done it the right way. She has a great marriage and two wonderful kids."

Gloria was clearly upset at the suggestion that she was somehow more approving of Morgan's sister. "I've never judged you, honey. We loved you both so much. Beth just took a different path." She patted Morgan's hand. "I know where your heart is. That's all that matters." She sighed and then continued. "I'm gettin' sleepy. Think I'll turn in." Gloria's eyes caught sight of a flash in the distance. "There's lightning in the north. Probably that Dallas storm coming this way."

Morgan could see that her mother was worried about Beth. After supper, they had seen television news reports of some of the damage. It was upsetting. When they first heard about the storm, Gloria tried to call Beth but could not get through.

"We'll try Beth again in the morning, Mom. The storm probably blew down some phone lines."

Morgan hated to see her mother looking so uneasy. As Gloria opened the screen door, she stopped, a thoughtful expression on her face. "I called her a few days ago, and Jenny said her mother was taking a nap. Beth never called back. Not a bit like your sister. I should've called her again."

"You know teenagers. Jenny probably forgot to tell her. Everything's fine, Mom. I'm sure of it." Morgan wished with all her heart that she could return a small measure of the comfort her mother always offered her, but her words seemed to do little to allay Gloria's fears. She felt completely helpless. "Good night, Mom."

"Good night, honey. Now, don't you go stayin' out here too long. That storm's gonna be movin' in. I can feel it."

Gazing into the night, Morgan's thoughts returned to her sister. Despite what she told her mother, Morgan, too, was worried about Beth—but for different reasons. Only two years separated the Carruthers sisters. It had been difficult for Morgan when Beth left for college, though having the bedroom all to herself was a huge perk. Within a week, Morgan missed Beth dreadfully. But distance had never harmed their friendship. Their relationship only grew closer throughout the years, fostered by letters, phone calls, and far too infrequent visits.

Morgan found herself thinking about their last phone conversation. Remembering the strange tone of her sister's voice sent a chill up her spine.

How strained and frightened Beth sounded. *What was really*

wrong? Morgan wondered. When Morgan called her, she had expected Beth to tell her to come straight to Dallas so Beth could comfort her. But she hadn't.

Morgan found herself overcome with the need to hear Beth's voice, to know everything was all right. She should have stopped to see her yesterday! Deciding she needed to know now, she jumped out of the swing and bolted into the house. It didn't matter what time it was. Storm or no storm, Morgan had to talk to her best friend.

Just as Morgan reached for the phone, it suddenly rang, startling her. "Who'd be calling at this hour?" she said out loud. Her eye caught sight of her mother standing apprehensively in the doorway to her bedroom. No one ever called the Carruthers' house this late at night. No one.

Ten

*E*vening, Dr. Valeske. Thought I'd be seeing you," said a tall, slender man in a gray guard's uniform. "They just brought the body in."

"Darn beepers. It's my wife's birthday, too. Electronic leashes, if you ask me." The small, middle-aged man with thinning brown hair, combed over the top of his head in a vain attempt to cover his baldness, wasn't happy about this late night call.

"Chambers had to pick tonight to have the flu." Taking off his glasses, Valeske pulled a handkerchief from his pants pocket and wiped away the fog that had formed on the thick, Coke-bottle lenses. "The evening's ruined, the wife's upset . . ."

"Bad night for the one in the bag, too. Huh, doc?"

The guard's humor was lost on Valeske as he ran his card-key through the slot on the side of the locked door. After a moment, the door automatically unlocked. He entered and started down a long, deserted corridor. His footsteps echoed eerily.

Unlocking the door to this office, he flipped on the harsh fluorescent light. He squinted as his eyes adjusted to the light. Hanging his tweed jacket on a wooden coat rack, he entered the sterile autopsy examination room. One overhead light brightly lit the black body bag waiting for him on the stainless steel examination table.

Dr. Valeske took a moment to put on a gown, gloves, and clear plastic goggles. Seeing the report left for him by the investigators, he automatically switched on the recording equipment and began to speak. "Thursday, March 6, 11:20 P.M. Dr. Sydney Valeske." In a voice so humdrum it could have been ordering a hamburger and fries, he continued, "We have a female car accident victim."

Through the thick lenses of his glasses, Dr. Valeske looked at the deceased's Texas driver's license. The picture of a pretty thirty-six-year-old woman smiled back at him.

"Beth Ann Woodsen. Nice photo," he said out loud. "Pretty lady." He tossed the license onto the report, unzipped the body bag, and reached for a camera.

❧   ❧   ❧   ❧

The bright lights of Morgan's rented Infinity sliced into the cool, damp darkness as it savagely devoured the lonely miles of Texas Highway 287. It was neither night nor day, but that time that exists only for the uneasiness of the soul.

Morgan's hands gripped the steering wheel so tightly her knuckles were white. She swallowed hard to keep from screaming. *It's not true! Beth is just fine. This is some kind of twisted joke. It's not true!*

It was quiet in the car, for there was little for mother and daughter to say. Each one was dealing with their own grief, and their pain was too deep for words. Morgan glanced toward her mother. Her small, aging hands twisted a tearstained white linen handkerchief.

Stunned, Morgan realized she would never talk to her sister again. Never hear her voice or share in her laughter and tears. Her mind searched for something she could depend upon, something that couldn't be ripped away from her in a cruel and inexplicable minute.

"She's gone, Morgan! Beth is dead!" Troy's voice had sounded unreal, the words disjointed and outrageous. He didn't believe what he was saying any more than Morgan did. *"How could this possibly be true?"* Troy offered incoherent, fragmented information. *"The storm. Some kind of car accident."* The police had just left, and it was too soon to know all the details.

Gloria had been the one to take the phone and tell Troy

they'd be there in a few hours. Then she quietly told Morgan, "Dear, we have to go. They need us in Dallas."

Morgan was relieved when she turned off the two-lane highway onto Interstate 45. "We'll be there soon, Mom."

Her sister's phone number kept going through her mind. *Why didn't I call her today?* Morgan had waited one day, one hour, one minute too long. She couldn't stop thinking that the time it took for that one phone call would have thrown off Beth's entire schedule—and her appointment with whatever twist of fate it was that caused the accident might have been missed.

Instead, Beth would have been waiting for their arrival in her comfortable kitchen with bay windows and French doors. The beautiful red-brick home on Jasmine Court would be full of life—not grieving. This kind of tragedy wasn't supposed to happen in that kind of neighborhood.

As she drove, memories pushed and elbowed their way into her awareness, so vivid Morgan could almost hear Beth's voice. *"Hi, sis! Y'all get outta that car and come on inside."* Her words always bubbled with a thick Texas accent, and she was all smiles and up to her elbows in flowerbed dirt. Like their father, she adored roses. Beth's hugs were warm and sincere and easy for her to give. She had been able to love with such freedom.

Morgan's eyes filled with tears as she remembered their last visit together. It was last fall and they had had such fun. Staying up after the rest of the house was quiet and sleeping, they had giggled about sister secrets and shared the remaining slice of Beth's famous double-decker chocolate suicide cake. It was that evening that Beth had said the words that now haunted Morgan: *"Sisters are very special, and nothing can come between us, Morgan. Nothing."*

Morgan shook her head. But something had! Their last phone conversation should have sent Morgan racing to Dallas. But she was so wrapped up in her own broken heart. *"We'll talk later,"* she had told her sister. But there would be no later for Beth and Morgan.

Driving toward the Woodsen's on the Dallas North Tollway, Morgan's fragile composure disintegrated. Without warning, her frustration and agony escaped in one loud, wrenching burst. "How could you let this happen, Beth?" Morgan questioned, her pain evident in the emotional tone of her voice.

Morgan's outburst startled her mother. Gloria tried to comfort her daughter. "We'll get through this, honey. We will." But Morgan was aware that the reality of their shattered world was coming ever closer. There was no turning back, only the gaping uncertainty of the days ahead.

Gloria's voice became very quiet and thoughtful. "I do hope your sister went to the store. I'm gonna need milk. I'll make breakfast. They're all gonna be starved. You know how little Michael loves my pancakes."

Then she took a deep breath and again turned to stare out the window at nothing.

Eleven

"Mornin', Les," said a well-built young man in sweats as he tossed a morning newspaper on the counter of the Cybersurf Café.

"So how's it going, Justin?"

"Great. Couldn't be better."

Les immediately put in Justin's familiar order. "Café mocha, a health-nut bagel. Toasted, no butter. Right?"

"You got it!"

"Anything interesting in the paper this morning?"

"That storm caused a lot of damage. Take a look at these pictures." Justin shoved the paper toward Les, then swiveled around on his stool, his green eyes scanning the cyberbooths as though he was looking for someone. He returned his attention to the man behind the counter. "I'm surprised you're doing so much business this early in the morning."

Les laughed, sitting the steaming cup of café mocha in front of Justin. "Can't keep those kids off the computers. They're turning into a bunch of little addicts."

"I can see you're really upset about that."

"Yeah. Hey, you on your way to the gym?"

"Already been there. When're you going to join me?"

Patting the generous stomach that made his belt invisible, Les let out a sputtering laugh. "Not me, buddy. I'm up before dawn as it is. This job's all the exercise I can handle." He wiped the counter as he added, "You through with this paper?" Justin nodded and Les tossed it into the garbage. "Your bagel will be up in a minute."

"Maybe you ought to keep the place open twenty-four hours a day," quipped a waitress who was busily operating the espresso machine.

"Why not? The Web never closes," replied another, adding two cups of steaming espresso to her tray, which already held an iced cappuccino. "Need two toasted sesame bagels, one strawberry and the other plain cream cheese," she called into the kitchen area.

The waitress expertly balanced her tray as she zigzagged through the tables to cyberbooth six. Without making eye contact with the occupant, she slid the iced cappuccino across the shiny tabletop. "Bon appetit!" She didn't even notice the computerized female voice saying, "Welcome to the Catacomb. Enter your password."

After taking a sip of cappuccino, the customer complied, typing *Cyclosa*. Then hitting the Enter key, the swirling vortex filled the computer screen. The sinister graphic of the Catacomb appeared for only a moment. A Private Chamber Chat window immediately overshadowed it.

```
ARA:  WB cyclosa ... word has reached me that
you took care of everything.
CYCLOSA:  Yes. You don't have to worry about her
any longer.
ARA:  i am well pleased :) now my spiderling ...
crawl into a dark, safe place and don't call
attention to yourself ... this will soon be
forgotten and we can continue increasing our
foothold.
CYCLOSA:  But what should I do? When will I hear
from you???
```

The questions were left unanswered as, without another word, the Catacomb connection was cut off and the Web connection severed. Worried and frustrated, the occupant of the cyberbooth restlessly tapped his fingers on the stainless steel tabletop and stared at the blinking cursor.

Twelve

*T*hree packets of sugar and a hefty dose of powdered creamer failed to improve a cup of ten-hour-old coffee. "Anybody notified hazardous materials about this?" wisecracked Dell Hancock, holding up his chipped, coffee-stained cup. The burly fifty-six-year-old homicide detective had easily deduced, unhappily, that the pot had been brewed sometime during the previous night's shift.

Walking briskly through the squad room, carrying a gym bag, he continued, "Ever try same day coffee? It's a heck of a concept."

"You volunteering to make a fresh pot, Hancock?" One of the younger detectives got in a friendly jab.

"In your dreams, Willie." The big bear of a man gave out a laugh that was a comforting and welcome fixture around the homicide department. It was hard not to like Detective Hancock.

Over the past six months, he'd taken an unprecedented interest in working out in the police gym, something completely abhorrent to him in years past. The results were apparent.

"Only a few more months and you'll be pickin' up fresh brew at Dunkin' Donuts," laughed another officer.

After working in the Dallas Police Department for the last twenty-two years and with the Chicago Police for six years before that, Dell was ready for his retirement. "Nine months, three weeks and"—looking at his watch—"six hours. Then I'm outta here! On my way to that sweet little fishin' boat waiting for me in the Gulf! But you can forget the donuts—I'm thinkin' I've lived this long as a cop, I'd like to enjoy a few of the good years." Giving a wink, he patted his shrinking and tightening stomach. "Not bad, if I do say so myself."

"Any chance of getting rid of you sooner, Hancock?" smiled Sergeant Hannah Lasser, the department head, as she leaned in the doorway of her private office. "We're all gonna miss that grumpy attitude you drag in here every day."

"No, you won't, Hannah, 'cause I'm leaving it here!" He flashed her a big smile. "Along with my high blood pressure and irritated colon."

Hannah Lasser had a sincere fondness for her senior detective. When she transferred into the department a couple of years ago, being only thirty-two, black, and female were just three of the things that put cautious distance between her and the detectives she would be supervising.

Her friendship with Hancock was forged during those first weeks when a tough case involving the senseless murders of two youngsters in South Dallas became her "trial by fire." At the grizzly, unsettling crime scene, it was Dell who spotted her throwing up her Chinese dinner behind an old dump truck. Their eyes met and what she found wasn't judgement, but compassion.

Dell tossed his well-worn sports jacket on the back of his swivel chair, sat down at his desk, and began his morning ritual of thumbing through the *Dallas Morning News*. After a few minutes he leaned back, putting his hands behind his graying head. "I don't get it. What makes 'em think the Cowboys deserve front-page coverage *every* week?"

"Twenty-two years and still a Bears fan?" His partner, Detective Ballantine, enjoyed jousting with Dell. "You can't live in Texas and not be a Cowboys fan, Hancock. It's unAmerican."

"I'm tellin' ya, Mayberry, this whole town's Cowboy crazy! You included."

When Detective Hancock met his new redheaded and freckle-faced partner some eight months ago, Dell kidded him about being from TV's Mayberry. The name had stuck from day one.

Chuck Ballantine waved off Dell's remark and returned to his computer. Chuck was thirty-four and sharp. He not only knew the police business, he knew more than most about the computer system that now operated throughout the department.

"Hey, you still getting those e-whatchamacallits from that gal in Community Affairs? It boggles my mind why she doesn't just pick up the phone, dial your extension, and talk to you. It's scary, Mayberry. You're turning into a computer nerd."

"What I'm doing is looking at mug shots on that Gonzales case, which, by the way, you might find interesting." Chuck looked amused as he turned his computer screen so Dell could get a look at it. "And those whatchamacallits are called email. And 'that gal' is named Trudy."

"You can just leave me outta this electronic age. As for ole Hancock, just call me up on the Alexander Graham Bell or lick a stamp." Amused at his own humor, Dell snickered and returned to his newspaper.

"Surprise!" Dr. Valeske announced as he strolled into the homicide department waving a plastic bag containing the corpse of a large black widow spider. The head medical examiner had garnered the attention of all the personnel in the office with his unexpected appearance.

"Hey, look at that. Valeske's got a new pet," Ballantine said as he took a closer look at the specimen.

Hancock interjected, "I think the spider's dead, doc."

"It's a latrodectus mactan, better known as a black widow. Interested in where it came from, Hancock?"

"Nope, not particularly." Dell turned another page of his newspaper.

Valeske's voice went up an octave as he announced. "It came from a body bag!"

"No kidding?" Sergeant Lasser smiled. "Your boys running out of the real thing?"

"That's too much to ask for, Sergeant." Becoming more serious, he continued, "Hannah, it was *in* the body bag *with* a body. I unzipped the bag, and out it crawled. Curious, don't you think?"

Dell slowly looked up from the newspaper that was still laying open in front of him. He tried his best to look interested.
"So, Doc, you taking the little lady around to meet everybody,
or is there some special reason you dropped in on us?"

Without a word, Dr. Valeske walked to Dell's desk. He
flipped the newspaper to the front page, and, with a grand gesture, dropped the bag. It landed, as aimed, next to a front-page
story: "Storm Claims Life of Woman in Car Accident."

"You must've gotten lost, Doc. This is homicide. Not traffic," Hannah replied.

"Oh, I'm in the right place. Traffic's putting this one in your
lap."

Dell picked up the bag and shook it. "Is this our suspect?"

"No. One bite from a black widow probably won't kill you,
but it'll make you so sick you'll wish it had. Dizzy, short of
breath, abdominal pains . . ."

"You've lost me. What makes this our problem?" the sergeant questioned.

Valeske sat on the edge of Dell's desk as he gave them the
details of the previous night's autopsy of Beth Ann Woodsen.
"Of course, seeing the spider, I immediately thought the victim
had been bitten and the shock probably caused her to lose control of her car. But when I did a thorough search of the body,
looking for the two identifying small, red puncture marks from
the spider's fangs, there weren't any. Could it have just crawled
into the body bag at the scene? Maybe."

"You're saying she wasn't bitten?" Ballantine asked.

"Right. Like I said, I didn't find two puncture marks. But I
did find one in the back of her neck," he said, pointing to his
hairline. "Right here. It had a red circle around it, same as a bite.
And the area was bruised."

"One fang mark? That makes it murder? Give us a break,
Valeske." Dell impatiently sighed. "Where's the punch line,
Doc?"

Annoyed at Hancock, as he usually was, Valeske continued,
"It wasn't a fang mark . . . it was a syringe puncture and the tip
was broken off, probably in a struggle. It was lodged in the tis-
sue of the neck, near the spinal cord. I've ordered a special tox-

icology report. It'll tell you *what* killed her. But it's up to you to dig up the *who*."

"Any other signs of a struggle?"

"No major bruises that could've occurred *before* she died, so I'd say no. Scrapings from under her fingernails are at the crime lab. We'll see what kind of trace evidence they come up with, but I'm figuring not much."

Hannah pointed to Dell. "This one's for you and Ballantine. Think of it as my going-away present."

"Thanks," the detective mumbled, pulling a small spiral notebook and pen from his shirt pocket and jotting some notes. "Keep us posted, okay, Doc?"

"Oh, there is one more thing. The victim was definitely dead, oh, I'd say twenty to thirty minutes *before* the car accident." They all reacted with surprised interest. "It was some trick if she was driving that car when it flipped into that ditch."

"Thanks, Valeske." Sergeant Lasser turned to Hancock and Ballantine. "Get that car checked out bumper to bumper. And while you're at it, stop off at traffic and pick up the records."

Thirteen

$\mathcal{E}$verything felt as though it was moving in slow motion. Well-meaning neighbors and friends stopped by with food, offering their condolences to the family. But Beth's death still seemed unreal to her sister.

Morgan and her mother had not yet seen Beth's body. Before Troy called Piney Bend last night, the police took him to identify her. But by ten A.M. the next morning, they had still not released the body to the family. Something about "completing the investigation."

As much as Morgan dreaded the moment, she knew that when she could touch her sister and say good-bye, acceptance would be inevitable.

Morgan was amazed at Gloria's strength. Her mother was able to find some temporary relief from her own grief by staying close to Jenny and Michael, providing them with spiritual and loving support. They had so many questions. Nine-year-old Michael clung to his grandmother, his eyes red and swollen. Jenny, wanting to be alone, sat quietly in the window seat in her mother and dad's bedroom. She held back the curtain and stared at the cars coming and going on the cul-de-sac.

Together, Troy and Morgan had mechanically gone through the excruciating task of making arrangements for Beth's funeral. Gloria had taken the responsibility of speaking with Pastor Shelby about the service at Beth's beloved Greenwood Baptist Church. Never in her deepest nightmares had Morgan ever thought she would be burying her sister.

The day had now become overcast and cold, but Morgan could no longer stay inside the house and face even one more visitor. Slipping a violet cable-knit sweater over her jeans, Morgan grabbed a mug of hot coffee and wandered out into the large backyard.

She was surprised to see Troy gazing motionless out over the wooded area at the back of their lot. He was such a big man, with broad shoulders and handsome features. Troy's dishwater blond hair, once a mass of curls, was now worn short and combed smoothly back away from his rugged face.

Morgan said nothing as she straddled the bench of the weathered redwood picnic table where so many wonderful family memories had been created. She nervously twisted her coffee mug back and forth, making meaningless circles in the afternoon dew that clung to the slatted tabletop.

Troy must have felt her presence. He turned and didn't seem surprised to find her there. She thought he was almost relieved. "Tough staying in there, isn't it?"

"Yeah." Morgan was glad Troy was coming to join her. "You were great this morning. I couldn't have gotten through that funeral home thing without you."

Troy put a cowboy-booted foot on the other bench and leaned forward on his muscular thigh. "It's real funny, you being here in Piney Bend . . . just when it happened. What are the chances?"

The strain of attempting to have a sane conversation in the midst of complete havoc was unbearable. Morgan looked away as tears came to her eyes. "Yeah, what are the chances?" she slowly answered, allowing the tears to come freely. "What are the chances, Troy, that Beth would be killed? I'm dying inside. Talk to me. Please. Why are the police keeping her body? Tell me what you really know—don't hold back anything," she implored him. "I have to know what happened!"

Troy cleared his throat, forcing back unwanted emotions. "I really don't know that much, Morgan. One minute I had a wife, and the next there's a knock on the door and . . . and she's gone."

Troy continued to grapple with words, sharing with Morgan

what little information he had learned from the police. Every sentence brought on more anger and disbelief.

"There were storm warnings! Sirens going off all over town! Why was she on the road, Morgan?" Troy's body stiffened with rage. "How could she do such a *stupid* thing?"

"There had to be something so important it didn't matter about the weather."

"She wasn't a child. She knew better."

His six foot two, well-exercised frame seemed to diminish in size under the burden he now shouldered. Morgan recalled how everyone who knew Troy and Beth had always been amused by the way he towered over her like a loving guardian. Beth had often said, *"He makes me feel so safe."* Beth adored Troy—and the feeling was mutual.

Anguish continued to accent Troy's words. "Apparently a tornado touched down only four miles away from where she crashed! There had to be a wall of debris blowing across the road." Running a large hand through his hair, he started pacing. "But there weren't even any skid marks. She just drove off the edge of the road! It's not like her, Morgan. Beth was an excellent driver."

Morgan listened with eagerness, prompted by her macabre need to know exactly what happened in the last seconds of her sister's life.

"The soft shoulder flipped her car over and it landed in that muddy ditch." Troy tightened his grip on a faltering composure, then took a long moment before he continued, unashamed of the tears filling his eyes. "She . . . was thrown . . . through the windshield. That's all they know. At least that's all they told me."

The terror of the picture conjured up by his words sickened her. Morgan's hands flew over her mouth and she tossed her head back in horror. "Oh, Beth . . ."

Troy's face took on a calm longing as he looked toward the back door. His voice became tender. "You know, I keep expecting to see her come through that door any minute." He turned to Morgan, his eyes pleading for her to make it so. "But I never will see her again . . . will I?"

Morgan could offer no consolation. Her own pain was so deep and searing she had nothing to give him. *Get up. Go to him.* The words echoed in her mind. That's what Beth would have done. She ached to do it—but Morgan could not move.

Studying his face, Morgan wished she and Troy were closer. Their personalities were so similar that Beth often said they were "two peas in a pod." Morgan knew Beth would be broken-hearted if she could see the two most intimate companions in her life unable to help each other through their pain. But Morgan, like Troy, held her emotions jealously—a far cry from her affectionate sister. Both Troy and Morgan openly shared their emotions with only one person—Beth. Now she was gone, and they were left with only each other.

I'll try, Beth, Morgan thought, closing her eyes. Her mind whirled with unanswered questions. "This whole thing is so queer—not at all like Beth. They told you she wasn't wearing a seat belt, but Beth always wore one. And she knew better than to flirt with Texas tornado weather. Could it be a mistake, Troy? Could it?"

Troy seemed unable to answer and simply said, "Our Beth is gone."

Morgan's anger broke through the barrier she had tried to build all day. "Our Beth? She hadn't been *our* Beth for months, Troy. I hardly recognized her when we spoke. Something was tormenting her, eating away at her—couldn't you see it? Were you blind?"

Her cutting accusation made him explode. "No! I knew something was wrong. I tried to talk to her, but she wouldn't tell me anything. I felt helpless—what could I do?"

"Help her somehow! You should've helped her. She sounded so frightened."

In anger, Troy took a step toward Morgan, then suddenly pulled back. Morgan watched as he ran his fingers through his thick hair. It was clear that Troy was struggling with his own demons. She knew he had little or no experience with helplessness, for Troy Woodsen made sure he was always in control. The pain of being able to do nothing while the most important person in his life desperately needed him was probably unimaginable.

Troy's strong arms came down hard on the table directly across from Morgan. His blazing hazel eyes made an intimidating connection with hers. "If you knew she was in trouble, why didn't *you* do something? Supposedly you two knew everything about each other. Or were you too busy being Miss Executive?"

Morgan felt suddenly guilty, as if he were a prosecutor pressing her for a murder confession. "Sure, I knew something was wrong, but . . . I was a thousand miles away." Her words carried a defensive tone as she rose to her full height, needing to break his unnerving gaze.

"You should have come, Morgan."

"Beth said she was taking care of it. That it would be over soon. I wanted to call you. I told her I would, but she made me promise not to." Her face grew hot and flushed. "Why are you trying to make this my fault, Troy? You were her knight in shining armor. Why was she afraid to come to you?"

"It was the two of you who had this special 'sibling club' that kept everyone else out. I thought you two talked about *everything*. She must've told you something—because she didn't talk to me. Beth could have come to me with anything. She knew that."

Morgan stared silently into her cold, half-empty mug of coffee.

"There's no confidence to break now, Morgan. She's dead."

Troy's words carried an angry edge. Morgan suddenly realized that he must have been carrying resentment about their close friendship for years. How could he have been jealous of her relationship with Beth?

"You saw her every day. Lived with her. If she needed help, why didn't you see that she got it? Why?"

"You didn't do anything and neither did I. We let Beth die, Morgan. You and I weren't there when she needed us!"

Morgan was coming apart at the seams. "I just don't know what was tormenting her. If I did, I'd tell you. What reason would I have to keep that from you, Troy?"

His anger was growing, overtaking him. His handsome, rugged face was twisted in rage, mirroring the unrelenting strain of the last twenty-four hours. "Morgan—we both let her down.

She was crying out for help. Maybe . . . she finally gave up.''

Troy's words took her breath away as surely as if he had slugged her in the stomach. Incredulously she uttered, "No! Beth would never commit suicide. I'll never accept that. She loved life. She loved us.''

Troy whirled around to face her. "Right now, I don't know what to believe.''

Frustrated, angry, accusing words spilled from her trembling lips. "I can't stand this, Troy. You want to know what she told me? I'll tell you.'' She attempted to shift the suffocating feelings of guilt. "She was lonely, Troy. She didn't feel like a necessary part of your life anymore.'' Morgan didn't stop there. "Where were you when she needed you? At the office? Out of town? How much time did you give her? That company got all your time, and you let your family have the leftovers.''

Angrily, Morgan slammed her cup of cold coffee on the table and lunged at Troy. Her fists pounded on his chest, again and again, as she screamed and cried. He did nothing to restrain her. Her heartbreaking words were barely audible, "You were supposed to take care of her. Where were *you*, Troy?''

As her physical assault subsided, Morgan dissolved into sobs of sorrow and despair, and an overpowering weariness overtook her. Troy's arms slowly closed around his sister-in-law. He held her while she cried.

"What will we do without her?'' His voice was soft and compassionate.

"Dad!''

Troy and Morgan turned to see Jenny hurrying toward them. She looked worried. For an instant, Troy appeared to lose himself in the beauty of his daughter, who resembled his wife so closely.

"What's wrong, honey?'' Morgan could see Jenny was confused and frightened.

"Two policemen . . . They're here to see you, Dad.''

Fourteen

r. Woodsen, I'm Detective Hancock of the Dallas Police Department, Homicide Division. And this is my partner, Detective Ballantine." Troy looked at their badges and shook hands with the two detectives.

"Please let us offer our condolences. We're sorry to bother you, but we've got some questions."

"Certainly." Troy nodded uneasily. He then realized that Jenny was standing beside him. "This is our . . . my daughter, Jenny."

Before he could introduce Morgan, she spoke. "I'm Morgan Carruthers. Beth's sister."

Detective Hancock shook her hand warmly. "I'm very sorry, ma'am. It's a terrible tragedy." Returning his attention to Troy, he quietly said, "Could we have a few words with you? Privately, please."

"Jenny, honey, I'd like you to go upstairs and stay with Michael and your grandmother."

She clearly didn't want to be sent out of the room. "But, Dad . . ." Her look pleaded with him to allow her to stay.

"Please, Jenny. Now," he insisted, his tone firm.

The young teenager, still reeling from the loss of her mother, responded emotionally. "It was my mom who died! Why can't I hear what they're going to say?"

Morgan leaned close to her niece. "We'll tell you everything, I promise. Every word."

"Dad . . ." Her pleas, however, were not going to change

her father's mind. Jenny, hurt and embarrassed by the tears that rolled down her cheeks, turned and ran up the carpeted stairs. After a moment, a door closed loudly.

"I'm sorry . . . we're all trying to cope the best we can." Troy motioned for them to sit. "Please. Have a seat."

"Thank you." Dell and his partner clumsily found seats beside each other on a flowery loveseat. Ballantine sat forward, so he wouldn't be pulled into the gap created by the weight of his much larger partner.

Morgan resolutely took a seat in a large, overstuffed chair facing them, her intentions clear. Even in jeans and a sweater, the young woman presented a cool, intelligent, and formidable presence.

Troy's words affirmed Morgan's actions. "Anything you have to say to me, my sister-in-law should hear."

"Fine," answered Detective Hancock. "That's your decision."

An air of anticipation hung heavily in the room. "Now, what can I do for you?" Troy asked, hoping to get this ordeal over with as quickly as possible.

"I know this has been a very hard time for you and your whole family, but I'm afraid we've got something rather disturbing to tell you." Hancock cleared his throat uncomfortably. "Traffic did tell you that an autopsy would be performed—it's a matter of procedure in an automobile fatality."

"Yes. We know." Too apprehensive to sit, Troy stood and shoved his hands into the pockets of his jeans.

Morgan broke in, "Has that been done?"

"Yes, it has, Ms. Carruthers." Dell dug around in his suit pockets, then pulled out the small notebook. "Here it is," he said, under his breath. They all watched as he thumbed through it.

The detective's earlier warning caused Troy to steel himself for what would obviously be unwelcome news about his wife's death.

Hancock shifted in the uncomfortable hole he had made for himself in the soft loveseat. "The medical examiner has concluded that the victim was already deceased when the accident occurred."

"What?" Troy slowly lowered himself back into the chair. "She was dead *before* the car accident?"

"That's ridiculous!" Morgan protested.

"Ma'am, your sister may have been in the driver's seat, but she was already dead when the car rolled down that embankment," Ballantine stated bluntly.

The shocking statement horrified Troy. "But . . . that's nuts! She was killed in that accident. That's what your people told me last night! Now you're telling me she was already dead!"

Detective Hancock took another look at his notes, then continued. "The ME's waiting for the results of the toxicology report. That could take a week or two, maybe longer. But we're not waiting. The department feels there's enough evidence for us to go ahead with a murder investigation."

"Murder?" Troy could barely say the word.

Morgan stood and walked toward the two detectives. "Evidence? What kind of evidence? What could possibly make you think she was . . . murdered?"

"You're talking about a beautiful young woman, the mother of two great kids. Who in the world would want to . . ." Troy's sentence broke off as he absorbed the horror of the possibility.

Dell worked his way out of the loveseat and got to his feet. "The autopsy findings were conclusive. Your wife died under suspicious circumstances and not in a car accident as we all had thought. I understand this is hard for you both to accept."

Ballantine added, "Yeah. This isn't the kind of news we wanted you to read in tomorrow's paper."

Troy asked, "But how can you be so sure? She went through the windshield . . . her neck—it was broken."

Hancock thumbed to another page in his notebook. "There were a number of things, Mr. Woodsen. For one, there was an absence of extensive bruising and blood loss normally associated with this kind of accident. If she had been alive at the time of the impact, the body would've incurred other injuries." He paused to give Troy time to take in what he was hearing. "Sir, the medical examiner is certain she had been dead twenty to thirty minutes before the impact."

Ballantine's youthful impatience brought him to his feet.

"We're surmising that the perpetrator was probably in the car with her. Either hiding in the back waiting for her, or she let him in. He—or she—killed your wife, then staged the accident to make it appear to be the cause of her death."

Dell shot an irritated glance at his young partner.

"No! You're wrong!" Morgan moved to Troy and took his arm. "They're wrong!" she said softly. Then she looked toward the detectives. "You've got to be wrong!

"Look at this home." Morgan grabbed a beautifully framed picture of the Woodsen family and shoved it toward the young detective. "Look at this family. You're in one of the best neighborhoods in Dallas. People like my sister aren't murdered!"

Troy, more in control of himself, put his arm around Morgan's shoulder and pulled her close. He knew no matter how long and hard she protested, they couldn't change the facts.

"I'm sorry, Ms. Carruthers. But the evidence doesn't lie. In this case, I wish it did." The detective was sincere. Murder didn't belong here. But years on the police force taught that no neighborhood was immune to the sudden, shattering violence of murder. It searched out the most unlikely victims.

Troy and Morgan quietly listened, doing their best to cope. Ballantine continued to present more of the evidence. The puncture wound. The probable struggle. The broken needle. Hancock and his partner had agreed not to mention the black widow spider. There was no hard evidence that it was anything but a coincidence.

"We're expecting the toxicology report will show that she received a lethal dose of some kind of drug prior to the accident. Once we know what it was, we'll have something more to go on." Detective Hancock continued, "In the meantime, I'm afraid we have to ask you both some questions."

Troy's analytical mind searched for some reasonable excuse for this totally unreasonable act of brutality. "Could it have been a robbery? Or a car jacking?"

"No, sir, we don't think so." Ballantine answered. "We believe it was an intentional act against the victim."

"The *victim* had a name. Beth . . . Mommy . . . daughter . . . wife!" Her voice dropped as she said her final word. "Sister."

Hancock took charge. "Ma'am, I realize this has got to be very hard for you. But we have to do our job. Whoever did this wanted to be sure your sister was dead. And they didn't want to take a chance that the car accident might not be fatal."

Without a beat, Ballantine jumped right in. "Do either of you have any idea who might've wanted to hurt Mrs. Woodsen?"

Troy couldn't imagine contemplating the young detective's totally absurd question. Incredulously he replied, "Detective, my wife was a wonderful, caring woman. Everyone loved her."

"Where were you yesterday afternoon, Mr. Woodsen?"

Hancock's question was not kindly accepted by either Troy or Morgan. "You couldn't possibly think that Troy could've . . ." Morgan's voice trailed off as she looked at Troy's fallen expression. He was destroyed by the very thought.

Troy spoke in a clear and controlled tone. "I was in my office until about two P.M. I was on the road to Fort Worth when the tornado warning came. Since most of the storm was behind me, I continued on to a three-thirty meeting with Phil Landers at Landers and Collins Architectural firm. I can get you the number."

"No, sir, that won't be necessary right now." Hancock made the notes in his small notebook. "Were you and Mrs. Woodsen having any . . . problems?"

Morgan was appalled. "You can't possibly think Troy's a suspect!"

"Right now everyone is, Ms. Carruthers."

Troy answered the detective's question. "We had a good marriage. Beth and I loved each other very much."

A distraught and angry Morgan went to the door and opened it with trembling hands. "This whole thing is ludicrous. I think you should both leave."

"We'll need to be talking with friends, neighbors, and people she worked with. Could you put together a list for us?" Dell requested.

"Certainly. I'll fax it to your office tomorrow." Troy walked the two men to the door.

Hancock took two business cards from his pocket and

handed them to Troy. "If either of you think of anything we should know, please call."

Halfway down the porch stairs, Ballantine added, "We may need to ask you some more questions. Please don't leave town."

As soon as the door was closed, Troy's stoic pretence melted. Placing an arm around Morgan's shoulders, he drew her close and began to weep.

Fifteen

*T*he day was warm, and fluffy white clouds played about in the brilliant blue Texas sky. It was the kind of day perfect for a family picnic or a leisurely drive through the Dogwood Trails—not a day meant for tears and final good-byes.

Floral arrangements of every size and variety filled the air with an intoxicatingly sweet fragrance. As she sat on the small wooden folding chair and closed her eyes, Morgan tried desperately to imagine herself lying spread-eagle in a field of Texas wild flowers. But try as she might, she could not close out the sounds, the words. . . .

"Father, into your hands we commend the soul of Beth Ann Woodsen. We ask your mercy and tender care for the loved ones she left behind. . . ."

Gloria's black-gloved hand tightened around Morgan's. Next to her, Troy sat with Jenny and Michael on either side. The young boy sobbed softly and laid his head on his father's arm. Jenny's tears were silent as Troy held his daughter's hand.

Behind the family were the many unfamiliar faces, pieces of Beth's life that Morgan hadn't shared. Each there to say their own good-byes. Each with a different memory of Beth, a different attachment. Morgan listened to the pastor, her eyes empty of tears. They'd been pushed aside by anger, which she could not release.

Local news cameras ignored the need for privacy. They stood behind gravestones gathering video for the evening news at six. Her sister's murder had made her and the family public property. Prying eyes at private moments . . . business as usual.

Her anger went beyond the continual press coverage and speculations about Beth's death. She was enraged that they were not burying Beth because some tragic accident had taken her. Instead they were lowering the flower-draped, bronze casket into the ground because some twisted mind had deliberately ripped the life out of her.

Pastor Shelby's voice seemed far away. "When the pain of this is too great for us to bear, you are there to help us through our grief. You carry us when we cannot walk, you are our comforter, our strength."

Morgan was almost surprised when she heard her own voice blending with the others, saying, " 'The Lord is my shepherd; I shall not want. He makes me to lie down in green pastures; He leads me beside the still waters. . . .' "

❧ ❧ ❧ ❧

Gloria busied herself in the kitchen, directing neighbors and friends as they helped put out all the food that had been dropped off at the Woodsen home. Filling their plates, the visitors gravitated into small groups as hushed voices speculated about the murder.

After greeting as many people as she could, Morgan went upstairs to freshen up and take a private moment. In her room, she sat down at the little dressing table and looked at her reflection in the mirror. With her fingers, she touched the mirror, as if she were touching the face she would never see again. It was the first time she was happy that she and Beth resembled each other.

"I'll miss you," she whispered. "You were right, Beth. Sisters are special. I'll never be one again." Morgan paused, then with total commitment she said, "I'll find out who did this to you. I promise you."

"Morgan."

Her mother's voice startled her. Turning around, Morgan managed a small smile. "How are you, Mom?"

Gloria walked into the room and sat down on the edge of

her daughter's bed. "I'll be fine. It's better now that the funeral is behind us."

"It's not going to be over until we know who did it."

"Morgan, vengeance will destroy you, honey. That's why God said, 'vengeance is mine.' Let *Him* take care of it."

Morgan looked away, turning back to stare into the mirror. "I can't, Mom. Maybe God will take care of it, but I have to be sure. For Beth."

Gloria got up and walked over to her daughter, resting her wrinkled hands on Morgan's shoulders and kissing the brown curls. "If only you could trust Him. You'd find Him faithful, I promise you."

Touching her mother's hand, Morgan turned and looked into her eyes and replied, "I wish I could . . . but where was He when Beth needed Him?"

"All our questions won't be answered, honey. Not here. Not now. But they will be one day. Don't lose the life you've been granted in a pool of hatred and revenge. It would break Beth's heart."

Troy didn't feel at ease with Pastor Shelby, even though he and his family had been attending Greenwood Baptist for over six years now. He thought of it more as Beth's church. Tom Shelby was a pleasant man in his late forties with a gentle, chiseled face and short, dark brown hair. He walked with a slight limp, a continual reminder of a misunderstanding between himself and a high-spirited stallion on his father's Austin ranch.

The two men, chatting casually, had wandered into Troy's study. It was warm and conducive to conversation, but this one was making Troy very tense. He had hoped there would have been a chance for him to slip off by himself, but he felt cornered.

"Thank you again for doing such a beautiful service, Pastor," he said. The formality of his words stemmed from never having a meaningful conversation with the man before today. "I . . . I mean the whole family appreciated the kind things you said about my wife."

He and the pastor sat down in matching high-backed,

stuffed chairs across from each other. "She was a wonderful woman, Troy. So giving and interested in others. This tragedy has affected more people than you know."

"Beth had a lot of friends. I was surprised at how full the church was today. But I wonder if some of it was due to all the publicity." The second the words were out of his mouth, Troy felt embarrassed. He had no idea why he had said such a thing.

"Sometimes that happens," replied the pastor, trying to put him at ease. "But today, I don't think that was the case at all. Were you aware of all the wonderful work Beth was doing with the teen group at the church?"

Troy shook his head, looking down into his empty coffee cup. "Truthfully, Pastor, I wasn't aware of much of what Beth did there, and I'm ashamed that I wasn't. You see, I've got a very demanding job and . . ." He gazed up, hoping for some kind of exoneration. "Beth understood. . . . At least I hope she did."

"Yes, she understood you were committed to your career. Beth loved you very much, and she was very proud of you." Tom Shelby smiled warmly at Troy. "Your wife and I talked quite a bit. I was glad when she came to me asking to be more involved. At first, I think it was because she felt somehow it would help to bring her and Jenny closer."

"She had talked to me about that just a few weeks ago. Jenny's a handful. I've never figured out how to reach her, not really. Beth understood Jenny. Now I don't know what I'm going to do." Troy didn't want to admit how frightened he was of the confused fourteen-year-old girl. But he was terrified, and Tom Shelby seemed to know it.

"Anytime you want to talk, you know where to find me."

Troy suddenly recalled something Morgan had said in the yard the morning after the murder. He could not stop himself from passionately asking, "Tell me, Pastor, was Beth . . . lonely? Did I let her down?"

Putting his coffee cup on the nearby table, Tom Shelby leaned toward Troy, his eyes filled with compassion. "Sometimes our priorities get a little out of line, Troy. The work Beth did at the church was good for her. And I think it helped her cope with the time you spent away."

Troy was distraught. "Then you think I let her down."

"No, Troy, I don't. I think you let yourself down by not connecting on a more profound level with your family—with God. There's so much love and satisfaction there just waiting for you to reach out and take."

Feelings of deeper loss than he had ever felt stirred Troy's heart. Tears were rushing to his deep hazel eyes. Troy swallowed hard, trying not to lose his composure. "But now it's too late." His voice broke.

He quickly got to his feet, turned away from the pastor, and moved to the window. Troy rested his forearm on the window frame, staring out into the twilight. Tears of regret and loss ran down his square jaw. He made no attempt to wipe them away. "She's gone."

"No. It's not too late, Troy." The pastor slowly walked up behind him, placing a strong, encouraging hand on Troy's broad shoulder. "You've still got Jenny and Michael. They're going to need you more than ever now. And God . . . well, He's the God of second chances. When you're ready, He'll be there."

Thoughts of his beautiful Beth flooded Troy's mind. "Oh, Beth!" His emotions laid bare, Troy buried his head in his arm and surrendered himself to wave upon wave of irrepressible sobs.

Sixteen

*T*he media had a field day with Beth Woodsen's murder. A week after her death, speculation and a continuing macabre fascination still surfaced on a daily basis in the papers and on the radio. "Who killed the suburban mom?"

As expected, it also brought the whackos out of the woodwork. The homicide department received countless confessions. Hancock and Ballantine had no choice but to check out each one; they couldn't afford to overlook anything. The entire department was frustrated at the lack of evidence in this baffling case. The wrecked Bronco had given up nothing of significance, and trace evidence was almost nonexistent. Interviews with family, friends, and witnesses at the scene yielded nothing. At every turn, they came up empty.

Hancock hit his huge fist on his desk. "Killers make mistakes! So did this one! Somewhere he screwed up and we're gonna get him!"

A young man delivering interoffice mail tossed a manila envelope on Ballantine's desk. "Something from computer services for Detective Ballantine," called the clerk as he moved on, adding mail, memos, and files to In-boxes throughout the squad room.

"Finally it's here!" Chuck lunged for the envelope and tore off the end. He dumped a zip disk out of it and waved it in the air. "The scans of the Woodsen accident scene photos, Dell."

Annoyed, Dell replied, "Traffic sure took their sweet time. They should've been here the next day. I thought computers were supposed to make everything faster." Despite his negative tone, Hancock was excited. He took several giant steps over to his partner's desk and expectantly stood behind Chuck, eager to see the computer screen.

"Somehow they got shuffled into the wrong stack. It happens. Computer services thought they'd already been done. A people mistake—not a computer error."

Teasing him, Hancock said, "I bet that gal you're dating—that Trudy—is really a computer. I hear they're doing that these days. Building computers to make humans obsolete. They don't make mistakes, you know."

"Very funny," Ballantine chuckled as he accessed the disk. "You're just being stubborn, Dell! Computers are fabulous. You'd enjoy 'em if you'd give yourself half a chance. And they *are* more fascinating than a lot of folks I know. Present company excluded . . . most of the time."

"Get off it, Mayberry. I'm not interested, okay?" Dell was showing his impatience. "If those pictures are on that little disk, then where the heck are they?"

"Here they come."

Both detectives were glued to the computer screen, as pixel by pixel the photos were revealed, one after another. Each gruesome picture contained a different angle of the smashed Bronco resting upside down in the muddy ditch. The mutilated victim was lying next to the car, near the shattered front window, her left leg twisted up under her body.

"An ugly scene," Ballantine remarked as he moved from picture to picture. "If she was gonna die, I guess I'm glad it was *before* this happened."

Hancock leaned over and poked the screen with his index finger. "Hey, zoom in on the victim."

"Sure." Ballantine clicked his mouse on the Zoom icon. Beth Woodsen's empty, ashen face became clearer and clearer. "How's that?"

Hancock said nothing, but his usual apathetic expression softned as he stared at the young woman. "They looked a lot alike."

"Who?" asked Chuck, confused by his partner's rather fatherly demeanor.

"Beth and Morgan. The two sisters."

The young detective was surprised by his unrelated remark. "Yeah, I guess they did. So?"

"Just thinking about the Carruthers woman. How protective and determined she is."

"Looks like she's going to be hanging around awhile. Mr. Woodsen mentioned that if we need to talk with either of them, we can find them at his house."

"She's not going back to Minneapolis anytime soon—I can assure you of that. I know human nature, Mayberry. And that young woman's got to know who did this."

"What makes you so sure?"

"Trust me on this one. What if that lunatic killed your sister?" Hancock's pointed question caught Ballantine by surprise. "Always think about that, Mayberry. Think about their families, the people who loved them. It'll kick you in the seat of your pants."

"You going soft on me, Dell?" Chuck asked, half-serious. Ballantine wasn't cold, but so far he'd been able to keep his cases impersonal—victims and perpetrators.

Hancock quickly added, "Some of 'em just get under your skin." His spellbound gaze, focused on the beauty of the young woman pictured on the screen, seemed to indicate that the Woodsen case was quickly doing just that.

"Everyone has the same story about her. She was a clean-cut, suburban mom. A church member active in the community. It wasn't a robbery or a car-jacking. . . ." Dell's voice trailed off as he frowned, perplexed by the inconsistencies of this case.

Ballantine moved to another picture. Then another.

"Hey! Let me see that other picture," Dell said with great interest. "The one just before."

With one click they were looking at a shot of the driver's door, almost torn off the car, and the victim's purse. Several pieces of mail were lying haphazardly on the grass.

"Zoom in!" Chuck clicked the mouse. "More! More!" Dell was getting very excited. He poked the screen. "There! What's that? What do you see, Mayberry? What do you see?"

The young detective's eyes widened as he zoomed in closer

on the photograph. Then he saw why Dell was so excited. "Spiders! Veleske's black widows." Checking back through some of the previous photos, it was unmistakable. "Black widow spiders are crawling out of the wrecked car. Weird, isn't it?"

"So, Mayberry, tell me—did Beth Woodsen's car just happen to roll into a spider nest, or did someone leave us a deadly message?"

Deep in thought, Dell Hancock returned to his desk and opened the Woodsen file, determined to search for the answer.

Seventeen

The fog that had engulfed Morgan lifted to a fine mist, and, for the first time since the funeral, she sensed a desire in her spirit to look beyond the confines of her sorrow. Small changes were taking place in the Woodsen home. Like tiny leaves pushing their way into the spring air, life struggled to find new hope, new reasons for going on. Seven days had passed since the murder, and this was the first day Morgan didn't have to imagine that last Friday, Beth was alive. Or last Saturday, she was working in her rose bed.

Flowers and cards had stopped arriving in droves. Gloria made sure all of the casserole and cake dishes were returned with proper "thank you" notes before Troy took her home to Piney Bend on Wednesday. She was planning to stay to care for her grandchildren and Troy, until Morgan announced she would not be returning to Minneapolis for a while.

"Is it okay with you if I stick around, Troy? I'd like to be here for you and the kids," she'd said, knowing what his answer would be.

Breathing a deep sigh of relief, he replied, "I didn't want to ask you to stay. I know what your job means to you, Morgan. But if you're sure . . ."

"I'm very sure," she added.

"You're an angel. A real angel. I can't tell you what it means to me—and to the kids. I don't know what we'd do without you." Troy's handsome face broke into the first real smile she'd seen since this ordeal began. Morgan's decision had postponed, at least for the moment, Troy's fearful and overwhelming new responsibilities.

Not surprisingly, Troy returned to work almost immediately. He'd come to Morgan only a day or two after the funeral apologizing. "I feel like I'm abandoning you and the children, but I have to go back to work. I can't stand being here . . . in this house. I hope you understand."

Of course she understood. Returning to the only place that helped ease the pain and memories was the sane thing for him to do. But Morgan wasn't anxious to leave her sister's house. Being around Beth's things, picking them up, touching them, brought an inexplicable comfort.

It also gave her tremendous joy to be needed so much. And then there was the promise Morgan had made the day of the funeral. *I'll find out who did this to you, Beth.* The words were not empty claims said in a moment of grief, but a promise between sisters—one she intended to keep.

With Michael and Jenny in school, the house felt empty and big. Living alone all of these years, she had become comfortable with apartments and townhouses. Empty houses had an entirely different feel. They were so silent. Unfamiliar sounds startled her. The refrigerator suddenly clicking on. The dryer buzzing when the cycle was complete. The creaking of a wall for absolutely no reason at all. All sounds that must have been commonplace for Beth.

Morgan longed to do something "normal," something to ground her and make her feel as though life was continuing. Noticing her laptop computer, Morgan realized she hadn't checked her email since she left Minneapolis.

Taking the computer to the table in the sunlit kitchen, she opened it, the screen automatically coming to life. While it loaded Windows, she fixed herself a cup of coffee. Adding two Sweet'n Low packets, she stirred it and took a sip. Screwing up her face, she said, "I hate coffee. Why do I drink it?" Shrugging, she took another sip.

Connecting the computer's phone cord to an extra kitchen phone jack, it took only moments for her modem to dial and access Heritage Design's private email service. She entered her screen name and password. The familiar female computerized voice said, "Welcome to Heritage Design. You have mail."

Morgan had sent Carl a brief email to inform him of Beth's death—she didn't want him to find out through the grapevine—and the firm had sent a beautiful arrangement to the funeral. Carl, of course, included a touching personal note. Opening her personal mailbox, Morgan knew she would find many condolence notes from colleagues but wasn't in the mood to read them. Her eyes scanned the list. When she saw *kwhitney@heritagedesign.com*, her stomach tightened.

She hadn't thought about Kevin much at all in the past week. However, she had half expected him to show up at the funeral. It was a great relief that he hadn't. She missed him but didn't feel like reading his note. Passing it by, she went directly to an email from Carl. With a double-click on the title, it opened.

```
TO: mcarruthers@heritagedesign.com
FROM: cmercer@heritagedesign.com
SUBJECT: Thinking of you

My dear Morgan,
    I decided not to call as I'm sure you have been deluged
with phone calls. But you know I am here for you, any time,
any hour. Word of this tragedy has stunned not only me but
also the entire firm.
    If there is anything at all I can do, please contact me.
Of course you are missed, but take all the time necessary.
I'm anxious for your return.
    My prayers are with you and your family.
    Your friend always--Carl
```

It was good just to read his words. Morgan had never been one to make a lot of female friends. Close relationships were not easy to come by for a driven career woman. That was one of the reasons Beth had continued to be her closest friend and confidant.

She moved her mouse to Reply, and a fresh email window popped up.

```
TO: cmercer@heritagedesign.com
FROM: mcarruthers@heritagedesign.com
```

SUBJECT: Many Thanks

Dear Carl,

The many flowers sent by the firm were greatly appreciated. But it was your note that touched me the most. I am blessed to have such a good friend and mentor.

Life here is difficult, at best. I'm missing Beth dreadfully, but find that taking care of my niece and nephew, as well as Troy, my brother-in-law, helps me to cope with my own grief.

I know you are aware that the police are sure my sister was murdered. This came as a terrible shock, and part of me still doesn't believe it. Yet I know it is true.

I've thought about returning, but, Carl, for now, I am needed here. I cannot even give you an estimate as to when I might return. Please understand I have things here that I must resolve before I can even begin thinking about coming back to my life there.

Please stay in touch, as your notes mean so much to me. I'll keep you posted on the continuing investigation.

Morgan

After reading through several other notes she thought important, Morgan deleted Kevin's unread email. She had just signed off when the phone rang.

"Hi, how's it going?"

Morgan was happy to hear Troy's voice. "It's quiet. Big house you have here."

"I thought it might be getting to you. Just wanted to check in." The cheeriness in his voice was false, and she knew it. But she adored him for trying.

"I think I might go out for a drive. Take a look around. Don't want you to worry." She didn't want to add any unnecessary concern if he called and didn't find her there. "Let me give you my cell phone number. I always keep it with me."

"I've got it. But, listen, if you leave the house . . . and maybe even while you're at home, turn on the alarm system. I gave you the code. The kids know it—they can get in."

"Okay. Try to have a good day. Things are okay here at home. Really. But . . . could you possibly tell me what the kids might eat for supper? I'm not much of a cook. How about Whoppers?"

He laughed. "They'd love it!"

"Then Whoppers it is! See you later."

She was glad their call had ended on an up note. Morgan grabbed her bag from the kitchen counter and headed out the door, first punching in the security system code. The long, steady beep indicated she had sixty seconds to open the door, exit, and close it.

Eighteen

I can't believe you actually gave up chicken-fried steak and country gravy!" remarked Ballantine as he and his partner returned to the squad room from lunch at Nettie's Diner.

"My heart thanks me by continuing to thumpity-thump-thump. You think it's easy, Mayberry?" Dell chuckled. "Wednesday's special was my favorite thing in the world, next to fishing and the Chicago Bears."

"You just might outlive all of us. Working out and grazing the salad bar—I've got to hand it to you. I never believed you'd stick with it." The young detective affectionately slapped his partner's broad back.

Hannah came out of her office with a stack of faxes. "Hey, fellas. The rest of the credit card records and bank statements came in on the Woodsen case."

A look of anticipation crossed Ballantine's round but attractive face as she handed them over to him. "Thanks, Hannah. Let's hope it's not another dead end."

"Detective Hancock." The voice was familiar, and the large detective turned to find Morgan Carruthers standing near the door.

"Ms. Carruthers . . ." He was obviously surprised. "What're you doing here?"

"Can we talk?" Morgan asked.

"Sure thing." The detective pulled up a wooden chair and motioned for her to be seated. "Ballantine, you want to join us?"

The young man eagerly pulled up another chair and greeted the young woman.

Morgan began by announcing, "I'm not leaving Texas until this murder is solved. Just thought you'd like to know."

"There's no reason for you to hang around here, not on our account. You and Mr. Woodsen have been cleared."

"I know, but finding out who killed Beth is the only way I can ever go back to my own life. She'd do the same for me." Morgan's face radiated the resolve and seriousness of her statement.

Ballantine shot a concerned look toward his partner, then spoke to her. "Ms. Carruthers, we're dealing with a cold-blooded killer here. I hope you're not intending to get personally involved in the investigation."

"I plan to do whatever I can. I'd like for you to keep me appraised of what you uncover. I think that's a fair request."

Hancock sat on the edge of his desk and leaned in toward the persistent young woman. "Detective Ballantine may not have made himself clear. We can't have you poking around with a deranged murderer on the loose. The guy's as nervous as a cat by now. You don't want to cross his path."

Morgan cocked her head to one side and listened, showing no sign of retreating.

Hancock continued, "It's commendable to see you so interested in solving this crime, but we're on top of it, I assure you."

"What progress have you made?" Morgan asked, knowing that at their last conversation with Troy yesterday, they were still quite in the dark.

Dell looked toward the ceiling, then, after a moment, his eyes searched out hers. "I'm sure it frustrates you that we don't already know who this animal is—but killers make mistakes. They always do. This guy's pretty clever, and right now he's thinking he may have gotten away with it."

"Has he?"

Ballantine jumped in. "Not on your life! We'll get him. But what gives us hesitation is that this creep could be carrying out your groceries at the local store or delivering your laundry."

"This isn't a game, Ms. Carruthers," Hancock tried once again. "Please, let us do our job, and we'll keep you up to date as we see necessary."

Morgan got to her feet, looking even more determined than she had before. She smiled pleasantly at Hancock, who knew what was coming, as she said, "Detective, you go ahead and do your job. And if I want to go to the corner store or send out the laundry—that's my business. I just thought it would be productive if we worked together. Obviously, you don't agree. Good afternoon."

Both men stood as Morgan turned and briskly walked out the door.

"Woo-wee. That's one headstrong woman." Ballantine shook his head in complete astonishment.

Dell's response was one of grave concern. "And she's just gutsy enough to get herself killed if she's not careful." He angrily sat down in his desk chair. "What did I tell you? I need this like a jelly donut à la mode."

Hannah approached from her office. "You handled it the best you could, Dell. We can't put a squad out to watch her every move."

"You might wish we had, Hannah." Dell grabbed the faxed credit card reports and started going over them.

"Stop trying to save the world, Dell. You can't do it," Hannah concluded.

Chuck took off his jacket and rolled up his shirtsleeves, remarking to the sergeant, "This one's really getting to Hancock."

Dell didn't look up from the faxes as he stated, "I just don't want to see the life of another young woman cut short by some maniac."

"It's okay to care about her, Dell." Hannah made the statement knowing he was the kind of man who made a difference because he did care—he never left a stone unturned. Putting him on the case was giving it to the best.

"Good luck," Hannah smiled sincerely as she turned and headed back to her office.

Dell called, "I'm not forgiving you for this. I thought we

were pals. How am I going to leave with that woman's name still on the victim board?"

She confidently gave him the thumbs up sign. "When it's time for you to head out, it'll be erased."

"Yeah, from your mouth to God's ears," he mumbled, returning his gaze to the reports from Visa, Master Card, American Express, Texaco, Mobil, and almost every department store in Dallas, including Neiman Marcus.

Chuck pulled up a chair and leaned his arms on Hancock's desk. "Anything interesting in those bills?"

"Not yet. But there's got to be something." He shoved half the stack toward Chuck, tossing him a yellow highlighter. "Here. Look for any activity on or around March sixth."

The young man stopped, staring at one of the bank statements. "Wow! Would you take a look at this bank balance!"

Hancock slowly looked up at his partner in annoyed disbelief. "Mayberry, I realize you're used to looking at overdraft notices, but could you please concentrate on the business at hand. March sixth!"

Dell examined the Mobil statement, running his finger down the list of transactions. "His was card one. Hers was card two." His finger stopped on a charge. "Looks like the last time Mrs. Woodsen used her card was on February eighteenth. Unless she kept that Bronco in the garage, she'd have to be pulling into a station in a week or so. But it looks like it wasn't at a Mobil."

They both continued to search for the important date. "Here, she filled up at Texaco on February twenty-seventh." He sighed. "Let's hope she did a lot of driving and filled it up one more time." But he found no gas purchase on either card.

"She could've used one of the other cards," Ballantine added, still searching the statements in his pile. With a big smile, he snapped his fingers. "Hey, Dell, here's an ATM withdrawal on March sixth at 12:46 P.M. for sixty dollars. It was made at Texas Commerce Bank's Preston Road branch. Troy Woodsen told us he didn't make any withdrawals that entire week."

Hancock found another. "Visa. March sixth at 1:12 P.M. Computer City, in Farmer's Branch. No one's said anything about her being into computers."

"Maybe it was for her kids."

"Who cares? Get on the phone and have a copy of that charge slip faxed over here . . . *now*! I want to know what Beth Woodsen was buying."

It wasn't long until the detective found another charge on March 6. The transaction occured at 10:32 A.M. "Hey, Mayberry, ever hear of a place called the Cybersurf Café?"

"Sure. It's one of those new computer cafés. You can rent time on their computers and surf the Web. It's a new twist to sell a cup of coffee."

"They serve food and stuff?" Dell was amazed.

"Sure. There are several of them around the area." He paused. "What was a classy lady like Beth Woodsen doing hanging out at a place like that? You know they've got to have one or two computers at that house."

Dell felt that the statements were beginning to give them some idea of Beth's movements the day of her murder, so he grabbed a Dallas map and pinned it to the wall behind his desk. "Now let's start looking at Beth Woodsen's day."

With a satisfied grin, Chuck motioned with his head and said, "Come here, Hancock. Let me show you something."

"I don't have time for a computer lesson. We're finally getting somewhere."

Chuck quickly brought up his computer system's mapping program. "I'm going to save you a lot of time!"

Begrudgingly, the big man stood behind Ballantine. He watched in amazement as Chuck accessed a map of Dallas. He zoomed in on the North Dallas area. "Now let's put a mark here at the Texas Commerce Bank." He clicked on his mouse, and a red *X* appeared on the map at that location. Beside the *X* he typed in the time Beth had been there, 12:46 P.M.

Chuck was getting excited. Snapping his fingers in the air, he called, "The next one. Give me the next one."

Hancock was always irritated by Ballantine's finger snapping gesture. "Hold on to your gigabyte."

Chuck shot him an amused glance.

"Surprised I knew that word, huh?" Dell replied. Reaching over and grabbing the Woodsen statements off his desk, he directed his young partner. "Okay, okay. Let's see. Computer City, Farmer's Branch."

Locating the exact address, Ballantine placed another red X on the map, adding the time, 1:12 P.M. The next one he added was the Cybersurf Café. Again a red X and the time, 10:32 A.M., were added.

Impressed, but not quite sure why, Hancock mumbled, "Okay, so now what?"

"Let's add one more." He put a red X at 458 Jasmine Court, the Woodsen home. "Now, the daughter told us that her mother took the nine-year-old to school that morning. Check your notes, Dell. What time?"

The seasoned detective was way ahead of him. He had thumbed through his little notebook. "She left the house about eight A.M."

Dell watched Chuck type 8:00 next to the red X. Then, using his mouse and a drawing tool, Ballantine drew a circle around the four X's. He saved the file under Woodsen and sent it to the printer.

In seconds, they had a map in their hands. "Here you go, Dell. Now, what do you think?" Ballantine asked with a smirk.

Dell was impressed, but there was no way he was going to give his young partner the satisfaction. Trying to hide a smile, he said, "The printout's a little fuzzy. But it'll do."

"You're something. But you're edging over to my side. And it's a beautiful sight."

"Don't push it, Mayberry. Just don't push it."

Nineteen

*L*ight from the computer screen spilled out into the disorderly bedroom, casting an eerie, otherworldly countenance. A small lamp on the bedside table was the only other light source.

Haphazard piles of computer magazines, books, and disks were scattered everywhere. The bed obviously hadn't been made for weeks. Clothing hung from the bedpost and chairs, and a collection of dirty cups and glasses had been negligently left on the computer desk.

Suddenly the door to the room opened and a figure quickly entered, closing it behind him. He went immediately to the computer. In seconds, his modem was opening the door to the Internet. He was making his way through cyberspace to the Catacomb Website.

The appearance of the underworld site fit the surroundings of its visitor's disheveled, dark domain. He nervously drummed his fingers on the tops of the keys.

"Okay. Where are you?"

He didn't have to wait long. Quickly a Private Chamber Chat window popped open.

ARA: i told you to lay low.
CYCLOSA: I'm scared. It's on the TV and the radio. Things are getting crazy here!!!! The police know the Woodsen woman was murdered! They're talking to everybody. What if somebody saw something? I thought they were supposed to

think it was an accident.

ARA: that was a long shot ... you knew that.
they're not as stupid as I'd hoped ... but now
it's so entertaining to watch them run around
chasing their tails ... oh how i enjoy this
<snicker>

CYCLOSA: But what about me? Now what do I do?!

ARA: you keep your mouth shut :-(

CYCLOSA: But what if they know something—you
know, something about what really happened?

ARA: sometimes it is necessary to sacrifice one
for the good of many...

CYCLOSA: Am I the sacrifice?

ARA: i will do what i can to protect you.

CYCLOSA: You lied to me!

ARA: FYI ... it is not wise to call me a liar.
they have not come for you ... have they?

CYCLOSA: Not yet. But I'm scared.

ARA: don't let panic make you do something
stupid ... you must continue to be a faithful
follower, my spiderling.

CYCLOSA: I did what you told me to do. I killed
her. Now what about me?

ARA: i chose you to do this small task for me
because you have proven to be a faithful member
of the Gathering ... trust me and you will
continue to thrive amongst us ... my
principality is growing day by day. i guide the
minds of many...

CYCLOSA: But there's trouble. Things aren't
cooling off. Beth Woodsen's sister is hanging
around. She's starting to ask questions.

ARA: AISI then perhaps she needs a little
message from me ... after her sister's
unfortunate ''accident'' i think we can easily
convince her that it is in her best interest to
leave this place ... you will take care of that
for me?

```
CYCLOSA:  Leave a message? Or kill her, too?
ARA:  it is i who tell you what to do ... it's
almost time for the Gathering—your fellow
spiderlings will give you renewed strength.
CYCLOSA:  When will it be? When is the
Gathering? Soon??
ARA:  you will be contacted.
```

Immediate disconnection from the Catacomb left the anxious visitor with an empty blue screen and a flashing cursor.

In an attempt to bolster his deteriorating confidence, he pushed up the sleeve of his T-shirt and gazed at the small tattoo of a spider on the inside of his upper left arm. "Ara is all powerful. He is my protector."

Soon the Gathering will take place, and the others can help me. The power of that thought lessened his fears.

๖๙ ๖๙ ๖๙ ๖๙

A hand inside a heavy, black glove moved through the darkness of a small metal storage shed searching for a familiar piece of dirty string. Finding it, a sharp pull turned on a bare overhead light bulb. The shed was a disorderly jumble of yard tools and boxes of all sizes overflowing with old clothing and toys no longer wanted by a child long past the age of innocence.

Artisans who work only in the dark had spun delicate, silken strands and created spiraling webs throughout a careless stack of discarded furniture. The damp dirt floor caused everything in the shed to rot, and the smell was sickening.

Affectionately, the gloved hand slowly stroked the curved tip of a blue fiberglass snow ski propped against the back wall with its mate. They were still tied with a red ribbon. A small folded card dangled from the bow, decorated with a smiling Santa face and a candy cane. A gift never given, or one not received. Unlike everything else in this foul chamber, the gift was still shiny and unsoiled, as though it had recently been dusted.

A small area on the ground had been cleared to make room for an overturned, slatted wooden orange crate. The colorful labels on the ends of the crate were ripped and faded, but the words *Valencia Oranges* could still be recognized.

Two gloved hands carefully reached for the crate and flipped it over, revealing two small Plexiglas cubes with very tiny holes punched in the top. The moment light hit the cubes they became filled with bizarre activity. The eight-legged inhabitants of the cubes frantically searched out the darkness.

One of the cubes contained several live, venomous brown recluse spiders, and the other housed six large black widow spiders. The visitor sat on a nearby box. He passed over the black widow cube and picked up the other. Holding it in front of him, he turned it slowly, observing his squirming captives.

With precise movements, he took a small brown envelope from his pocket and opened the top of the cube just far enough to allow one captive to escape. Putting the envelope next to the opening, he watched with pleasure as the spider crawled into it, sensing the darkness.

Immediately replacing the cube, he covered his treasured collection with the orange crate. A sharp tug on the dirty string, and darkness reclaimed the musty shed.

Twenty

Morgan was thrilled when Troy told her their cleaning lady, Celetia, would be coming back. After what had happened, he wasn't sure she would.

"You've done a wonderful job." Morgan was complimenting Celetia in the upstairs bathroom when she heard the loud, excited voice of her nine-year-old nephew coming from somewhere down the hall.

"Get him! Kill him! Yeah!"

"Michael! What's wrong?" She ran down the hall toward the sound of his voice.

"You're dead! You're dead!" he hollered. He was in Jenny's room.

Terrified, Morgan rushed in. "Michael! What's wrong?" She stopped short. Michael was mesmerized by the bloody, violent, animated action on the computer screen, cheering on a gory battle between nightmarish monsters.

Morgan took a deep breath. She wanted to yank him away from that violence, but instead she took a moment to regain control of herself. Walking up behind him, she said, "Honey, what's that you're playing?"

"Death Planet. It's cool, isn't it?" He never looked up but continued working the keys and the joystick like a pro. "Yeaaaaa! Gotcha!" He thrust his right fist into the air. "I'm the champion! Look at that score, Aunt Morgie!"

Morgan forced a smile, realizing he had no idea why this would upset her. Kneeling down beside his chair, she pushed his light brown hair out of his eyes. "Where did you get this game?"

"From Cody. He let me use it. It's really neat, isn't it?"

"I don't think you should be playing this game, honey. It's too violent." She tried not to sound judgmental or harsh.

Michael spun the desk chair around so he was looking directly at his aunt. "Mom wouldn't let me play it, either. But now it doesn't matter what I do. Who cares?"

He looked so lost, so vulnerable. Morgan took his small, cherub face in her hands and kissed his forehead. "Oh yes, it does matter, honey. Your dad cares, and so do I. We care very much."

He jumped up. The same angry look came across his face, the look she saw when he was playing the game. "You're not my mother! Jenny says you're trying to take her place. She says we don't have to listen to you. So don't try to tell me what to do." He began to sob. "My mother's dead! I don't have a mother!" Michael ran from the room yelling. "If she loved me, why did she go away?"

Morgan was stunned at his angry words. She hadn't realized the hostility both the children felt toward her. "How can I help them?" she said out loud. The shock of their mother's death had now become loss and fear. All the mindless activity of that first week had left them totally unprepared for the cold reality of their day-to-day existence without Beth.

Morgan sank into the desk chair in complete despair. Her words, first intended to be only thoughts, took form and became despondent pleas. "Beth, I can't do this! I don't know anything about taking care of children." She felt her own anger growing. "How could you leave me with all this responsibility?" Morgan's frustration peaked, then going limp, she plaintively asked, "What am I supposed to do?" She was overwhelmed at the void she was trying to fill.

Regaining her composure, Morgan removed the CD game disk and returned it to its case. She'd have to speak with the mother of Michael's friend.

As she was leaving Jenny's room, she almost collided with her niece, who was rushing in from school.

"You're early," Morgan exclaimed, checking her watch.

"Cade gave me a ride." Jenny looked irritated at finding her there. "What're you doing in here?"

"I was just talking with Michael. He was playing a CD and I—"

Jenny exploded. "He's not supposed to be in my room unless he asks me first."

"Calm down, Jen. You have to be more patient with your brother right now. He's going through a tough time."

"And I guess I'm not?" Jenny moved to the window and stared out. "I don't like people just coming in here anytime they please. He wouldn't have done that if Mom were still here."

Morgan was in for a battle if she was to reach Jenny. Remembering how rebellious she herself had been as a teenager, she knew this was not the time to lose her temper. With restraint she said, "I understand how you feel, honey."

The young girl whirled around angrily. "No, you don't! You don't have any idea how I feel about anything. Mom didn't understand, either, so how could you?"

Before Morgan could gather herself together from this unexpected attack, the phone rang. Jenny grabbed the receiver. "Hello." Her expression changed and her voice softened. "Hi—just a second." Turning to her aunt, "Do you mind if I have some privacy? Or is that changing, too?"

Shaking her head in bewilderment, Morgan left the room, closing the door behind her.

❧　❧　❧　❧

Later that afternoon, Celetia went to the kitchen doorway and called out in broken English, "I am finish, Miss Morgan!"

Morgan ran downstairs and entered the room just as Celetia was gathering her purse and jacket. "I go now to the bus."

"Thank you so much, Celetia. You did a wonderful job."

The friendly but quiet woman, who had been coming to the Woodsen home for over four years, had tears in her eyes as she said, "I am so sorry, ma'am. Miss Beth, she was such nice lady. Too good for such a bad thing. She always helping everybody."

"I'm happy you thought so much of my sister," Morgan replied with a warm smile. "And thank you again for coming back to help me take care of things around here." As Celetia collected her things and headed for the laundry room door, Morgan asked with a touch of pleading, "You will be back on Saturday?"

The cleaning woman nodded her head. "Yes, ma'am. Tuesday and Saturday, every week. Good-bye."

Celetia grabbed a bucket of soapy water to dump into the sink in the laundry room on her way out. As she reached around the corner and turned on the light in the small room, her eyes caught the rapid movement of a large spider crawling on the floor near her feet. A scream erupted as the bucket fell to the floor, splashing water in all directions.

Racing to the room, Morgan found Celetia frozen in her tracks, pointing wildly toward the darkness under the sink. "Spider! *Big* spider!"

"Get back!" Pushing Celetia out of the way, Morgan grabbed a broom from its wall clip. As the spider scurried toward a dark corner, she brought the broom down on it with a powerful thud.

Celetia was shaking. "Spiders . . . they scare me."

"They don't exactly thrill me either, Celetia." Morgan turned the broom over and was relieved to find the spider's remains stuck to the bristles.

"Don't touch it!"

Startled by the deep male voice, Morgan dropped the broom and found herself staring at a tall, handsome young man standing in the laundry room doorway. He had obviously entered through the open garage door.

"Are you all right?" he asked.

"I was until you snuck up on me." Morgan was breathless.

Celetia answered in a gasping, terrified voice. "Big spider!" She held up her hands in the exaggerated gesture often used by weekend fisherman to describe their catch. "Mucho grande!"

Taking a look at the eight-legged intruder, which was now stuck to the broom, Morgan replied, "Well, mucho grande somehow seems a bit too 'mucho.' "

The man smiled. "I guarantee he was more frightened of you than you were of him. Spiders are looking for much smaller prey."

"Lucky for us. Well, thanks for coming to our rescue, Mr. . . ." Morgan said, tipping her head quizzically, fighting the urge to stare into his emerald green eyes. "Mr. . . ."

"Oh, I'm Justin Maguire." He offered his hand to Morgan. Cautiously, Morgan moved back. Justin self-consciously pulled back his hand and jammed it into his blue jean pocket. "I'm doing some construction work for Lynn Stiles," he replied, making a motion with his head. "A couple of houses down. You know, Cade's mom."

"Oh yes, Jenny's friend." Her body language relaxed somewhat.

"Sorry I frightened you."

As the two talked, Celetia quickly wiped up the spilled water and then stated, "I'm going to miss bus, ma'am." She picked up her purse and rushed passed Morgan.

"Good-bye, Celetia!" Morgan called to the still-shaken woman hurrying through the garage and down the driveway. "Gosh, I hope she comes back." She laughed nervously, giving the broom handle one more push with the tip of her finger. "Just making sure."

The two strangers looked at each other for an awkward moment. She broke the silence with an offer she really had not intended to make. "Could I offer you a glass of iced tea? It's the least I can do—for my knight in blue jeans."

He was visibly pleased. "Sure. That'd be great. You must be Morgan—Mrs. Woodsen's sister."

"Yes, I am."

He followed her into the kitchen and straddled a barstool at the island counter as if he'd been there a million times. "You two sure look alike—in the face, I mean."

"I guess we did. But in so many other ways, we were very different." Morgan paused. For some unknown reason the young man made her uncomfortable. "Did you know my sister?"

Having made a large pitcher of her mom's honey-sweetened tea earlier in the day, Morgan now took it from the refrigerator. As she sat it on the kitchen island, she could feel him watching her every move.

"I only met Mrs. Woodsen once, but Lynn talks about her all the time. Everyone thought she was a terrific lady."

Wishing she had not made this offer, Morgan got two large tea glasses and filled them with ice from the dispenser in the refrigerator door. "Could you do me a big favor, Mr. Maguire? Would you get that spider out of here?"

"Sure thing." He hopped off the stool and pulled a pair of work gloves from his back pocket. Putting on the left one, he picked up the spider carcass and dropped it into the garbage can just outside the laundry room door. "You did him in alright. I wouldn't want to be on the receiving end of one of your swings. Hate to tell you, but looks to me like he might've been a real troublemaker."

"What do you mean?" Morgan inquired, pouring the tea and offering him a glass.

He perched himself back up on the stool. Morgan stood on the opposite side of the island. "I think it was poisonous."

"Wow. Lucky Celetia saw it."

"She's lucky you're such a good shot with a broom." He paused to take a drink of tea. "But Texas and spiders sort of go together. It's a good thing we've got a lot of other things to offer—like bluebonnets and barbecue."

"Hi." Troy's well-built frame nearly filled the doorway between the laundry room and the kitchen. His suit coat was draped over his right arm, and his huge, satchel-type briefcase overflowed with papers, building plans, and folders.

Justin was visibly disappointed as he quickly climbed off the stool. "Howdy."

Troy's unexpected arrival brought an easy smile to Morgan's face. She could tell he was tired. "Hi, Troy. How about some tea?"

"Sounds great." Troy immediately walked over to the young man, extending his hand. "Troy Woodsen."

"Justin Maguire." The two men cordially shook hands.

"Justin's doing some construction over at Lynn Stiles' home. He sort of came to my rescue a little while ago."

Troy looked worried. "Rescue?"

"Aw, it was just a little unexpected visitor in the laundry

room—a brown recluse spider.''

"Are you all right, Morgan?''

She nodded her head. "I'm fine.''

"The little lady took care of it all by herself. A very resource-ful gal. Didn't need me at all.'' Justin gave her a shadow of a smile, then returned his attention to Troy. His voice became se-rious and sincere. "Mr. Woodsen, please let me offer my con-dolences. I'm very sorry about what happened.''

Troy quickly said, "Thanks,'' then changed the subject. "Morgan, I'll be in my study. Got a few calls to make.'' His voice was a bit cooler as he said, "Nice to have met you, Mr. Ma-guire.'' Picking up his coat and briefcase, he left.

Morgan got another glass, filled it with ice. "I think he could use some of this tea. Thanks for your help, Justin.''

The young man finished his tea in one long swig. "Anytime, Morgan. I'm around a lot. Hope I'll be seeing you.'' He started to leave. Then he stopped and turned to her. "You staying for a while?''

"Yes. There's still a lot to do here. And Troy—'' she paused to correct herself— "the whole family needs my support. And I need theirs.''

"Then I'm sure we'll be seeing each other. Bye.''

"Bye. And thanks again.''

Morgan slowly closed the door, turning the deadbolt. She raised her eyebrow slightly as she thought of those emerald green eyes. But it was a fleeting thought that left her in an in-stant.

The door to Troy's study was closed. Morgan listened, and he didn't seem to be on the phone. She knocked. "Troy?''

"Come on in.''

She entered and took the cool glass of tea over to him. "You look like you could use this.''

"Thanks.'' He took the glass and drew in a long, deep breath, letting it out very slowly. "The days aren't so bad, you know. I'm busy, and people have finally stopped getting that pit-iful look on their faces and asking, 'How are you doing?' '' He paused. "But coming home . . . that's the worst part. Turning into the cul-de-sac. Not seeing her car in the garage.'' His voice sounded a little cheerier when he added, "But it was great to see your car there."

Today had certainly been a day for looking at life without Beth. Michael, Jenny, and now Troy. Without thinking, Morgan said, "I don't think any of us realized what it would be like to try to get back to life as usual. Those first days, there were so many people around, so much activity. We didn't really have time to think."

"I didn't want to think about life without her."

"Neither did I." Morgan sat on a nearby chair.

For a while they just quietly gathered their thoughts. It felt so nice to have him home; the house was so empty when Troy wasn't there. How much worse must it be for him, without Beth?

"I hope this isn't the wrong time to bring this up, Troy, but I need to talk to you about Michael and Jenny."

For a moment Troy looked overburdened, and Morgan thought perhaps she should wait. Then he leaned forward, putting his arms on his thighs. He intertwined the fingers of his strong hands and gave her a warm, open smile. "Of course. You can come to me anytime. I sometimes forget the tough position you've been tossed into."

She heaved a sigh of relief, thankful he was making this a lot easier than she thought it would be. "You know, I was a pretty good sister."

"Pretty good? You were terrific."

"But I'm afraid I'm a lousy 'fill-in' mom. I'm used to being the visiting aunt who pops in with a gift and a hug. Spending a little time with the kids, having fun. Then packing up and splitting."

"The day-to-day stuff getting you down?" He understood.

"It's frightening. I want to do the right things, Troy. But now the gift they need from me . . . well, I'm afraid it's something I might not be able to give."

He sat back in his large, brown leather chair and looked toward the ceiling. "Boy, do I understand. I'm as scared as you are."

"That's not exactly what I was hoping to hear."

He looked into her eyes with compassion. "Morgan, we're quite a pair, you and I. You see, the truth is I spent so much time away from my kids that I don't have any answers for you. Beth was always there them. Oh, I don't mean I never did anything with them or had to discipline them, because I did. But over the long haul, it was Beth. I depended upon her so much. Much more than I ever realized. Morgan, this is probably the toughest thing I've ever faced."

Her voice feigned reassurance she wished she felt. "Then we'll just make it through as best we can. Mistake by mistake."

Troy reached out and took her hand. "You're really something. Why did we spend so many years avoiding each other?"

Morgan gently clasped his hand in a silent response.

Twenty-one

*D*edra Koehler marched through the newsroom at a brisk pace. Even though she was a rather short, heavy-set woman of fifty-four, she radiated energy. Gray was attempting to take over her thick head of black hair, and it was winning. She wore it cut very short, so it was all but impossible to hide the square bandage near her hairline that was being held in place by two strips of white medical tape. Her skin looked red and inflamed around the injury.

With her thick Texas drawl, she cheerfully stated, "Howdy, everyone! I'm back!" Heads popped up, and voices returned her greeting. It was obvious that she was well liked.

"Welcome back, lady of leisure," one fellow reporter shouted.

"Couldn't stay away from the smell of the ink, could you?" laughed Molly Hansford, the food columnist for the *North Dallas Daily News*.

"It's a sickness, Molly. A real sickness. I reckon I'd just move right on in here if they'd let me."

"We missed you." Molly went to hug her friend and immediately noticed the bandage. She held her back at arms length. "So what did you do to yourself, Dedra? Will you look at that! All red and puffy."

"Oh, it's nothin'. You know I'm hardly ever at home, and I guess some visitors moved into my bedroom. Spiders. Two of 'em that I could find."

"My goodness. You were stung by a spider?"

"Bitten is the correct term, Molly. Trust me, it's bitten." She crooked her index finger and her middle finger and moved them toward Molly. "They've got these two little fangs!"

"Ooooww! Get away from me. I hate spiders." She brushed her clothing, as though they were crawling on her. "How'd it happen?"

"I guess they must've been near my bed. I was almost asleep and *zap*! One of the little guys had a late night snack." She touched her neck. "Hurt like the devil, too, I'll tell you. Even got a little sick to my stomach. But I'm fine. Gonna be just fine."

Molly shivered and put her arms around herself. "Isn't that the strangest thing. Now, thanks to you, I'll never be able to get into my bed again without shaking the sheets. Dedra Koehler, you've done it now. You've turned me into an arachnophobic."

"I keep forgetting you're such a worry wart. Shouldn't have told you." Dedra became agitated as she continued. "By the way, I'm not looking to take any more forced vacations, either. I've fired my doctor. He couldn't quite get the concept that my work *is* my life. Who needs 'em anyway? My grandmother lived in Waco, the middle of nowhere, and she never had a shot or a cough drop. Lived to be eighty-nine. I'd say that's just about long enough for anybody."

Molly, obviously still a bit bothered by Dedra's experience, wandered slowly over to her desk. Dedra headed for her office. Her two-week vacation had been exasperating, and she was furious about it. She simply didn't know what to do with herself when an editor wasn't waiting for a column and she didn't have a deadline. They had even blocked her phone messages so she couldn't pick them up from home. She was livid.

She had counted the days until she could get back and give her editor a piece of her mind. If she didn't love her job so much, she would have quit. But today she could get back into the swing of her popular column, "In the Know."

A leading investigative reporter, Dedra had a tendency to grab hold of a story and shake it like a mad dog until it gave up every last buried bone. The last thing anyone with something to hide wanted was to be the subject of one of Debra Koehler's investigations.

She entered her small office and immediately felt at home. It was one of the few with a window, and she'd earned it. Wading through stacks of magazines, books, and papers, she tossed her makeshift briefcase on the messy desk and flipped on her computer.

In reality, her "briefcase" was a large, stained, and faded yellow canvas bag that sported the words "I just look mean!" Her daughter gave it to her ten or so years ago, well before a drug addiction claimed her life. Dedra missed her daughter dreadfully. The last eight years of Nancy's life had been a battle against an evil force so strong she couldn't defeat it. At age twenty-eight, she finally surrendered.

Dedra's coworkers knew this was the driving force behind the many stories she wrote on the need to protect children. The most recent subject to pique her interest was the Internet. And she'd taken it head-on with a continuing series of articles.

In an "In the Know" column printed just before her vacation, Dedra had once again confronted the issue: *The World Wide Web, touted as the greatest learning tool in the history of the world, is all too often overlooked as the doorway to pornographic, obscene, and hate-laced information—only a click away from innocent eyes.*

As she sat down in her well-worn chair, Dedra punched in the code to retrieve her phone messages. Seventeen messages were waiting. Giving them her full attention, she listened, jotting down names, numbers, and information, before erasing them.

The ninth one began with the computerized voice saying, "March 5, 12:14 P.M." Then the message started. "Ms. Koehler, you don't know me, but . . . I've just got to talk to you, immediately! There's no time to lose. It's very, very important. It's urgent!"

There was a short pause, and Dedra sat forward in her chair. Something compelling and frightening drew her to the woman's voice.

The message continued, "You can help. I know you can. I can't leave a number. But . . . tomorrow at two P.M., please meet me—on the first level of the Galleria Mall . . . the circular, marble bench outside Saks Fifth Avenue. I'll recognize you. Oh, please come! I'll be waiting."

Swirling her chair around to face her wall calendar, Dedra jabbed her chubby finger on March 5. That entire week, and the next, were marked *vacation*. "I'm gonna kill that editor!" She hit the Replay button and listened to the heart-wrenching message once more. She chose to save this one.

Why hadn't the desperate woman left a name? A number? Something? Dedra was totally frustrated. *I would've been there.* She listened closely to the remaining messages, hoping each one might be another from the faceless voice reaching out for help. But none of them were.

Who was she? And what had been so urgent?

Twenty-two

Morgan spent the next week finding out all she could about her sister's last days. She went to see Pastor Shelby, then, using Beth's address book and remembering which friends she'd met over the years, Morgan dropped in on one or two of them. The main theme she heard from everyone was, "Beth became reclusive. She seemed frightened." But none of them could offer any clue as to the source of that fear.

Morgan had systematically gathered every newspaper article she could find about the murder. And sitting in jeans, cross-legged on her bed, Morgan spread the newspaper clippings before her. Using a yellow highlighter, she scanned each one looking for anything that stood out, anything that might help.

The frustration of finding nothing significant set her pacing the room. Glancing out the window, she saw Lynn Stiles sitting in her yard watching Justin dig a hole for a new red leaf plum tree. She immediately recalled how anxious Lynn had been for her few minutes of fame when Channel Eleven interviewed her the day after the murder. All of the other neighbors had declined.

Knowing Lynn loved to talk, Morgan thought she'd seize the opportunity and called her, offering to share a cup of coffee. Though surprised, Lynn soon arrived, and, where others had seemed reserved and careful about what they said to Morgan, Lynn spoke easily about her neighbor.

"This is just the most comfortable house on the cul-de-sac. Your sister had such an eye for decorating."

Smiling, Morgan replied, "Yes, she sure did." Settled at the kitchen table, Lynn launched into a conversation.

"How do you like our little community, Morgan?"

"It's very nice. I've been here often, but this is the first time I've spent more than a couple of days."

"I hope we're going to have you around for a long spell this time. Troy just looks so forlorn. He's going to be lost without Beth." Lynn brought the cup to her lips and looked pleasantly surprised. "Mmm, it smells good. Truthfully, Morgan, I'm not much of a coffee drinker."

"Me either," added Morgan. "This is chocolate pecan."

"Decaf, I hope. I don't need anything to hype my nerves— they're janglely enough." She smiled, vibrating her hand in front of her. "Now, if you need anything, you must pop over. I'm home most all the time."

This was what Morgan had counted upon. She smiled warmly. "I'll do that. Thanks." She didn't want Lynn to think she had invited her over just to pump her for information, so she initiated a new vein of questions. "Lynn, what does your husband do?"

Morgan was immediately aware she had chosen an unfortunate subject when Lynn's voice took on an edge of anger. "I'm divorced. After almost sixteen years of marriage—*poof*— he up and left me. A fine how-do-you-do, don't you think?"

Afraid she had opened a can of worms, Morgan searched for a way to put the top back on. "I'm sorry. I didn't know."

"I just assumed Jenny told you. Cade tells the girl everything. He thinks the world of your niece." Lynn smiled slyly. "If she were a little older . . . well, that boy of mine would definitely be lovestruck."

Morgan recalled Beth wishing Cade wouldn't spend so much time with Jenny. Her sister had never been really comfortable around the teenager, who dressed in somber, dark colors and always looked as though he needed a haircut.

"This coffee's really wonderful, Morgan." Lynn looked around the familiar kitchen, seeming a little overwhelmed. "I hear you're some kind of big executive in Minnesota. I never did much with my life. Got married right out of high school.

Had Cade. Then . . . well, here I am, about to be an empty-nested divorcée. Not too exciting, I must say." She paused just long enough to take a breath. "Do you have children?"

"No, I've never been married." Morgan didn't feel like going into her private life.

"Too bad. And you're so beautiful," Lynn said with a sweet smile. "Guess you career women just have it all. Great jobs, handsome, powerful men, and freedom. What more could you ask for?" Morgan's answer probably would have surprised her, but Lynn didn't give her a chance to reply. "You know, it's just terrible trying to raise a teenage son without a father. Not that Bruce was much of a father when he was around."

Morgan picked up the coffeepot. "Would you like another cup?"

"Just warm it up." Lynn held out her cup.

Morgan noted that she would be quite attractive if she didn't overdo everything. Her jeans were too tight and her makeup too heavy. Lynn was definitely going into her middle-aged years kicking and screaming. Despite this, she found Lynn charming in her own way and thought perhaps she had stumbled upon the right information source.

"You know, Morgan, I'm worried about Cade. And I know Beth was worried about Jenny, too." Lynn was heading the conversation in the very direction Morgan had hoped she would. "Kids today are getting into drugs and doing things we never even thought of when we were their age."

Morgan agreed. "Beth thought Jenny was growing up too fast."

"But Beth had that church. And it made a difference." Lynn paused, seeming a bit regretful. "Maybe I should've taken Cade to church. Do you think it would have helped?" She looked plaintively at Morgan.

"Beth and I were raised in the church, since our father was a minister. But I think it always helps."

Lynn looked lost. "It's way too late now. I can't get him to comb his hair, let alone go to church. I don't even know who his friends are, except for Jenny and her friend Rebecca."

Morgan continued to unearth any information Lynn Stiles

might have. "Beth didn't actually think Jenny was involved in drugs, did she?"

"Oh no. But she was getting headstrong and gave Beth a lot of worry. Your sister wasn't one to stick her head in the sand. No siree. I guess you already know she was working with the teens at the church."

Morgan and Lynn continued talking about Beth's interest in the teenagers and her motives. Whatever Lynn thought, Morgan was sure her sister was looking for a way to reach Jenny, to strengthen their relationship.

"The pastor told me she stopped coming. He didn't know why. Do you, Lynn?"

A serious look came across Lynn's brow. "Not really. But during those last weeks, before . . . well, before *it* happened, your sister changed. She didn't go out much. Her car was always in the garage. Sometimes I didn't even see her drapes opened until afternoon."

"But you said 'not really.' Did Beth tell you something, Lynn?"

"She said there were a lot of terrible things out there, things trying to get to the minds of our kids, and she had to do something to stop it. I know the world's changed, Morgan, but when Beth talked, she sounded sort of paranoid."

"Maybe Cade knows something. Did he keep coming over to see Jenny during that time?" Morgan wanted every drop of information or observation Lynn could provide.

"Yes. But usually just to pick her up. Jenny always wanted out of the house, so the two of them spent more and more time together. I asked Jenny about her mom, 'cause I was really worried, but she just said Beth wasn't feeling well." Lynn leaned in toward Morgan with deep concern. "Honestly, Beth looked just terrible. You know, the way people look when they don't get much sleep. We didn't talk at all during that last week, but I think she was sick and nobody knew it."

Lynn's words jabbed at Morgan's own guilt. Morgan's stomach tightened. *I should've known. Troy should've known.* "I appreciate your concern, Lynn. Did you see anyone strange hanging around Beth's house? Or cars you hadn't seen before?" she asked hopefully.

"No. Nothing on the outside. But if you ask me, I think whatever was frightening her was inside this house."

༃ ༃ ༃ ༃

Upstairs in her bedroom, Jenny giggled as she sat at her computer reading posts from her cyberfriends. She then eagerly joined the chat in a familiar Internet teen chat room.

```
TINKER:  You all are sooooo weird! I've been
lurking in the background, but couldn't resist
joining in. You make me laugh.
BESTBUD:  Noticed you lurking the last few days.
JESTER:  Welcome back.
KIP:  Hi, cutie. :-)) Glad to see you!
JESTER:  LTNS. We've missed you. What's up?
TINKER:  Nothing.
BESTBUD:  Something must have been keeping you
silent. You always have something to say!
<snicker>
```

Despite how she really felt, Jenny knew no one there knew who she was or what had happened. Here she could be anyone she wanted. Here she didn't have to face up to life as it was. With her computer she could have it any way she wanted.

```
TINKER:  Everything's great here.
OPDYJUDY:  Glad to hear it. I've been told that
Dallas is a wild place. Any good music groups
around there that aren't hay-chewers?
```

Jenny was typing in her response when a chime sounded and an Immediate Message window popped open. "Cade? Stay outta my face," she said out loud. Jenny was sure it had to be him.

But as the words crawled across the small IM window, she was surprised to find that it wasn't Cade but the stranger who had contacted her weeks before.

```
ARA:  REHI jenny ... remember me?
```

TINKER: Sure. But who are you?

ARA: your secret friend :) i'm always here for you ... i told you i would be getting in touch ... sorry to hear about your mother.

TINKER: How did you know about that? Did you know my mom?

ARA: very well ... it must be very lonely for you now :(

TINKER: How would she have known you?

ARA: i know a lot of people.

TINKER: Look, whoever you are, this is really creepy. How did you find me? And how do you know who I am?

ARA: LOL ... oh, i know every time you go online ... it's really quite easy for me ... you can't keep secrets from me, Jenny ... so don't bother trying.

TINKER: You're weird. I don't think I like this. You're scaring me.

ARA: :-(too bad, because i'm not going away ... you'd be surprised at the things i can offer you. FYI ... those who are my friends find me very useful indeed.

TINKER: I don't know what you're talking about. I'm out of here!

ARA: soon you will know a lot more about me ... soon, sweet jenny ... soon.

Twenty-three

$\mathcal{E}$aster arrived, and the family faced the first holiday without Beth. Gloria came up from Piney Bend on the bus, and they all attended church on Easter Sunday. Everyone did their best to get through the day without crumbling.

Morgan enjoyed helping her mother make the traditional Easter dinner of ham, roasted new potatoes, and string beans. Nearly a month had passed since Beth's death, and Morgan was happy to see her mother. Most of all, she was happy to see how well she was handling the loss. What a wonder she was.

Doing the dishes together gave Morgan and Gloria a chance to be alone. Needing to tell someone how she was feeling, Morgan shared with the only person she really could talk to. "I hated today. I'm glad it's almost over." Her tone was forlorn, and she slumped down into a kitchen chair, fighting back hot tears. It was so good to finally let it out. "Everyone was dreading it. And the police are getting nowhere. They're not any closer to finding her killer than they were weeks ago. It's just never going to be over. If you hadn't been here today, Mom, I don't know if we'd have made it."

"You would've done just fine."

"I love you." Morgan's heart was filled with so much admiration for her mother. "I wish I had your strength, but I don't."

"It's not *my* strength, honey. You know that. Why, I couldn't do anything on my own strength."

Her mother's strong faith in God always seemed to carry her

through the worst of times. Morgan had heard this speech a million times. "I know, Mom. I need to pray more often. But my
prayers don't seem to be going any higher than the ceiling. I
just don't feel that God's here." She wiped away tears. "I'm still
so angry."

"I know you are. But you've got to let it go, honey. Being
angry with God isn't going to bring your sister back—it's just
going to make you bitter and push you farther away from Him."

In her heart she knew her mother was right. "Every time I
listen to you pray, Mom, I'm amazed. You always pray as though
you expect an answer."

"I do!" Gloria took off her apron, folded it, and sat down
at the table with Morgan. "Tell me about you, honey."

"Me? Oh, I'm doing okay. The kids are getting back into
school activities. Michael's still afraid to be home alone, so I
make sure I'm here."

Gloria noticed Troy playing catch in the backyard with his
son. Going to the kitchen window, she remarked, "I guess he's
doing 'okay', too? You two are quite a pair of little liars. Troy's
going through the days as if he had blinders on. He needs your
prayers, Morgan. That man's so full of pain and anger he's about
to burst."

"I know." Morgan joined her at the window. "But he won't
talk about it. Every time I bring up her name, he changes the
subject."

"Make him talk. He needs to talk about her."

Morgan softly smiled as she watched him laughing and playing with Michael as though it were any other Easter afternoon.
"Look at him, Mom. Would you believe he's scared to death of
those kids?"

"Yes, I believe it," she answered with a knowing nod. "He's
being forced to get to know them. They're strangers to him."

Looking into her mother's caring blue eyes, Morgan shook
her head in amazement. "Is there anything you don't know?"

"Oh, my lands, yes!" Gloria laughed softly, patting her
daughter's cheek. Then a more thoughtful expression appeared
on her lovely, aging face. "Having you here with them is the best
thing in the world for them, but I'm concerned about you. You

seem so focused on your sister's death and your sister's family. . . . What about your life, Morgan? When are you going to get back to your life?"

※   ※   ※   ※

The next morning, Troy drove Gloria back to Piney Bend. Morgan waved until the car disappeared around the corner. It had been good to spend time with her mother. Remembering what Gloria told her about making Troy talk, Morgan realized she must break through the wall he'd built around himself. *But how?* The relentless question demanded an answer.

Morgan, emotionally drained from the day before, stopped fighting and allowed her thoughts free reign as the beautiful morning enticed her to remain outside. She soon found herself walking along the path in front of the house, where Beth's rose bushes were eagerly coming into full bloom. Buds of soft pink and vibrant yellow peeked through with no idea that the one who loved them so would not be here to see them this year.

Reaching to touch one of the buds, she carelessly pricked her forefinger with a thorn. "Ouch." Morgan brought her finger to her lips and tasted the tiny drop of blood. She closed her eyes and smelled the fragrant morning. And there, in the midst of Beth's rose bushes, Morgan silently asked God to help her reach Troy.

A short while later, as she sat quietly in the garden's wooden A-frame swing, her tennis shoes dragging along the worn dirt patch, a tiny smile crossed her pretty face. Morgan had prayed, and she expected an answer.

※   ※   ※   ※

Although she was exhausted, sleep did not come as easily that night as Morgan had hoped. She heard Troy come in, returning from Piney Bend. Since he hadn't slept in his and Beth's bedroom since the murder, Morgan didn't know if he went straight to bed in the downstairs guestroom or into his study. Her guess was the study.

Morgan turned first one way and then the other, trying to find a comfortable position that would coax her body into oblivious sleep. Finding it impossible, she turned on the bedside lamp. Getting up only long enough to grab her laptop computer and connect the modem phone line to the wall jack, Morgan crawled back under the covers. She scrunched two pillows behind her back and opened the computer.

After it loaded Windows, she logged on to the Heritage email server. As she thought, her mailbox was full. An email from Carl was waiting, as she thought it would be. He asked about how she was, never really coming right out and asking when she would be back. But it was implied, with a slight nudge.

Moving the mouse to the Reply button, she clicked, and a new email form appeared on the screen, already addressed to Carl Mercer.

TO: cmercer@heritagedesign.com
FROM: mcarruthers@heritagedesign.com
SUBJECT: Needed to talk.

Dear Carl,
   It's so late I didn't want to call and wake you. But I needed to talk. You asked if I was missing my work—I guess the answer is somewhat. I'd be lying to say not at all. But things here still remain in turmoil. So much is unresolved.
   After almost four weeks, the police have nothing. They've talked to everyone, but clues seem to be found only by detectives in mystery novels and TV shows. The toxicology report should be back any day. Then maybe we'll know more. Maybe it will expose something that will help.
   Detective Hancock seems to be very thorough, but he certainly doesn't know how to return phone calls. I know he's avoiding me. They carefully searched Beth's car but didn't find anything—not even fingerprints. They keep hoping to discover some mistake this guy made somewhere.
   The policemen asked—no, demanded—that I stay miles away from the investigation. Not getting involved, as you well know, is an impossibility for me. So I've been doing some detective work of my own. I must admit I don't have the

vaguest idea what I'm doing. But I can't give up. Whatever was frightening my sister is here, in this house. I have to find out what it was.

I'm getting sleepy, which is a blessing. Good night, my friend.

Morgan

Clicking the Send button, she closed the top of the computer, returning the telephone cord to the phone jack. Writing things down always helped clear her head. She and Beth kept diaries when they were growing up. Maybe she still should. Morgan sighed and turned out the light, snuggling down into her warm bed.

One thought resounded. *Beth's tormentor is in this house.*

Twenty-four

"Will you be here when I get home, Aunt Morgie?" Michael's big blue eyes were filled with worry.

Morgan wished she could take his anxiety away, but only time would do that. He lived in constant fear that while he wasn't looking, someone would swoop down and steal away another vital piece of his life.

"Yes. Yes, honey, I'll be right here, waiting for you." Morgan gave him a big, warm smile and swept the nine-year-old into her arms, hugging him tightly. "I'm not going anywhere. I promise." Kissing the top of his head, she walked with him to the back door.

"See ya this afternoon." Michael reached up and grabbed his keys from the peg. On the boy's key chain with his garage and house keys was a plastic robot, missing a left arm, and a bright red security whistle his mom had given him.

"Have a great day! Bye, sweetheart!" Morgan called. "I love you."

She stood in the doorway where he could see her, knowing he would keep looking back as long as he could. Just as he reached the edge of the lawn, another boy called to him, "Hey, come on. We're gonna miss the bus!" Morgan was relieved to see Michael happily running to meet his friend.

Jenny, looking bright and perky in a green miniskirt and a pale yellow sweater, ran into the kitchen. "Sorry. I don't have time to eat. I'm late." A car horn blasted in the drive. "That's Cade."

Morgan quickly took a half-pint of orange juice from the refrigerator. "Here, at least take this with you. You have to have something. You're getting too thin.''

"Not hardly. Stop worrying about me." Jenny took the juice and grabbed her keys from the peg on the way out the door. Morgan watched as the attractive teen ran toward the circular drive, then turned and called, "I might be late. I'm meeting friends after school. I'll get a ride home."

Morgan was infuriated that she had waited until it was all but impossible for her aunt to say anything before announcing her plans. "Jenny!" Morgan called. But her niece pretended not to hear as she jumped into Cade's Wrangler and was gone.

She sighed and slowly closed the door. What in the world would she do with her? No wonder Beth had been so worried. So far all of Morgan's sincere efforts to get close to Jenny had failed miserably.

Well, perhaps they wouldn't be friends, but Morgan had to take control of this situation. The ringing phone interrupted her thoughts, and she grabbed it, answering, "Hello."

"Good morning, Morgan."

"Hi, Troy. I'm glad it's you." Morgan held the portable phone between her cheek and her shoulder as she loaded the breakfast dishes into the dishwasher. "Sorry I missed you this morning, but you get up with the roosters." She was glad to hear his voice, for it reminded her she wasn't alone in this. It had been one of those overwhelming mornings.

"Sounded like you were surprised to hear from me. Expecting someone else to call?"

"Oh no. Not really."

"Listen, I just had a call from Detective Hancock."

"I don't believe it. Finally!" Morgan didn't try to hide her annoyance. "He called you? I've left at least five messages. He won't even give me the courtesy of a call back."

"Whoa, there. Just calm down. I guess they didn't have anything to tell us until now."

The possibility that they might have something substantial about the murder excited her. "So what did he have to say?"

"The toxicology report is back. He apologized that it took so long, but they were waiting on some special tests. He wants to see me. I was sure you'd want to be there."

"Did you tell him that?"

"No, but I'm sure he's figuring you'll be with me."

"Of course I want to go." Morgan shut the dishwasher with a thud. Flipping the switch to On, she started the pre-rinse cycle. Not realizing it would be so noisy, she quickly moved to the other side of the kitchen "What time?"

"In about an hour. Can you make it?"

"I wouldn't miss it."

He paused a moment, then suggested, "Afterward, maybe we can pick up some lunch. Then we can talk."

"Sounds great. Then I'll be back by the time Michael gets home. I gave him my word."

"Got the address?" he asked.

She removed the yellow pushpin holding Detective Hancock's card to the small message board. "Yes, it's right here. I'd better get going. See you there."

Quickly, Troy interjected, "And set the alarm. Bye."

It's about time we heard from that detective, she thought as she hung up the phone. Noting the clock, she was glad she didn't have to take extra time to get dressed. That morning she'd thought about going out for a while, perhaps to the mall, and had slipped into a casual, long denim dress. The line and shape enhanced her figure, and Morgan smiled. She was attractive, and she knew it.

Her high, brown suede boots were by the back door, where she had placed them earlier. After she slipped them on, Morgan reached for her keys, which were hanging on a hook with the extra set of house keys.

Glancing down, Morgan noticed a powdery substance on her hand. On closer inspection she realized it was from the extra keys. She examined the spare set more closely, noting that bits of something putty-like stuck to several of them, especially on the key to Beth's car.

Intrigued, she took a moment to find a plastic sandwich bag and dropped the keys into it. Grabbing her leather shoulder bag, Morgan punched the code into the alarm system, turned the inside lock on the door, closed it, and hurried to her rental car. She was full of expectations and subtle fear at the thought of what they were about to discover about her sister's death.

Twenty-five

*T*roy and Morgan walked swiftly down the corridor, following the directions given to them by the officer at the door of the building. Morgan had not told Troy she'd been here to see Detective Hancock before. But now seemed the right time.

"Troy, just a second," she said, clearly concerned about how he'd take her news flash. "It's nothing terrible or anything at all, really . . . it's just that, well, I dropped in on Detective Hancock a few weeks ago."

"You what? Why didn't you tell me?" Troy was totally surprised.

"I just didn't think to bring it up. And the only reason I came down here at all was in the hopes that maybe there would be something I could do to help . . . you know, with the investigation." Troy was not pleased. Morgan hoped to win him over as she continued. "What could be wrong with pooling our resources? Who knows, I could find out something . . . you know, a clue or some piece of information." She flashed a mischievous smile his way and waited.

"Morgan, don't get involved. What are you thinking?" He was clearly disturbed by her confession. "Promise me you'll stay out of it?"

Knowing she couldn't give him such a promise, she quickly looked at her watch. "We're late. Come on, follow me."

After a few minutes of brisk walking, Morgan said, "There." She pointed to a sign at the end of the hall. Homicide Division.

Troy's tension was apparent in the brisk, long strides he

took, seeming not to care that Morgan had to take two for each of his.

Morgan tried to make conversation. "Since he didn't want to talk on the phone, they must have something important, don't you think?" She caught up to him, taking hold of his arm. "I just want this to be over, Troy."

His look softened as he smiled at her. "So do I, Morgan. So do I."

The two entered the squad room, and Morgan immediately spotted Detective Ballantine at his desk. "There's Hancock's partner."

Chuck looked up from his computer screen and spotted them. Getting to his feet, he shook hands with them. "Mr. Woodsen . . . and Ms. Carruthers. Have a chair." He scurried around, grabbing an extra straight-backed wooden chair and pulling it up next to his desk.

"Detective Hancock called and asked me to meet him here." Troy's eyes searched for the familiar figure, but he wasn't there. "I understand you've got some news?"

"Yes. We've got the medical examiner's toxicology report."

"Where's your partner?" Morgan asked. She was feeling a bit uneasy, having been brushed off the last time she'd seen them. "I assumed you knew I'd be coming with Troy."

Ballantine smiled. "Glad to see you. I know it's been tough waiting, not knowing what's going on down here. But we're on it," responded Ballantine politely, obviously stalling for time. "Would you like some coffee?"

"I'd advise against it," a familiar voice stated. "Nobody around here's a Mr. Coffee, if you know what I mean." Detective Hancock suddenly appeared behind them. For such a large man, he moved like a cat. "Ms. Carruthers, how nice to see you . . . again."

Morgan got the meaning in his tone, and quickly retorted, "Just out of curiosity, Detective, do you ever return your phone calls?"

"Didn't know you called, ma'am. My apologies."

Hancock's desk was only steps away from his partner's. He leaned over to it, grabbed a file folder, then pulled up a chair and joined them.

"Five times."

Ballantine tried unsuccessfully to stifle a smile. Then he offered up a defense for Dell. "My partner finds using the computer message system . . . inconvenient."

"What he's saying here is that I loathe high technology and refuse to become conversant in its use or jargon. I know it's become indispensable and probably rightly so, but I'm not going into the computer age. So if you need me, call my partner here. He'll see that I get the message." He turned to Ballantine. "Written in longhand, on a piece of paper." He glanced at the medical report inside the folder marked *Woodsen, Beth Ann*. "Now, for the reason I called, Mr. Woodsen. We've finally gotten the toxicology report."

Morgan could tell Troy's apprehension was becoming unbearable. She spoke with a decided urgency. "What does it show, Detective?"

"Your wife was given a lethal injection of a drug called fentanyl."

"Fentanyl? What is that?" Troy inquired.

Ballantine interjected his recently acquired knowledge. "Usually it's used in surgery by the anesthesiologist. Its pharmacological action is similar to morphine. Too much, and it suppresses the breathing and heart functions, which is what happened to your wife." This was a kinder way of saying that Beth suffocated.

The very thought set Morgan shifting nervously in her chair, and some of the color drained from her face. Hancock noticed and looked concerned. "Are you going to be all right with this, Ms. Carruthers?"

"I'm fine. Go on, please." Morgan grasped the sides of the chair.

Troy never took his eyes off the report in Hancock's hands. His voice reflected the strain of the past weeks. "I kept hoping the report would end this idea that Beth was murdered. It's harder to accept, you know . . . that someone took her life." Troy anxiously rubbed his forehead. "It's so inconceivable."

"I wish I could've given you other news. This wasn't something I wanted to discuss over the phone." Detective Hancock continued. "We picked up one piece of luck. Our medical examiner had a crazy hunch. He tested for something that wouldn't show up in a normal toxicology report—and he was right on."

Morgan asked quickly, "What do you mean? There's more?"

"I'm afraid so. It's the craziest thing. They also found a large amount of poisonous spider venom in your wife's blood."

"Black widow venom, to be exact," Ballantine added. "One was accidentally brought into the lab with the body."

The thought of the large spider she had killed in the laundry room flashed across her mind. It sent a shiver through Morgan. "A black widow?"

Troy stiffened in his chair betraying a growing outrage. In a frustrated and frightened voice, he shouted, "Spider venom? A lethal drug overdose? Which was it, Detective?"

"Sir, the fentanyl killed her, we're sure of that." The large detective rubbed the back of his thick neck, revealing his own disappointment at the lack of solid information in this case.

Leaning forward in her chair, Morgan's eyes connected with Hancock's. "You're right, crazy is the word! This is crazy. If the fentanyl killed my sister, then what did the spider have to do with it?"

Hancock, aware that he had two very volatile people hanging on his every word, tried to lessen their confusion. "The medical examiner inspected every inch of her body and couldn't find any spider bites. If she had been bitten, there would have been two telltale puncture marks surrounded by a red inflamed area. He only found the one puncture."

"Are you saying the venom was in the injection?" Morgan's bright, quick mind was grabbing at every piece of information.

Hancock shook his head. "Yes. That's the only explanation."

"But you said you found a live black widow. . . ." Troy's voice trailed off. But then his strong jaw tensed as he shared his speculations. "She must've gotten into her car, not knowing someone was waiting for her. Then she felt the sting in the back of her neck." He paused. "Oh, Beth. You were all alone and terrified. I'm so sorry, Beth."

Morgan put her hand on Troy's arm. Then she looked toward Detective Hancock with a plaintive gaze. "Is that how it happened? Was he hiding in the car?"

"Probably."

"It was quick. I don't suppose it's much comfort, Mr. Woodsen, but that much fentanyl, administered so near the brain . . . she was out in seconds." Ballantine was trying to help. "The spider and the venom? Well . . . we're not sure about that."

"Most likely it was some kind of 'signature.' Killers often do that. They like to play with us. Sometimes they even want to be caught." Troy and Morgan listened intently as the lead detective shared more information. "We've run a check throughout the country looking for crimes involving venom like this. But we've come up empty-handed. I'd be willing to bet he's done it before, but this time we picked up on the venom. If that live spider hadn't been with the body—we might never have known, either."

"That was the special test you've been waiting for?" Morgan asked.

"Yes, ma'am." Ballantine added, "The bite of one black widow spider wouldn't kill a healthy adult. But the amount of venom in the victim's body was drawn from a lot of those creatures. The killer had to actually take the time to collect venom."

"You've got to find this monster!" Morgan's passion to know who the killer was all but jumped out and grabbed Hancock by the collar.

Troy spoke. "We know you're doing everything you can. I guess we thought by now it might be over." Troy was calm, and his voice was steady and clear.

Nervously, Detective Hancock got to his feet, turned his chair around, and straddled it. Then, folding his arms over the top of the chair back, he continued. "Hard evidence is almost nonexistent. But we'll get him. Bottom line is, we're sure the venom and the drug were given to her with a syringe. The presence of the venom explains the red circle found around the puncture mark. No trace evidence in the car or on her body."

Hancock got to his feet. "I wish there were more, but right

now, that's all we've got." Hancock closed the file and tossed it on Ballantine's desk. "Trust me, we want to see this murder solved as much as you do."

Morgan wasn't able to get the picture of her dying sister out of her mind. "There's no way you could know what it's like to lie there night after night knowing that murderer is out there walking the streets. Find him!" Morgan's voice was tense and demanding. "You can't let him just walk away."

"Take a look at that board, Ms. Carruthers." Hancock pointed to a large whiteboard mounted on the office wall. On it were names and dates. "Every name is a murder victim. The name doesn't come off until the crime is solved." Hancock leaned across Ballantine's desk, balancing on his palms—eye-to-eye with Morgan. "There's nothing I would like better than to wipe that board clean." His passion was growing with every word. "And when I lie in bed at night, I dream of the hollow clang of a prison door, shutting and locking. I want to see every one of those murderers behind bars!"

Morgan did not respond but sat back in her chair. The sincerity in his voice and the look in his dark eyes convinced her he would do everything he could to close this case.

Hancock spoke compassionately to Troy. "We've got Mrs. Woodsen's personal effects. I was sure you'd want to have them."

As if on cue, Ballantine opened a lower drawer and took out a large, plastic bag labeled *Woodsen, B.* Troy's face went ashen. Morgan's stomach tightened.

The young detective laid the bag on the desk next to a clipboard holding a release form. It contained a list of all the items in the bag. "Just look through these and then sign off right here, Mr. Woodsen. We're finished with them."

Troy put his hand on the bag and hesitated a moment, steeling himself before opening it. Unable to bring himself to touch any of the items, Morgan hesitantly went through them: Beth's bloodstained clothing, her keys, shoulder bag containing the usual things—makeup, wallet, pen, and address book. Also in the bag were Beth's rings, her watch, and the fourteen karat gold necklace Morgan gave her last Christmas.

"Her clothing wasn't torn. Doesn't appear to have been a struggle. The bloodstains match up with the wounds her body received in the accident," Ballantine said, handing Troy a pen.

"Is there anything missing? Anything you know she would have had with her, Mr. Woodsen?" Hancock watched as Troy read through the list once again.

"Did you find a small red notebook? About this size?" Troy indicated four inches by two inches.

"Nope. Didn't find anything like that. Where would it have been?"

"Probably in the glove box, maybe in her purse. She kept a gas mileage log. You know, fill-ups and oil changes."

A bit puzzled, Ballantine asked, "Your wife kept precise records of her gas purchases? A little strange, for a woman."

Troy explained. "I asked her to. I do it, too. Our accountant uses the records for taxes. Beth wrote down the date, odometer reading, and sometimes even where she bought the gas, if she didn't use a gas card."

Ballantine said, "I'll call the lab, see if there's any chance they overlooked it or didn't give it to us."

"We've checked all the credit card statements. We know she didn't use one of them to buy gas that day. But, if we can find that book and if she bought gas that day, this would be a lucky break for us." Hancock looked encouraged. "It would give us more information on just where she was."

"I'll check out the house and my briefcase. She might have left it for me. It is tax time, you know."

"Get back to me if you find it," Hancock replied. He then handed Troy a small brown envelope. Inside were all of the credit cards Beth had with her. "We've reconstructed your wife's actions that day, but nothing pinpoints her location about the time of the murder."

Troy quickly closed the bag and signed the release form. Getting to his feet, he shook hands with the two detectives. "I'll look for that log. But I don't understand why it's missing. She kept it with her all the time."

Dell turned to Morgan. "I hope you've taken our advice, Ms. Carruthers. If you run across anything we should know, let us check it out. Don't do it yourself."

"Sure," Morgan replied as she started toward the door.

Troy added, "I've told her the same thing." He tentatively took the plastic bag containing his wife's belongings.

"We appreciate you coming down." Hancock shook his hand, then watched with interest as the two left the squad room. Shaking his head and sighing deeply, he mumbled, "She's gonna get in trouble. I can feel it in my bones."

Twenty-six

*T*hey had barely gotten seated in the comfortable, round booth when a young waitress approached. "Hi, I'm Kelley. May I bring you something to drink?" Her smile was a bit tired. The lunch crowd must have been heavy that day.

"Yes, I'll have an iced tea, please. A large." After their meeting with Detective Hancock, Morgan needed a quiet place to cool down and collect her thoughts. She used her long, slender fingers to massage her neck.

"Sounds good. Tea for me, too. And bring lots of lemon."

The waitress hurried off. Troy gazed at Morgan thoughtfully. "You okay?"

She sighed deeply as she laid her head back on the booth. "I'm fine. Just a bit overwhelmed with everything."

"You're not alone." He reached across the table, offering her his hand. She took it.

"I know." A gentle smile softened her melancholy demeanor. "Troy, I don't think any of us can really move on until we know the truth . . . all of it."

Troy released her hand and put his arm over the back of the booth. "I thought it would help somehow to get that report. I'm not sure what I thought it would tell us. But it didn't help at all. It just made it worse."

"It would have been so much easier, for you and the children, if it had been a car accident. For me, as well."

Morgan ran her hand over the crisp, white tablecloth. "Do you think we could talk about something else?" Candlelight flickered from the small, cut-glass votive, making ever-changing shapes. The conversation stopped.

"I'm not very good at small talk," Troy replied truthfully, fumbling for some way to keep the conversation going without talking about Beth.

Morgan let her eyes wander, gazing at the small, pleasant restaurant. "Italy's Garden. It's a lovely place. And I'm sure the food is scrumptious."

"I've never been here before. One of my clients raves about it," he replied as tenseness began to drain from his body ever so slightly. He opened the large menu. "Order whatever you want. But I'm a spaghetti man myself."

"Spaghetti? In a white shirt?" she asked playfully. "You're also brave."

"What if I tuck in my napkin?" Troy opened the large, red-and-white checked napkin with a flourish, tucking one corner into the collar of his white shirt. "That is, if you don't mind, ma'am."

Morgan couldn't help herself and began laughing. It had been weeks since she had allowed herself to indulge in laughter, abandoning the sorrow she often carried. It felt so good. "You're a wonderful guy, Troy Woodsen. I'm so happy and proud to be your sister-in-law."

He didn't take compliments well. "Hey, don't jump to conclusions. Actually, I was thinking the other day that we barely know each other."

Before she could respond, their conversation was interrupted by the waitress serving their iced teas. The girl pulled the pad and pencil from her apron pocket, poised to take their order.

"You order for us both." Morgan put down her menu. She wasn't in the mood to make decisions.

"You do like to live dangerously, don't you?" Troy stated, then ordered spaghetti marinara, a side order of meatballs, and a Caesar salad for two. As the waitress walked away, he added, "No anchovies!"

Morgan stirred her tea thoughtfully. Bringing the glass to her lips, she looked over at him. "Do you think it looks funny . . . you know, me staying at the house so long?"

"I thought we settled that, Morgan. I need you. The kids need you—" Before he could finish his thought, his cell phone rang. "Sorry." He pulled the phone from the inside pocket of his navy double-breasted suit coat lying on the seat next to him.

Flipping it open, he pushed the Talk button. "Troy Woodsen here." His voice was very businesslike, low and commanding. Completely different than it had been moments earlier. There was much more to Troy Woodsen than met the eye. It was true—she didn't know him. Not really.

She watched him, not wanting to stare, but finding his business persona very fascinating. He was in his own little world, lost to her for the moment. Out of habit, Morgan poured two packets of Sweet'n Low into her tea. The long silver spoon and the ice cubes made a tinkling sound on the sides of the glass as she stirred.

She thought of the first time she'd met Troy. He had always been a handsome man, but watching him now, she realized that age had added a self-confidence and style that fit him like a fine leather glove.

Morgan smiled as she suddenly became aware that she was feeling quite comfortable with Troy.

While he was still on the phone, Troy checked his watch. "I can't make it for at least two hours. I'm tied up in a very important lunch meeting." He smiled at her, completed the call, and replaced the phone in his jacket pocket. "Lunch used to be a time to get away. But not any more. They track me down everywhere I go."

"Thanks for not rushing off," Morgan replied. Then, looking him in the eye, she surprised herself by saying, "I needed some time to talk with my best friend."

Troy cocked his head, a look of surprise on his face. "Best friends? I like that, Morgan. It works for me." He paused, squeezing five pieces of lemon into his glass of tea.

"Sure you didn't want lemonade?" She asked with a slight giggle.

"Great. You see there, you can loosen up." He leaned toward her. "Morgan, teasing aside, I know how hard this has been on you. To tell you the truth, I've been very worried. Is it all too much? You can tell me."

"Sometimes I feel like it is. But, Troy, you and the kids . . . you're all I have left of Beth." Lightening up, she smiled, "What if I promise to call you before I completely fall apart? Deal?"

"Deal." Troy tapped his fingertips on the table and then changed the subject. "For a minute there, at the station, I thought you were going to bite Detective Hancock's head off."

She felt a little embarrassed. "I just have to know who did it."

"We all need to know. But, Morgan, they're handling it. You have another life in Minneapolis. Beth wouldn't want you to give that up. And what about Kevin? What does he think about you staying here?"

Morgan turned her eyes away from Troy and toward an ivy-framed window that looked out on a small patio furnished with small tables for two. Their waitress delivered their lunch, and after a brief moment, she returned her gaze to him. "Kevin and I . . . well, he left me. He's marrying someone else."

"He left *you* for someone else? What an idiot." Troy's response was out before he weighed his words.

"He met a woman in Cincinnati. They were falling in love right under my nose. I guess I was too busy with my career to notice. Now who's the idiot?"

"Maybe you and I are more alike than we thought." Troy reflected on Morgan's words. "I don't know if people like us are very good relationship material. Seems we don't see the big picture. Too focused on where we're heading to notice where we are."

"Kevin was looking for a wife . . . and children. Something I could never—"

Troy broke in. "I know, Beth told me. . . ." Troy nervously fidgeted with the meal before him, unaccustomed to sharing such a personal conversation. "You can't have children, and here I am with two I barely even know."

"Beth thought you were a terrific dad . . . and your children love you very much."

Her words didn't seem to reassure him as regret still laced his reply. "Jenny's a handful. Don't let her get the best of you. She'll try." His concern for Morgan was genuine. "I know Beth was having all kinds of trouble with her. She asked me to talk to Jenny several times. But I was always too busy, too late coming home, or too wrapped up in Woodsen Development. That sound like a 'good dad'?"

Morgan wished she could help him but knew that some of what he was saying was true. He *had* buried himself in his company. It was as if he hid there. But why? Beth hadn't ever blamed him. He was Troy—her Troy, and she loved him so. "You made Beth very happy, Troy."

Not wanting to talk about the past, Troy quickly changed the focus of their conversation. "I'm sorry about the breakup."

"Me too."

"Kevin seemed like a nice guy. Beth thought you two would be getting married any day."

"Then we were both surprised." Morgan turned to retrieve her purse from the seat beside her. "Funny, isn't it? I mean the way things don't turn out at all the way we plan." The words had barely escaped her lips before she realized how thoughtless and cruel they were.

Troy pulled back from continuing their conversation. Catching the eye of the waitress, he snapped his fingers, motioning for the check. "Come on, let's get out of here." He slid out of the booth and offered his hand to help her. Morgan took it more to experience his touch than because she needed the assistance.

They walked silently to the parking lot where she had left her car. Troy held his jacket slung over his left shoulder—his right hand in his pocket. The pleated trousers were perfectly pressed and broke just at the top of his dark brown Gucci loafers. The collarless shirt he wore accentuated his large, muscular neck. Troy hated ties and rarely wore them.

"Better get going. Michael's going to hold you to your promise."

"You're right." Morgan dug around in her purse looking for the car keys. Her fingers felt the plastic bag holding the house keys she had intended to show to Detective Hancock. She'd forgotten all about them. "I don't want to let him down."

Troy took her keys and opened the car door. As he placed them in the palm of her hand, she noticed a shadow of a smile cross his face. "Thanks for everything, Morgan." He slipped on his jacket. "I hope you know what it means to me to have you here." His look became very serious. "But, Morgan, when you need to leave—go. Promise me you will."

"I promise." He had nothing to worry about, for she wasn't leaving any time soon. There were too many unanswered questions, and her heart and mind were far removed from the life that only weeks ago had been so important to her. Could she ever be *that* Morgan again?

For a brief moment, Morgan felt he wanted to hug her but just couldn't allow himself to do it. Instead, he simply said, "Bye," turned away from her, and hurried off toward his own car.

She'd really enjoyed this time with him. For brief moments, they had actually talked about normal, pleasant things. But as she slid into her car, the sight of the plastic bag containing her sister's belongings brought Morgan abruptly back to reality.

Twenty-seven

When Morgan arrived at the house it was midafternoon. She decided to leave the plastic bag on a shelf in the garage so there was no chance Jenny or Michael might find it.

Glancing at the kitchen clock near the refrigerator, she was surprised to see it was almost 2:35. She'd just made it. Michael would be home in about twenty minutes. She quickly thumbed through the stack of mail she had pulled from the mailbox on her way in. A few condolence cards were mixed with bills and magazines. Then her eyes fell on a small brown envelope addressed to *Beth Woodsen*. There was no return address.

Without questioning her action, she tore open the top. Inside she found a handwritten note and a small notebook. The knot in Morgan's throat tightened as she opened the note.

> *Dear Mrs. Woodsen,*
> *I tried to stop you, but you were already pulling out of the station when I found this little book on the floor. Luckily your name and address were inside. I was sure you would want it.*
> *Hope you'll stop in again.*
> *Hal*
> *Manager, Sheldon's 76 Station, Preston Road & Woodley*

Morgan opened the cover of the small notebook. She immediately recognized her sister's handwriting. It was the missing gasoline records.

Her hand shook as she dug through her purse looking for Detective Hancock's card. "You'd better answer this time," she said, grabbing the phone. She dialed his direct number.

It rang only once and he answered. "Detective Hancock."

"Thank goodness you're there. This is Morgan Carruthers." She knew her voice was trembling.

"What's wrong? Are you okay, Ms. Carruthers?"

"Fine. I'm fine. I've got the records! The gas records."

"Great! Where'd you find them?" he asked.

She explained, reading him the note and giving him the address of the 76 Station.

Hancock replied, "She must have used cash. Look in the back of the book. Did she enter the transaction?"

Morgan turned the pages. "The last complete entry was on February twenty-seventh at Texaco. But wait a minute, she started an entry at the bottom of the page. March sixth . . ." Her voice trailed off.

Hancock responded with great enthusiasm. "That's it! We got a big break, Morgan. Did she write down the mileage?"

"No. Nothing more."

"Well, it's something we didn't have before." His disappointment was evident.

Morgan's mind was racing with questions. "She always wrote down the transaction record. This is the only one that's not complete."

Detective Hancock thought aloud. "Something must've interrupted her." He quickly thanked Morgan and said he would keep her posted. "If you're going to be home, we'll stop by and pick up the book."

"Okay. Sure." She hung up, still staring at the small book. "Where were you going in such a hurry, Beth?"

Knowing Troy was on his way to an important meeting, she decided she'd tell him about finding the book when he got home.

A blinking red light on the answering machine caught her eye. There were messages. Morgan pushed the Replay button and sat down to listen as she removed her boots and wiggled her toes. The tape rewound, then began playing:

"Hello, this is Marge King, Teddy's mother. I wanted you to know I picked up Kenny and Michael at school. We stopped by to tell you, but you weren't in. Don't worry, Michael's over here playing. Beth used to . . . I mean, well, we're good friends of the Woodsens. Please call me at 555–0218." Then she added, "Michael's fine. Bye."

The next message began. "Hi. Just me. I'm calling from the car. Wanted to tell you I enjoyed lunch. Don't know what time I'll be home, so don't wait dinner. If you want to reach me, call my beeper. I'll be out looking at some property. Later. Bye."

Morgan smiled at the upbeat sound of Troy's voice. Funny, even though she'd known him for over sixteen years, she'd never had a relaxed one-on-one conversation with him. Her time spent with Beth's husband had always been at family affairs, bustling with activity. For some reason, they had never gotten to know each other very well. He was a man's man and perfectly satisfied to simply know Morgan as his sister-in-law, and nothing more. Everything she knew about who he was she had learned from Beth.

Living here day in and day out and struggling through this devastating loss together had definitely brought them closer. Troy had few relationships that could be termed "close." His life was Woodsen Development and his family. Period. Beth had been his soul mate and his closest friend. Obviously Troy adored Jenny and Michael. But at lunch he had admitted, *"I don't really know them."* Remembering his words made her sad. In her heart, she knew Troy felt truly alone.

Morgan was now beginning to understand some of his words that shocked her that cold spring morning weeks ago. In his anger and despair, Troy admitted jealousy of Beth's relationship with Morgan. Now she realized Troy had wanted Beth to need him—and no one else. Troy Woodsen needed to be needed, something Morgan would never have guessed in a million years.

Before she did another thing, Morgan phoned Marge King. Yes, it would be fine for Michael to stay and play with Kenny. It had been weeks since the boy had spent time with his friends. Morgan breathed easier. Was this an indication that her nephew would be all right?

Picking up Beth's small notebook, Morgan's interest was

aroused. She quickly phoned Marge King once again to ask if it would be an imposition for Michael to stay for supper. They all seemed pleased, and Michael was happy about it. Good. She would see him later.

Hurriedly, Morgan jotted a note on the blackboard in the kitchen: *Jen, out for about an hour. Be back soon. Aunt Morgie.* Then Morgan pulled on her boots and grabbed her bag and keys. After setting the alarm, Morgan ran out, closing the door behind her.

Twenty-eight

Morgan knew the North Dallas area well enough to find the 76 Station on Preston Road. She and her sister had been in this neighborhood many times for lunch and shopping sprees. As she drove her rented Infinity, she glanced again at the handwritten note.

Why had Beth been in such a hurry that day? What interrupted her? Was it the murderer? The ringing of Morgan's cell phone startled her. She had dropped it in her bag. *Keep ringing!* Driving with one hand, she dug around in the large purse, but the heavy traffic near the Galleria Mall was demanding all of her attention.

Luckily it continued to ring. "Okay!" She glanced down for one second, and when she looked up, the light was red—and the car in front of her had stopped. Morgan's quick reflexes took over, and she slammed on the brakes, stopping inches from the back bumper of a silver Chevy van.

The force of the stop flung her bag to the floor on the passenger side, dumping its contents onto the floor mat. There was the phone! And it was still ringing. Whoever it was must *really* want to talk to her. She grabbed the phone and hit the Send button. A bit shaken, she said, "Hello."

"I know the Infinity is a big car, but six rings?" Troy's laugh was something she seldom heard.

"You nearly caused me to have an accident! Never mind, it's a long story. Oh, thanks for lunch. I enjoyed it, too." The light changed and the line of cars began to move.

"I was checking to be sure you got home before Michael. But you weren't there."

She wasn't sure she like the idea of being checked up on, and that's exactly what it felt like to her. "I was home. But Michael's having supper at the King's. Something came up, and I had to run an errand."

"If you needed something you could've beeped or tried me on my cellular." He seemed hurt that she hadn't called.

"I know, but this was something I needed to do myself, Troy." She was intentionally not telling him where she was going or that she had found the gas book. "I'll be home in an hour or so." She spotted Woodley, and there on the corner was the 76 Station. "Oops! Gotta run, Troy."

He obviously wasn't ready to hang up. "Morgan . . ."

She turned into the drive of the small station, her voice hurried as she said, "Don't worry, I'm fine. See you tonight. Bye." Morgan closed her cell phone and tossed it on the passenger seat.

She parked next to the building and observed the station. It wasn't one of the new, automated scan-your-card-fill-'er-up-and-drive-off operations. Instead, there was a small store and one island with four pumps. A customer would have to go inside to pay for gasoline.

Morgan took the note and headed into the store, not at all sure what she thought she would discover there. Behind the counter was a tall, very thin man of about seventy. He used a twisted wooden cane to move about.

A welcome smile greeted Morgan. "Afternoon ma'am. What can I do for you?"

"I'm looking for—" she looked at the note—"Hal." She turned the note so he could see it. "The man who wrote this note."

"You found him. I'm Hal Sheldon. My son, Willie, owns the place now. I just help him out now and then. Meet lots of interestin' folks." He squinted his eyes, then adjusted his glasses. The afternoon sun was streaming through the glass doors, and they backlit the tall, willowy figure who had entered his store. Morgan moved closer.

"Say, you're not the lady who left—"

She anxiously interrupted him. "No. You sent this notebook back to my sister, Beth Woodsen."

"Oh yes. Shorter. Blond lady. She left it here a few weeks back. Good thing she had her name and address inside."

"I'd like to ask you some questions about her."

He reacted as though he might be in some kind of trouble. "Sorry I didn't get it back to her sooner. You see, I put it here—" he indicated a shelf under the counter—"and then forgot about it. The memory, it's not what it used to be."

Morgan could only hope that was just a figure of speech. She needed to know what he remembered about that day. Hal Sheldon may have been the last person to see her sister alive. "Thank you so much for sending it back. It's very important."

He hobbled out from behind the counter, just as an old-fashioned grandfather wall clock chimed with an odd, tinny sound. It was 3:15. The clock's orange face, a 76 ball, was just the kind of thing she'd expect to find in this little store.

"Folks just aren't as interested in helpin' each other any more. Not neighborly like they used to be. But I remember that lady. She was a nice lady. And mighty pretty, just like you. You say you're sisters?"

Morgan's smile faded as she replied, "Yes, sir. We were. But my sister, Beth, was murdered the same day she was in your store."

The man's eyes widened in horror and disbelief. He looked a bit unsteady and leaned both hands on the top of his cane. "Murdered? My lands, the world's goin' crazy." He shook his head in despair. Looking at Morgan with sincere sympathy he said, "I'm so sorry, ma'am. So sorry."

"Afternoon, Ms. Carruthers."

"Oops." Morgan rolled her eyes as she immediately recognized the annoyed voice of Detective Hancock. She'd been so involved in her conversation with Mr. Sheldon she hadn't noticed the unmarked police car pulling in. Slowly she turned around, knowing the disgruntled look that would confront her.

"Well, looks like we both had the same idea." She smiled as she greeted Hancock and his partner.

Mr. Sheldon looked confused and not at all sure of what was going on in his little store. The two detectives showed Hal Sheldon their badges. "I'm Detective Hancock. This is my partner, Detective Ballantine. We're with the Dallas Police Department, Homicide Division. We'd like to ask you a few questions, Mr. Sheldon."

A young customer entered to pay for gas and a root beer. Hal said, "Excuse me. Gotta tend to my son's business." He hobbled back behind the counter to wait on the young man.

"Does Mr. Woodsen know you're out here nosing around?" Hancock inquired.

"I don't have to check with him or anyone, including you. I called you, didn't I?"

Hancock's retort was almost out of his mouth when a sweet-looking middle-aged woman entered with two young children. He swallowed the words he was about to say. Taking a deep breath, he spoke emphatically, keeping his husky voice low. "It would *really* be appreciated if you would let us do our job."

Morgan, not wanting to create a scene, spoke through clenched teeth. "I would, Detective, but after all these weeks, you're not one inch closer to finding the murderer, are you? I'd think you'd welcome the help."

"Look, I know you're only trying to help, but your meddling could hamper our investigation. Is that what you want?"

Morgan stood her ground. "What I want, Detective Hancock, is to see my sister's murderer behind bars! And if there's anything I can do to make that happen, I intend to do it!"

Ballantine had been standing several paces back, watching as the two exchanged words. The smile on his freckled face made it easy to see that he was amused to watch Hancock locking horns with Morgan. He noticed more customers entering the little store and moved to the counter. "Sir, is there anyone else around who could help you out here so we could talk?"

"My son's out back checking in supplies." All of this excitement was making Mr. Sheldon apprehensive. He stammered, "I'll . . . I'll get him."

The young detective smiled reassuringly. "Thanks. I think that would be a good idea."

Mr. Sheldon hobbled off as quickly as he could, disappearing into the back room.

Their conversation cooled, Morgan showed the small notebook to the detective. Standing next to him, she pointed to the last entry. "I think you're right about something happening. Maybe something frightened her."

He looked closely at it. "Wish she'd just finished that odometer reading. Then we'd have a good idea of how far she drove before she was killed."

Ballantine and Hal Sheldon joined the other two. "His son is taking over. Let's step outside and talk." All four exited the glass doors and walked to the side of the store where Morgan had parked her car.

"Ms. Carruthers tells me you remember seeing her sister on March sixth." Hancock realized the old man was nervous. "Could you try to think back, Mr. Sheldon? Was there anything strange about her actions or anything she said?"

The old man slowly sat down in a battered and torn lawn chair shaded by the awning of the store. The others stood. "Well, like I told her"—he pointed to Morgan—"she was a nice lady. Pumped her own gas. Then she came in to pay."

"Did she seem nervous or agitated?" Ballantine asked.

The old man shook his head. "Not at first. She paid in cash. I remember because I told her nobody uses cash anymore. Everything's plastic. Hard to get to know a piece of plastic." He continued. "After she paid me, she took that little notebook and a pen out of her bag. She asked me how many gallons she'd gotten. I read it off the meter. I can't remember how much it was."

"That's all right. Go on, please," Hancock coaxed him. "Something must've happened, something that caused her not to finish writing in the book. Was anything special going on that day? It was March sixth, a Thursday. Around noon."

Ballantine added, "The day of that big storm."

Mr. Sheldon's eyes suddenly looked clear and alert. He leaned on his cane, rising to his feet. "Yep, now I remember. The lady was writing in that book, and then the clock . . . the one behind the counter, it started to chime. She looked at the time and then at her watch. She was upset. Said something like,

'It's stopped.' Meaning her watch, I think. And she rushed out to her car.''

Morgan asked, "Do you know what time it was?"

"Yep, I sure do. It was 1:30. I remember because I was signing for a delivery from the Frito Lay driver, and he had just asked me what time it was." He proudly repeated. "Yep. It was 1:30.''

Morgan wanted to hug the old man but held herself back. "Thank you!"

Hancock looked pleased as he wrote in his own notebook. "You've helped us out a lot, Mr. Sheldon." They had another vital piece to the puzzle. "When did you notice the book?"

"Oh, right away. It was lying on the floor where she'd been standing. I tried to stop her, but as you can see . . ." he tapped his lame leg with his cane, "I can't do much hurryin' these days."

"Thanks, Mr. Sheldon. You've been very helpful." Detective Ballantine shook the man's fragile hand. "If you think of anything else, give me a call." He pulled a card from his jacket pocket and handed it to the old man.

Morgan walked with the two detectives toward their car. "Sounds like your sister had an appointment. Some place she had to be either by 1:30 or near 1:30." Detective Hancock stopped and looked around the area. "She's got to give us just a little more. Who was she meeting?"

"Where do women go on Thursday afternoons—suburban women who have time on their hands?"

Ballantine's question annoyed Morgan. "You make her sound like she was a fancy-free lady of leisure. She wasn't."

"Sorry. Didn't mean to imply . . ."

Detective Hancock threw his hands in the air and walked away muttering. "You're making us crazy."

Morgan hurried to get alongside him. "I want to help. I *need* to help."

Hancock shook his head as he looked at her. "You're going to get yourself in too deep one of these days, Morgan."

She was pleased to hear him call her Morgan, instead of Ms. Carruthers. She actually thought he was sincerely concerned about her safety. "I'll be careful."

Turning his attention to his partner, he said, "Let's get back to the station, Mayberry. I want to add this to that computer map."

Morgan followed Hancock and Ballantine to their car. "Look, what do you say we call a truce, Detective?" She held out her hand to Hancock.

The big man leaned back on his car and crossed one foot over the other as he studied her. "Meaning?"

His look, while not unfriendly, was very businesslike. She pulled back her hand. "Meaning . . . we work together. I don't want to sneak around behind your back, but you know I'm not going to just sit back and wait."

His large body heaved a sigh. "Look, I'm not wanting to find another murder on our hands, Ms. Carruthers."

"Morgan. I liked that better, okay?"

"Okay. Morgan, if that weirdo's still hanging around—and we can be pretty sure he is—he knows you're poking around. You don't want to meet up with that kind of slime. Trust me on this one."

"Why, Detective, you sound honestly worried about me." Morgan smiled.

Dell quickly turned away and opened the passenger car door. "Look, little lady, I'm just months away from retirement. I've done my time. There's a little boat calling my name, and I can smell the sea breeze." He narrowed his friendly eyes and pursed his lips. "Nothing—and I mean *nothing*—is going to keep me from heading straight for that sweet little craft as soon as my time's up. So if you go and get yourself hurt, or worse, I'm gonna be hooked here until I take care of the creep who did you in. I'm asking . . . no, I'm pleading. Morgan, stay out of this investigation!"

He moved the bulk of his large body into the car and closed the door. Morgan smiled as she leaned into the open window.

"I'm so glad to know you care, Detective. See ya."

As they pulled away, Morgan remembered the house keys she had for him in her purse. She began waving her arms and whistled loudly—a bit out of character, but effective.

The detective's car stopped and she ran up to Hancock's

window. Holding out the bag containing the keys, she said, "Thought you might be interested in looking these over. They're the extra set of house and car keys."

"Thanks. Now this is more like it," Hancock replied.

"See that powdery stuff? Just looked funny to me," she added. "Anyway, didn't want you to think I was holding out on you. Bye." She smiled at him and ran to her car.

ॐ ॐ ॐ ॐ

Morgan was exhausted when she finally returned to the house. The day had been an emotional roller coaster. If she could stay awake, she'd wait for Troy and tell him about the notebook and probably about her excursion to the 76 Station.

The Kings brought Michael home, and he had gone to bed early. Jenny finally showed up after nine. Her aunt's requests to know where she could have been all those hours met with a stubborn refusal to yield to Morgan's supervision. Morgan wanted to confront her, but, after the day she'd had, she was in no mood to handle what would most certainly turn into an unpleasant conversation.

Morgan fell asleep in a big, overstuffed chair in the den. When she awoke, her left arm decided to remain asleep. She awkwardly shook it, until the prickly feeling let her know the blood was returning to that appendage. She checked her watch. It was 11:30. Troy still wasn't home.

More than a little worried, Morgan headed upstairs to her room. When she heard the phone ring, she ran down the hall to grab it, hoping it didn't wake the rest of the house.

"Hi, I'm in Austin."

Morgan looked comically quizzical. "Austin? Texas?"

"The very same. I was about to tell you when you so rudely hung up on me this afternoon."

Morgan yawned, then defended herself. "Sorry, but I was in traffic."

"Apology accepted. I hope I didn't wake you."

"What are you doing in Austin?" She felt strangely uneasy about him not being in the house that night. It was the first time she had been there without him.

"I'm an investor in a mall down here. There's a little trouble with the contractor."

"So they called you—Mr. Fix It." Morgan took off her gold, heart-shaped earrings as she talked. "Woodsen to the rescue. When will you be coming home? Tomorrow?" she asked hopefully.

"I'm afraid it will be a few days." She felt sadness at hearing his words. "I keep a 'quick trip' suitcase at the office."

He gave her his hotel phone number, and she jotted it on a pad near the bed. "If you need to reach me, use the beeper, Morgan. Or call Marlene at the office. She'll know where I am all the time. You all going to be okay?" he asked.

She didn't want to add to his worry. "We're just fine. Michael and Jenny are in bed, sound asleep, I hope." There was no need to worry him with Jenny's late arrival. For now, Morgan would have to figure out how to handle that situation herself. She yawned again, "I'm falling asleep, Troy. Gotta go."

"Okay. Good night, Morgan. Tell the kids I love them."

Slipping into her nightgown, Morgan remembered she hadn't told Troy about the gas book or her little journey to the 76 Station. But there were no new breakthroughs. When he returned would be soon enough.

She was asleep almost as quickly as her head hit the pillow.

Twenty-nine

"B ye, have a great weekend," Jenny called to one of her friends as she and Rebecca ran out of the school.

"Any plans?" Rebecca asked.

"Dad's supposed to be back by tomorrow. Aunt Morgan's always watching me. I feel like I can't even breathe without her checking up on me."

The two walked toward the bus. "Did you ever think that maybe, after what happened, she's worried about you? I mean, you have been sort of . . . weird to her. I think she's kind of nice."

"That's because you don't have her hovering over you like a mother hen!"

The sound of a familiar car horn got their attention. The girls looked up and saw Cade's Wrangler pulling up behind the bus.

"Come on, let's go with him." Jenny started to run toward the car.

Her best friend grabbed her arm. "I don't know. My mom's expecting me home."

"Then we'll drop you off. Come on!" They jumped into the car.

"Hi, ladies!" Cade said as he put the car in gear and pulled out and around the bus. The afternoon was warm, and he had the top rolled back. "How about stopping off at the Cybersurf? It's usually hoppin' on Fridays."

"Great!" Jenny replied. She didn't really like hanging out

with Cade that much, but she was so glad not to have to go right home. It seemed so sad there. With her friends, she could at least pretend nothing had changed. To keep herself from getting stuck alone with Cade, Jenny talked Rebecca into coming with them and giving her mom a call from the café.

Cade surprised the girls by renting computer time. He'd never done that before when they were with him. "Let me take you surfing. I'll give you a look at some cool Websites."

This was Jenny's first time to actually go online with a Cybersurf computer. She'd been here a few times with Cade, but only to hang out and grab something to eat. Jenny had a computer at home, so why pay for time on this one? It never made a lot of sense to her before.

Both girls felt excited to be there with Cade, who seemed such an insider in this cybersociety. Soon he had Jenny chatting away in a couple of different teen chat rooms.

The Teen Love Shack, known to all the kids as *the* place to meet cyberfriends, was new to Jenny and Rebecca. The chat rooms Jenny visited were much tamer. She hadn't done a lot of looking around on the Web. The whole idea titillated her.

The home page of the Teen Love Shack stated clearly that it was for teens sixteen to nineteen. Rebecca was reticent to sign on. "But we're only fourteen—well, almost fifteen."

"Who'll know the difference?" Cade replied, urging them to join the chat. Each of them signed on with their screen names. He switched them to the Dallas chat room. "You might as well start out with the home boys."

After watching the chat for a while, Jenny decided to jump in. It took only a few minutes before she was feeling at ease there.

WHISTLER: Dallas, dude. Looking for Texas
chatter box.
MENACE: There are plenty of them around. Howdy,
little ladies. I'm the MENACE! Email me and I'll
get right back with a list of far out Websites.
Don't be shy. Looking for that mail. ;-)
TINKER: Dallas is the place, Whistler. You chat
in this room often?

```
WHISTLER:  Mostly at night. But today, I'm glad
I signed on earlier. BTW, where do you go to
school, Tinker?
TINKER:  RHS.
WHISTLER:  How old are you?
TINKER:  Eighteen.
```

Cade was so right about their anonymity. On the Web, Jenny could be anyone she wanted. Any age. Any personality. The freedom was electrifying.

Rebecca was getting more and more excited. "Can everyone in the room see what you're saying?" Rebecca asked.

"Sure. But that's the fun of a chat room." Cade turned to Jenny, urging her on. "Go ahead. Say whatever you want. They don't know who you are."

Without warning, Pam Ruston slipped into the booth next to Rebecca. "Hanging out with 'children' again, Cade?"

"Hi, Pam." Cade sounded annoyed.

"I was in the same chat room. Sometimes I just go into the rooms and lurk. Shame on you, Cade. What are you doing taking them to 'forbidden' places?"

Cade didn't respond, and Rebecca clearly didn't like this new addition to their booth, saying, "If we ignore her, maybe she'll go away."

"Not just yet." Pam reached over and pulled the keyboard away from Jenny.

"Hey, I was using that!"

Pam began to type with her brilliant pink porcelain nails. The tiny spider painted on her right index finger appeared to hop up and down as her fingers flew over the keys.

```
PINKY:  Hi, guys. Pinky's here. Just wanted you
all to know Tinker's a ''child''—don't waste
your time.
BUGSY:  Why, Pinky, it sounds like you're
jealous.<wink>
```

She pushed the keyboard back to Jenny. "See ya!"

"Not if we see you first," Rebecca called as Pam ran back to her friends in another booth. "That spider on her nail must be a self-portrait. Here, let me chat. It's my turn."

Les stopped by, peering over the booth. "Hey, good to see you, Cade. Stop by my office before you go. I've got that information you wanted."

Cade appeared uneasy as he replied, "Okay. Sure. Thanks."

Jenny was impressed. "I didn't know you were friends with the manager of this place."

"Sure. I hang here a lot. He's got some software I'm gonna borrow. Want to try it out on my own PC."

Jenny gazed around at the busy atmosphere, so different from what she experienced at home. "Thanks for bringing us here."

"I figured you needed a little R and R. You've got friends, Jen. Friends who care about you . . . like me." He looked at her meaningfully.

Please don't, Cade. It made Jenny nervous when Cade made comments like that. She knew he wanted more than just friendship, but she wasn't interested. She'd tried to tell him a million times, but he never gave up. Jenny quietly said, "You're a great guy. And a . . . good friend."

Knowing what she was trying to imply, Cade quickly interjected, "Hey, what time do you have to get home?" He glanced at his watch, realizing the afternoon had become evening. He was used to the strict rules at the Woodsen house.

"When I get there," Jenny said with a new-found feeling of freedom. "Dad's out of town."

"What about your aunt?"

"Since when do I have to answer to her?"

Rebecca was lost in cyberspace. "This is terrific. My folks sure wouldn't let me do this at home."

"Next time, I'll show you a really bizarre site where they do role playing," he told them. An impish smile made him look almost sinister. "It's a fantasy playground. You'll dig it." He turned and whispered in Jenny's ear, "Let's grab something to eat. I'm starved." Jenny nodded in agreement. They slid out of the computer booth, leaving Rebecca to fend for herself.

"Over there," he said, pointing to a small table in the corner.

When she was seated, he said, "I'll be right back. Go ahead and order something to drink." Jenny watched as Cade went to the door marked *Manager's Office*, located down the hallway near the restrooms. He knocked, then entered, closing the door behind him.

Sitting there alone, Jenny thought about calling home. Just to check in. But then she pushed the thought aside defiantly. "I'll have a Dr Pepper," she told the waitress.

The crowd was growing larger, and all of the computers were taken. Jenny noticed that her friend was still online. Then her eye caught sight of Pam entering the Manager's Office, but it didn't strike her as odd. Les seemed like a nice guy. He appeared to be friends with a lot of the kids.

Jenny was half finished with her soft drink when she saw the office door open. Cade emerged looking unnerved. He was putting a computer disk into his shirt pocket.

His words were brusque as he took Jenny's arm. "Come on, Jen. I've got to get you two home."

Thirty

Several lights were still on in the *North Dallas Daily News* building. One of those was in Dedra Koehler's office. As usual, she was there long after most of her cohorts had taken off for the weekend.

The *Daily* did not put out a weekend edition, but Dedra was lost in her work and writing ahead on several of the following week's "In the Know" columns. The overhead light was off, and she was working by the light from her desk lamp and the glow of her computer screen. She saved the document and ran her hands through her short hair, commending herself for her hard work. "Dedra, you pulled together a beauty here. If this doesn't make 'em think, they're brain dead."

Pleased with herself and wired from her continuous coffee drinking, she stood up in front of the window and gazed at her reflection in the dark glass. Putting her hands on the back of her waist, Dedra stretched her short, chubby body. "Oh, that feels good." Then alternating one arm at a time, she reached toward the ceiling. "And a one! And a two!" She then chuckled aloud. "Sweetheart, I think it's *way* too late for the Thigh Master!"

Dedra then walked to the printer to retrieve the pages it spit out. She was such a fast thinker and rapid typist that sometimes her fingers outpaced her thoughts or vice versa. Being a perfectionist, she always read her columns aloud to be certain they said exactly what she meant. Pacing her office, she began reading the section she'd just written.

"Critics say that censoring material available to adults on the Internet is unconstitutional. They are also professing that it will not be effective in protecting children from objectionable material.

"In reality, it doesn't matter whether our government moves to pass laws regarding Internet content, since offensive material is easily stored on and accessed through computers outside of our country.

"Public libraries, schools, and parents will continue to struggle with finding the best way for children to use the Internet. The many filtering software products I've mentioned in previous columns are continually being upgraded in an attempt to keep up with growing technology, while not blocking the educational and social opportunities the Internet offers.

"Alarming as it may seem, you must remain aware that even though you, as a parent, keep a watchful eye on your child's Web surfing habits, computers used at school, the library, or at a best friend's home may not be supervised or filtered. The protection of your child is in your hands.

"Stay alert and 'In the Know.' "

With a sigh of satisfaction, Dedra pulled out her grandfather's gold pocket watch—more out of habit than because she cared one whit about the time. It was almost midnight. She shrugged, filled her coffee mug for the umpteenth time, and plunked back down in her chair. Signing onto the Web server, she could hear her modem dialing in.

The connection was made, and her fingers flew over the keys as she entered her screen name, Meany, and then her password. She immediately went to a search engine to continue her quest for information. Dedra started a search by typing the words *Children Access,* then hit the Enter key.

Before the search even began, it was interrupted by the sudden appearance of an Immediate Message window.

"What the devil is this?" Dedra asked aloud, totally surprised.

ARA: working late aren't you, dedra?
MEANY: Who are you?

```
ARA:  i rarely have the opportunity to speak to
one so well known ... you're quite the writer...
MEANY:  Look, I'm in no mood to play games. Who
is this?
ARA:  let's just say we've already had a little
run-in :)
MEANY:  How did you know I was online? And my
screen name?
ARA:  LOL ... that's the easy part ... i've been
watching you gathering information for your
internet articles for weeks now.
MEANY:  The Web is full of nuts like you. I'm
outta here!
```

"Deranged crazies! The whole place is full of 'em." She darted her mouse to the disconnect icon, but before she could click on it to rid herself of this unwanted intruder, the mysterious chat powerfully snared her attention.

```
ARA:  spider bites can be so alarming ... but
then I guess you know that first hand. <grin>
```

Her eyes narrowed and her breathing increased. "Spiders?" Dedra touched the back of her neck where the spider bite was healing. She didn't like the queasy way she was feeling. The palms of her hands began sweating as she returned her attention to the chat. The cursor blinked. Ara lurked in the background waiting for her reply. Disconnecting him was no longer an option.

```
MEANY:  So you know I was bitten. Big deal!
Look, anyone around here could've known about
that.
ARA:  but i'm not around there. i'm out here—in
cyberspace...
MEANY:  I bet you're some joker right here at
the paper. If I get my hands on you, you're a
goner!
ARA:  you won't have that pleasure, precious
dedra ... but IMHO you are good ... very, very
```

```
good ... and i do hope you've written a really
great column tonight ... it may be your last :(
MEANY:  Don't you threaten me!
ARA:  it's no threat ... the first bite was a
warning ... don't you see how easy it is for me
to get to you?
MEANY:  The spiders? Were you in my house?
ARA:  you were fortunate dedra ... i wish i
could say the same for beth...
MEANY:  Beth? I don't know anyone named Beth.
ARA:  you and she were so much alike ... beth
thought she could stop me too ... what a shame
... but she left me no other choice ... just
like you.
```

Dedra knew there was no way she was going to let this maniac off. She had to keep him talking. Quickly she began to log the session, saving it to her hard disk. Maybe Ara would say something, anything that might help her discover who he was. She wanted to look at this chat again, with a cooler head.

```
MEANY:  Who is Beth?
ARA:  you would have liked her ... so concerned
about the poor innocents ... trying so hard to
be a protector ... a valiant effort, indeed ...
but i'll win in the end ... i always do :) it's
too bad—the two of you would have been quite the
adversarial pair for me.
```

Dedra's investigative spirit had shifted into high gear. If only I could draw him out—cause him to slip up. Adrenaline urged her to continue.

```
MEANY:  Tell me about Beth. Who is she?
ARA:  poor sweet beth isn't around any more
<grin>
MEANY:  You seem very proud of yourself.
ARA:  SICS
MEANY:  I'd like to know more about Beth.
ARA:  so would a lot of people ... you think
```

```
you're smarter than me ... don't you, dedra?
well i'm the one in charge ... don't forget that
:-(
MEANY: Ara, tell me...
ARA:  i do hope you have enjoyed this little
chat ... i do hate to lose an enemy as clever
and cunning as you ... it's a stinging thought!
good-bye, precious dedra.
MEANY: Ara, wait ...
```

Suddenly Dedra's connection to the Internet was severed. Angrily, she slapped the keyboard. "You come back here you . . . you . . ." Dedra was furious that he had the ability to somehow find her and control her computer—and she had no earthly idea who the intruder had been.

She became very quiet, her mind sifting through the information he had given her. In the eerie glow of the empty computer screen she wondered, *Who was Beth?*

A car parked in the darkest end of the building's parking lot became silent as the engine was turned off. Light from a distant source allowed the driver to see Dedra Koehler's picture on the banner of her "In the Know" column in Friday's *North Dallas Daily*. Nervously looking at his watch, he began impatiently jiggling his right leg as he watched her at her desk. "Come on, lady! Come on!"

Stopping abruptly, he reached into the glove compartment and removed a small manila envelope. He smiled as he shook it and heard a rustling, scratching sound. Life stirred inside. "Pretty soon, we'll go for a ride," he whispered, laying the envelope on the other seat.

Glancing back up to Dedra's window on the second floor, he exclaimed, "Yes!" It was dark.

His breath was visible as he quickly pulled plastic gloves from under the car seat and began to nervously pull them on. He then reached carefully into his jacket pocket and slid out a capped syringe filled with a milky liquid. Examining its contents, he turned it slowly in the light.

It worked before, and it will work again, he thought, attempting to calm himself.

❧   ❧   ❧   ❧

Molly Hansford pulled her late model red Buick LeSabre into the *North Dallas Daily News* parking lot. She wouldn't normally be there on a Saturday morning, but she was on her way to a wedding in Tyler and had left the gift in her office. She was surprised to see Dedra's old pickup still parked where she had been the day before.

She parked next to it and got out. *Hope she didn't have car trouble*, she thought as she walked past the car. She then saw Dedra's reporter's notebook lying halfway under the car, near the driver's door. "That's strange, she never lets this outta her sight," Molly said as she bent over and picked up the notebook.

The building was locked for the weekend, so she fumbled with her keys and punched her code into the alarm system. In moments, she was in the building and hurrying to her office space on the second floor. *I'd better drop this off*, she thought, remembering she was carrying Dedra's notebook. It was always so strange in here on weekends . . . so quiet.

Passing her own cubicle, Molly hurried down the hallway leading to the few real offices. Suddenly she heard footsteps coming up behind her. Gasping, she whirled around, dropping the book. Molly's knees went weak.

"Howdy! What the heck are you doing here?"

"Dedra!" Molly felt as if she were about to faint. "Don't *ever* sneak up on someone like that! You almost gave me a heart attack!" She was on the verge of anger.

Dedra, wearing the same clothing as the day before, took her friend by the arm and scooped up the notebook. "There's that thing! Thought I'd gone and lost it. Here. I think you better sit down." She helped her into the cluttered office.

It took Molly a minute to regain her composure. "What're you doing here?"

"Didn't you see my truck outside? The thing decided not to start. I guess I forgot to turn off my headlights when I came in early yesterday. And facing the building like it does, guess no one saw it."

"Then you stayed here last night?"

"Yep, that sofa in Cecil's office isn't half bad. A little on the narrow side, but I've used it before."

Molly pointed to the notebook. "How'd that get in the parking lot?"

"It's funny, but when I went out to the truck, it was pretty late. It didn't take a rocket scientist to see that the thing was dead—I knew the moment I opened the door and no lights came on. I guess I went a little nuts and started swinging at it with my bag! Guess that's when it must've fallen out."

Molly watched Dedra as she gazed out her window at the parking lot. She looked puzzled.

"What's wrong?"

"Ah, nothin' really." Her hand moved to the healing spider bite on the back of her neck. She turned and looked at Molly. "Last night was sorta spooky. . . . Ah, forget all that. Look at you, you're all dressed up and heading to . . ."

"Tyler." Molly got up and headed for the doorway. "For my brother's wedding. We never thought he'd get married."

Dedra went back to the window and replied in a distant, almost preoccupied tone, "Then you go and have a wild ole time. I'll call and get a jump."

As Molly pulled out of the nearly vacant parking lot, she could still see Dedra framed in her office window.

Thirty-one

*T*he weekend had been a rocky one for Morgan and Jenny.
Business had kept Troy out of town until Sunday night.
After Friday night, Morgan had grounded Jenny and told her
she was not to ride with Cade again until she gave her permission.

Over the weekend, despite Morgan's continued efforts to
talk some sense into the young girl, the cold war continued. But
she said nothing to Troy when she spoke with him on the phone.
What could he do from Austin?

Morgan called her mother on Sunday to say hello and to ask
for some advice. "How did you do it, Mom?"

Gloria, surely hearing the desperation in her daughter's
voice, replied, "Your father and I worked together. You and
Troy are going to have to do the same thing. You can't let her
think she can go around one of you to get to the other."

"Jenny's not acting like a girl who just lost her mother. She's
pushing everyone away."

"But you can't see her heart, honey. I can tell you, my
granddaughter's lost without her mother. Even though Beth
didn't think so, that girl looked to her for love, comfort, and
rules. Now she's gone, and Jenny's not sure where she's going
to get all that."

Gloria's words rang true. But it was hard to see Jenny as a
lost little girl when she resembled an angry tigress.

"If you ask me, she's giving you a hard time because she's
being protective of her mother. Even though she's not there

anymore, Jenny's still protecting her place in the family."

Gloria's words remained in her thoughts when five days of Jenny's attitude had almost made Morgan decide to pack and head back to the business piranhas in Minneapolis. Her toughest account had never confounded Morgan more than this rebellious fourteen-year-old.

"I know what you're doing, Jenny," Morgan said to her niece that morning at breakfast. "You're testing me."

"Why don't you just go home?" Jenny knew her father had already left for the office and wouldn't hear her outburst. "You're not my mother! So don't boss me around."

"If this is a battle of wills, you've got competition," Morgan called as Jenny grabbed her books and rushed off to catch the bus. She shook her head. Jenny was growing colder and more distant.

Morgan had to have some time with Troy tonight. Jenny was not the only thing they needed to talk about; there was also the gas book and her meeting with Detective Hancock at the 76 Station. She only prayed that by the time she told him, it wouldn't be old news.

After her morning shower, Morgan slipped into her jeans, a blue plaid cotton shirt tied at the waist, and white tennis shoes without socks. She had just finished making up her room when she heard the security system keypad in the upstairs hallway begin to beep. Panicked, Morgan grabbed for the phone.

"It's just me!" Troy called out.

She let out a big sigh of relief and ran out into the hall and down the stairs. Since his hours were so erratic, Morgan seemed to hardly see him on weekdays unless she made an effort to wait up for him or got up with him before dawn.

Morgan tried to hide her excitement when she greeted him, but it was futile. "Hi, there," she said, a bit breathless.

"Morning. Or should I say afternoon?" Troy was standing in the doorway to his study. His crooked smile made his face even more handsome.

"Just because you get up in the middle of the night doesn't mean everyone does. And it's morning. What are you doing home?" She followed him into the study.

"I left a site map here, and I need it for a meeting. Just stopped off for a minute." She was watching him rummage through some rolled-up maps sticking out of a small wicker wastebasket. He must have felt her eyes on him, because he turned and looked straight at her. "By the way, this isn't trash. Just an easy place to store these." Then he laughed.

Morgan felt a bit embarrassed and self-conscious. "What's so funny?" Her hands checked her hair, her shirt buttons. Everything was in place.

Troy leaned his arm against the corner of the bookshelf and cocked his head, studying her. She felt her face flush. "Is this a private joke, or are you going to let me in on it?"

He realized she was uncomfortable. "I'm sorry, Morgan. You just look so . . ."

"So what?" she urged.

He gathered up his briefcase and stuck the map into it. "So young. You know, the jeans. The tennis shoes." He paused. "It's cute."

"Cute?" She didn't know whether to be upset or not. "I've got a lot of work to do today, and I don't always . . ."

He waved off her statement. "It's just that in the past I've always seen you dressed up. I like this. It's . . ."

"Cute?" She laughed, forgiving his bumbling and charming effort to compliment her.

"Okay, now you're laughing at me!"

She covered her mouth, trying desperately to stop. "No. No, I'm not. Really."

"Turnabout's fair play." He started to leave the room. "Got to go, Morgan. I'm going to be late." As he passed her in the doorway, he reached up and gave her ponytail a jerk.

"Hey!" If she was looking "young," he was certainly acting like a schoolboy. She followed him into the kitchen. As he was about to leave, the front doorbell rang.

His voice took on a tone of apprehension. "You expecting someone?"

"No." The bell rang again. "Just a second." Morgan hurried to the front door. Looking through the small peephole, she saw only a field of yellow. Morgan opened the door to find a florist deliveryman holding a beautiful arrangement of yellow roses.

"My goodness, what's this?"

"Morgan Carruthers?" he asked.

"Yes, I'm Morgan."

Troy walked into the living room and was watching with interest as the man handed Morgan the extraordinary arrangement in an obviously expensive, tall cut-glass vase.

"Have a nice day," the man called as he ran down the sidewalk to his truck.

Morgan closed the door. "Yellow roses are my favorite!" She whirled around and saw Troy looking strangely disturbed.

"Who sent those?"

"I don't know. That's why there's a card." She smiled as she nuzzled them. "But I guess that question removes you from the list." The aroma was intoxicating, and the velvety texture of the petals felt cool on her cheeks.

It was obvious Troy was not leaving until he knew who sent her the flowers. Morgan sat them on a nearby table and pulled the small white envelope from its holder. "I adore getting flowers. It's so . . . so . . . ."

"Romantic?" he asked.

"It can be, when they're from the right person. But I was thinking more along the lines of . . . special."

Sliding the card from the envelope, her expression turned from cheerful to stunned.

"What's wrong, Morgan?"

She could barely believe what she saw on the card. "They're from Kevin."

Troy's face told her everything she needed to know. He was shocked and suspicious of Kevin's sudden reentry into Morgan's life.

"I thought you two were finished."

Morgan didn't answer as her eyes scanned the message on the card.

Dear Morgan,

Can you ever forgive me? I've made a mistake. It's you I love with all my heart. I always have. I can't live without you. I'm coming to Dallas tomorrow so we can talk in person. Please see me.

With all my love,
Kevin

Morgan looked up slowly, her eyes moist and her hand nervously rubbing her shoulder. Troy waited. "The note says he still loves me. He's coming here tomorrow." She paused, trying to take it all in. "It's just crazy."

Troy's eyes looked away, and he pretended to straighten some papers sticking from his briefcase. "Are you going to see him?"

Morgan sensed a coolness in Troy's words. His questioning eyes drifted back to her.

"The guy's obviously nuts about you. He was an idiot to leave you for someone else. I guess he came to his senses."

He seemed to want some kind of response from her, but she had none to give. A few minutes ago, Kevin was out of her life, as if he'd dropped off the end of the earth. Now she wasn't sure how she felt about seeing him again.

"Well, are you?"

Morgan took the flowers and headed for the stairs. "I don't know, Troy. I have to think about it. We'll talk when you get home tonight. We have a lot to discuss. Let's do it then, please."

In her room, Morgan set the roses on the dresser and walked to the window. A few moments later, she watched as Troy went to his car with hurried, almost angry steps. Sighing, she read the note once more and felt her knees buckle. Putting her right hand on the dressing table chair, she let herself down slowly. Incredulously, she read and reread the note. "Kevin, you can't do this to me. Not now."

For nearly two months she had been successful in pushing him into the background. But now his words frayed her nerve endings. Visions of Kevin's handsome face and winning smile forced themselves into her thoughts.

If she were still in Piney Bend and Beth hadn't been murdered, Morgan would not have been able to rid herself so quickly of the pain from this lost relationship. But that anguish had been brutally replaced by another kind of violently painful loss. Morgan had loved Kevin for so long, but he had broken her trust with words of betrayal so cutting and torturous, she'd thought she would die.

I'm not ready to see him. She knew Kevin could be very persuasive, and she was vulnerable these days. The timing was completely wrong. It wouldn't be fair to either of them.

She tore the card into pieces and let them drop to the floor. "I hate you for doing this to me," she whispered aloud.

Thirty-two

Going to the meeting had been a waste of time, for Troy found it almost impossible to concentrate on the new Hurst project. The meeting hadn't gone well at all, and before it was finished, he excused himself and drove back to his office.

He spent the better part of the day getting absolutely nothing done. Troy stared at his phone, wanting to call Morgan. Was she going to see Kevin? *Why did he care?*

His hand reached for the phone and he began to dial. Unnerved by his feelings, Troy slammed down the receiver and rushed out through the front office without even bothering to take his suit coat.

"I'll be back after a while." Troy spoke briskly as he passed his secretary, Marlene. She had been with Troy Woodsen since he started his company over ten years ago. She'd watched it grow from a one-man operation to the successful development firm it was today. And she'd watched Troy grow with it.

Surprised by his unexpected exit, Marlene ran to the door calling, "Troy! You've got meetings!" But Troy was already driving off in the company's white Ford Explorer. Returning to her desk, she checked his appointment book, then began to cancel Troy's appointments for the rest of the day.

The Explorer moved quickly in and out of traffic on Interstate 30, through downtown Fort Worth. Just outside of the city Troy turned, following the signs to Weatherford. He was driving much too fast, as he always did when he was upset. It was childish and dangerous, he knew. But lately Troy found it harder and harder to control his reactions to the stress he felt. His usually crystal-clear thinking was blurred. Emotions of any kind made Troy uneasy. *Don't let them control you. Be strong . . . hold it in*, he told himself.

Troy felt like he had lost control of so many things in his life lately. Where was the control he always had over his emotions? He was tired of pushing down his own rage and sadness so he could be strong for Michael and Jenny. And for Morgan. Maybe he didn't know how he really felt anymore.

He was also angry at how he'd reacted to the flowers. *Why is it bothering me? Go back to Minneapolis, Morgan! Go back to Kevin! There's nothing here for you but heartache.* Troy's strong hands twisted the steering wheel tightly.

His foot heavy on the gas pedal, he turned onto a small farm road that wound back into acres of beautiful ranch land. Here was a place where he could be alone, with no one needing anything from him. Having no expectations. Troy knew exactly where he was going. He yearned to see the piece of land he and Beth had purchased last year.

They were both excited about building a beautiful ranch house, but Troy knew it was much more his dream than hers. He thought of his wife and wondered, *Did I make you happy, Beth?*

He knew she was thrilled at the thought of getting the children out of Dallas and into the country. However, Jenny had been devastated by the thought and had cried for days. But he and Beth were a team. In their hearts they knew that a home built here, in the Texas countryside, would be wonderful.

If only we had done it then, Beth. You'd still be here with me. What am I supposed to do now?

Ahead was the white ranch-style fence they'd built along the border of their land. He turned the Explorer sharply into the gravel driveway. Hopping out, he opened the big gate, then continued down the rutted, small dirt road about a half-mile up into the trees to the spot Beth had chosen for their home. Turning off the engine, he sat quietly, his hands still on the steering wheel.

He bowed his head, resting it on his hands. Troy's strong,

deep voice broke as he spoke softly, tears filling his eyes. "God, help me. I don't know what to do. You've handed me something I can't handle, and I hate it. I have no idea what's happening to me . . . to my life."

After a long moment, he climbed down out of the four-by-four and began roaming aimlessly across the land. An afternoon breeze had come up, and it was cool and refreshing. Beth would have said something lyrical such as, "It's God's touch for a broken heart."

He stopped and smiled. "Now, I'd never have thought of something like that to say. Was that you, honey?" he said, half expecting to hear her voice. He could feel Beth's presence, and it brought him peace, the way her touch cooled his brow and her kiss set his heart on fire.

Troy must have walked for over an hour before he became aware that his thoughts had shifted from Beth to Morgan. What would she tell him tonight? Was she going to leave? He didn't want her to go.

If Morgan left, he'd be alone to deal with Jenny and Michael. Was that it? Had he come to depend upon Morgan as a nanny for his children? "The woman's got a life!" he shouted, so he could hear it loud and clear. The longer she stayed at the Woodsen house, the more difficult it would be to let her leave. "My children aren't Morgan's responsibility."

His own words echoed in his ears. Pensively he stopped beside the fence, put a foot on the bottom rail, and leaned forward on his knee. "Leave now, Morgan, or I might not be able to let you go." The words were quiet and full of a truth he wished with all his heart he could deny. Hot tears filled his eyes.

Beth, I'm sorry. I don't know what's wrong with me. I miss you, honey.

Morgan had been a part of his life for years. She was his sister-in-law. But they'd barely gotten to know each other. Thinking about it, it almost seemed like she'd made a point of staying clear of him. He couldn't remember even one time when the two of them had spent time together, alone. It just never happened before now.

Morgan was interesting and he liked her. It was strange the

way two sisters could come from the same upbringing and turn out so differently. Beth had been a great wife and mother, openly affectionate and caring. He had been completely happy with her. There was no doubt in his heart that he loved Beth. Their marriage worked, and he would have contentedly spent the rest of his life with her—if only violence hadn't changed everything, leaving Troy to face the future alone.

Morgan was a dynamic, successful businesswoman who had broken through the glass ceiling and gone right to the top. He admired her greatly. She was beautiful, just like Beth, but more striking. And her affections, like his, were not as accessible. *Had she been that way with Kevin? Is that why he found someone else?*

Troy scooped up a handful of stones. He threw them, one by one, hitting the top rail of the fence. *I'm jealous.* The startling thought rocked him to his very being. "God, forgive me. I've lost my mind!"

He whirled around and ran through the open field toward the car, chastising himself with every step. "I'm crazy. I can't be jealous. This is ridiculous. I'm trying to replace Beth with someone who looks like her. That's all. That's all there is to it."

Jumping into the Explorer, he started it with a roar. His hands turned the wheel violently and he floored the gas pedal. The car spun in a ninety-degree turn throwing dirt, dust, and rocks in all directions. *That settles it*, he thought, *the sooner Morgan leaves, the better.*

The sun setting behind him, he drove back toward the office feeling more in control. Trying to settle the issue in his mind, he said to himself, *It will be good for Morgan to get back with Kevin. Morgan deserves to be loved.*

Thirty-three

Yes, Kevin. Thank you, they're beautiful." Morgan couldn't believe she was actually speaking to Kevin. His card had left her with no option but to call. If she didn't, he would, and she didn't want to risk being taken by surprise at an awkward moment.

"Honey, I know you've been through so much. I left emails, but you never answered."

He sounded so sincere, and she knew the pain she heard was real. "I couldn't. There was no reason to answer, Kevin. Please . . ."

"I miss you. I'm a fool. Forgive me. I'm sorry I hurt you, honey. Please, see me tomorrow, Morgan. We'll talk it out. We had something really good, and I know we can get back on track. I know we can. Please. I love you."

Morgan had made up her mind before she called. This time, he wasn't going to get what he wanted. "No, Kevin, don't come. I can't see you. Not now. And you have no idea what I've been through here. Things have changed—nothing's the same. For you to think you can just come to Dallas expecting to patch things up . . . It's insane!"

"But we have to talk, Morgan. Please."

"Don't come. I can't see you, Kevin." She was pleading with him and on the verge of tears. "Don't put us both through that."

"I know it's been horrible for you, sweetheart. But, please . . ."

"Don't you understand? I can't and that's the end of it."
Morgan's resolve surprised even her. She had always been such
a pushover for him. "You can't just walk back into my life and
expect me to drop everything. I've got responsibilities."

"Don't throw everything away, Morgan. I'm going crazy
without you."

She would have given anything to hear those words two
months ago—but now that was a lifetime ago. It no longer carried the same significance it once had. For her, it was over.

Kevin sounded hurt and disappointed. "When will you be
back? Carl said he's not sure you *will* come back."

"I don't know, Kevin. I'm not even thinking about that
right now." How she wished she could give him the answer to
the question that truly haunted her. *When will I know who killed
my sister?* Perhaps that would be the thing that released her to
return to her old life. "There are things here I have to do. People who need me."

"I need you."

Morgan held tightly to her decision. "Kevin, please. Don't
do this." She paused. "I'll be in touch, but I've got to go
now. . . . Good-bye."

"Morgan?" He spoke quickly to keep her from hanging up.
She knew he didn't want their conversation to end. "Take care
of yourself. If you just need someone . . . call."

"Good-bye, Kevin." Morgan hung up the phone, surprised
that she wasn't emotionally destroyed as she had expected to be.
A flood of relief gave her spirits a needed lift.

❧   ❧   ❧   ❧

Morgan was curled up on the sofa reading a magazine as she
waited for Jenny to show up. Apparently nothing she said to her
niece seemed to get through to her. But Morgan wasn't ready
to give up.

It was now after nine, and she knew Troy would blow up if
Jenny didn't get home before he did. Then she heard the back
door open, and the alarm began beeping. She jumped.

"It's me," Troy called the second he was in the door.

Glad I'm not Jenny, Morgan thought, then said aloud, "I'm in the living room, Troy." Morgan was anxious to see him. Her day had been filled with a disturbing variety of feelings, things she couldn't explain. What worried her most was the mood he was in when he left earlier. He had been so cold, so distant. They needed to talk.

He slowly walked in the room, the top two buttons of his dark green collarless shirt already undone. He looked very tired, the features on his handsome face tense. Morgan yearned to run to him and give him a hug, but instead she bit the side of her lip and kept her seat, not knowing what to expect from him.

Morgan smiled warmly. "I'm glad you're home."

"Me too." He flopped down in the chair directly across.from her. Stretching out his long legs, he used his toes to slip his feet out of the dark brown leather loafers.

They both were at a loss for words. When he finally spoke, he chose his carefully. "Did you speak to Kevin?"

She closed the magazine and laid it beside her. "Yes."

"So what time is he arriving tomorrow?" He nonchalantly put his hands behind his head.

Morgan leaned forward. "I asked him not to come. I'm not ready to see him."

Troy, surprised at her response, pulled in his outstretched legs and leaned forward. "That's sort of what I want to talk about, Morgan. About what's going on here."

Her stomach tensed, anticipating his words.

"I've been thinking about everything . . . and I think you should go on back to Minneapolis."

There it was. The words she had dreaded hearing. After lunch the other day, she thought they had agreed she would stay on for a while, at least to help with the children. "But, Troy, I told you I wanted to stay. It was all right with my office and you . . . and the children—"

Interrupting her, he said, "Morgan, I'm not throwing you out. I just think you've given up too much for us. And that's not necessary." He paused to be sure he put a non-threatening emphasis on his statement. "I think it would be best if you go back. There's really nothing more you can do here."

She squirmed in her chair. "Is this because of the flowers? Because if it is . . ."

"No. You're a big girl, Morgan. Whatever you decide about your relationship with Kevin is up to you. But I feel guilty keeping you here."

Morgan got to her feet and looked down at him in the chair. "You need me here and you know it, Troy Woodsen. I may not be much of a 'fill-in mom' for these kids, but I'm doing the best I can. And you can't be thinking of just bringing in a stranger to take care of them."

"Whoa . . . now, hold it," he said, totally surprised at her reaction. Motioning with his hand, Troy continued. "Sit down. Relax."

She went back to her chair and sat down, but she didn't relax. The thought of leaving here was more painful than she ever imagined. Morgan began thinking of reasons why she couldn't possibly leave. "And the police . . . well, they need someone to stay after them. When I saw Detective Hancock the other day . . ."

Troy looked surprised, his eyes glaring at her. "You saw Detective Hancock again . . . after we saw him?"

Morgan had put her foot in it now. Why hadn't she told him everything the other day? "Yes. I ran into him at a service station."

Troy clearly knew there was more to this story. "And?" He never removed his gaze from her.

"We just haven't had time to sit down and talk. The night I was going to tell you all about this, you ended up in Austin. Then you were gone, and what were you going to do about it in Austin? So that's why—"

"I'm not going to jump down your throat. At least not yet. So you better fill me in."

"Okay. The missing gas book—the one Beth wrote her fill-ups in—well, it showed up in the mail. You see, this station manager found it. Her name was inside, and he sent it back. Naturally when I saw a hand-addressed letter to Beth, I opened it."

Troy raised his eyebrows, saying nothing.

She continued, "Anyway, I went to the station to talk to the man. To find out what he remembered about that day. About Beth."

"And of course you told Detective Hancock about this book?"

"Of course I did. But who knew he'd run right over there, too?"

Troy smiled as he lowered his head and shook it in disbelief. "That's his job! You're something. Beth would be very proud of you. But I'm furious!"

Standing up in his stocking feet, he towered over her. She looked up at him from her chair. His face and his voice let her know in no uncertain terms that he was not kidding. "Are you trying to get yourself killed? What were you doing, going to that station? How do you know what their involvement might have been in the murder? For a really intelligent woman, you're awfully stupid sometimes, Morgan."

She wanted to stand up, but if she did, she'd be right in his face, so she didn't move. Morgan was trapped, but she continued to defend her actions. "I just wanted to talk to him."

"I bet Hancock was thrilled."

"Well, he wasn't exactly happy. But before he left, I got the feeling he's okay with my involvement. Really."

Troy turned and walked away. "Well, I'm not! This is just another reason why I want you to go back to Minneapolis. You're just crazy enough to get yourself in big trouble." He paused, then turned back to find her standing right behind him. He put his hands on her shoulders, and his voice softened. "Morgan Carruthers, I care what happens to you. I'm just getting to know you after sixteen years, and I'm liking it." He became more serious. "Please, stay out of this. Leave it to the police. If anything happened to you . . ." He put his arms around her protectively.

Morgan leaned into his embrace, enjoying the comfort and security. It had been such a long time since she'd been held.

"I'm home!" Jenny called out as she ran into the living room. When she saw her father holding Morgan, she stopped dead in her tracks.

Troy immediately released Morgan and turned to face his daughter. She looked shocked. He looked very angry. "Jenny! Do you know what time it is?"

"I was just out with some friends. I can't stay in this house forever."

"You've got to check in with me or your aunt." His words were stern, but it was easy to hear his concern.

"Well, you're never home. And I didn't know I was supposed to answer to *her*." Jenny glared contemptuously at Morgan, then turned and hurried up the stairs. At the top, she stopped and looked down at her father. "Just because of what happened to Mom, I'm going to be a prisoner for the rest of my life. That's what's going to happen, isn't it? Well, I can't help it that Mom's gone. It wasn't my fault. So don't just lock me in my room and throw away the key!" She ran into her room and slammed the door.

Troy looked hurt and emotionally exhausted. "It's almost ten and Jenny wasn't home. Why didn't you tell me?"

"I was going to."

"Well, it seems like you've been keeping a lot of things from me. Why, Morgan?"

Morgan knew that Troy's need for control meant he didn't like being kept in the dark about anything. She was feeling fortunate that he didn't hand her a ticket for the next plane to Minneapolis.

Troy continued to unleash his frustration on Morgan. "She's fourteen years old, Morgan. Do you have any idea where she was tonight?"

Morgan had hoped Jenny would show up before her father got home so they could avoid this very scene. "No, not exactly. I've been trying to get control of this situation, Troy, but Jenny's so headstrong and . . . well, this mothering thing's a little new to me, too."

"I know." He paused, conquered by frustration. "But it shouldn't be new to me. I'm her father, and I don't know anything about her. I don't know who she hangs out with or what she does after school." Disheartened, he continued. "What if I'm not able to do this, Morgan?"

"But you can. I know you can."

Thirty-four

Morgan awoke around midnight, and despite over an hour of tossing and turning, she could not go back to sleep. A glance at the little clock on the bedside table revealed it was 1:34 A.M. Unable to lie in bed a second longer, she rose and walked to the dressing table. Sitting on the small chair, she looked at her tousled reflection in the mirror and, without thinking, picked up an oval, silver-handled brush and slowly pulled it through her tangled brown hair.

The house was almost silent. Peaceful to some, Morgan wasn't fond of this time of night, for it always made her feel alone. Setting down her brush, she suddenly thought she heard someone crying. Quickly slipping into her multicolored silk kimono, she hurried toward the children's rooms. Michael must be having a nightmare.

Nearly to his door, Morgan stopped and turned around. The crying was coming from behind the closed door to what had been Beth and Troy's bedroom. At that moment, she realized it wasn't Michael or Jenny—it was Troy. "Oh, Troy," she whispered, her heart aching at his loss. Morgan knew he hadn't slept in that room since Beth was killed.

Her first instinct was to return to her own room. But she was torn, feeling drawn to go to him but unable to find the courage to knock on the door. He had been so convincingly strong. *"Lean on me,"* he told everyone, including Morgan. *"I'll take care of everything."* But she had known the day would come when it would be too much for him to bear. Would he be angered by her intrusion into this private moment?

Turning away from the door, Morgan began to walk back to her own room. But the sound of Troy's soft sobbing pulled at her heart. Something her mother had said came to her mind. *"The only way to heal a hurt that's this deep is to share it. Carry it together. It's too much for one heart to bear."*

Morgan returned to the door and softly knocked. "It's Morgan." She opened the door slightly. "May I come in?"

Troy, barefooted and in jeans and a white T-shirt, sat on the edge of the big bed. His hair was tousled, his head cradled in his strong hands. The tears weren't bitter or angry—they were a soulful mourning. She waited.

After a long moment, she realized if Troy didn't want her there, he would have told her to leave. She took his silence as permission to enter. She softly closed the door. "Troy, is there anything I can do?"

Morgan followed her instincts and moved closer to him. Making no attempt to hide his tears, Troy raised his head and looked up at her. "I miss her. Oh, God . . ." Again, he buried his head in his hands. The sobs were strong and yet quiet, and his large, muscular body shuddered from the force of his sorrow.

Morgan noticed packing boxes stacked near the large walk-in closet. Several dresses and other personal things that had belonged to Beth were lying on the floor. She gently stroked Troy's sandy hair. "You don't have to do this alone."

Troy got to his feet and picked them up, one after another. "I thought I could pack her things." He turned to Morgan. "But I can't."

Morgan had asked him a few weeks after the funeral if he wanted her to pack Beth's things, but Troy wasn't ready to even discuss it. She had been waiting for him to let her know when the time was right.

"How do I do this, Morgan?" He raised pain-filled eyes to hers.

"I'll help you, if you'll let me."

He looked down at the boxes, his hazel eyes glistening with tears. "It's time."

"I'll begin tomorrow, while the children are in school."

"Are you sure? It's going to be hard for you, too."

Morgan was truthful when she answered, "I want to do it, Troy. Really, I do."

He surprised her when he reached for her hand. She gave it willingly. Tears rolled down her cheeks, and she did nothing to stop them or wipe them away.

"You're not going to be alone, Troy. I'm not leaving." Somewhere she found a smile. "Unless you're trying to get rid of me."

"Morgan, believe me—you're welcome here as long as you want to stay." He paused and looked into her dark brown eyes. "We need you." The sincerity in his voice touched Morgan deeply.

"It's wonderful to be needed. And I need all of you . . . more than you'll ever know."

Sighing deeply, Troy looked around the room that once had been filled with so much love. "I think I'll sleep here tonight."

Morgan nodded in understanding, knowing he needed to say good-bye to the last visible traces of the wife he loved so much.

❧   ❧   ❧   ❧

The next day, as she had promised Troy, Morgan began packing Beth's things. She had thought that by now it would have been easier, but packing away a life was more stressful than she could ever have imagined. Memories besieged her throughout the afternoon. First she'd cry, then laugh. Beth left her with so many treasured moments.

"Well, I'm almost finished," she said, putting her hands on her small waist. There was a finality to this that would probably help them all in their healing. Troy planned to talk with Jenny and Michael, to let them know what had been done.

He'd picked out several special things for both of them, things he knew Beth would have wanted them to have. Troy kept only her wedding ring and a gold locket of two intertwined hearts, one larger than the other, and neither one whole without the other. Other than pictures, he wanted nothing else.

Almost all of the boxes had been filled and taped shut. Folded neatly on a top shelf, she found Beth's favorite sweaters. Morgan gently picked up a familiar pink lamb's-wool pullover. She smelled it, recognizing the scent of Beth's favorite perfume, and held it close to her cheek. It was just last Thanksgiving morning when Beth, a vision in pink wearing this sweater and matching pink wool slacks, stood at the gate, waving as Morgan and Kevin walked up the ramp from their flight to Dallas.

Now Morgan gently and lovingly placed the sweater into the last box. She shook her head. The large walk-in closet looked so empty with only Troy's clothing remaining. She spread out his suit jackets, slacks, shirts, and jeans to take up as much of the large closet as possible. Noting his wonderful taste in clothes, Morgan recalled Beth saying she rarely had to pick out anything for him. But even his array of clothes did little to hide the emptiness.

After taping each box closed, she stacked them near the door. "There!" Morgan sighed with relief and sadness as she took one last look into the closet. Realizing she hadn't checked the custom-built drawers, she began to do so, knowing it was important that she didn't overlook something that might be found unexpectedly.

After cleaning out the top two drawers, she opened the bottom drawer expecting to find more of Beth's things. When her eyes fell on the contents of the drawer, Morgan stood for a moment, her hand inches away from a pair of exquisitely tailored men's silk pajamas. Monogrammed on the pocket were the initials *TJW*. Troy James Woodsen.

She slammed the drawer shut, her hand flying to cover her mouth. *What's wrong with me?* she thought. The tiny flutter in her stomach made Morgan feel like the young college girl who had met Troy for the first time that weekend so many years ago. The knowledge that even then she'd felt an overwhelming feeling of attraction to him frightened her.

Denial wouldn't help much, though. "What kind of person am I?" she said aloud. Leaning against the closet doorway, Morgan slowly let her body slide down the wooden frame until she was sitting propped up between the sides of the entry, her arms wrapped around her knees.

Somewhat ashamed, Morgan knew her attraction for Troy began the first time she laid eyes on him. *Was that why I never tried to be friends with him? To get to know him better?* She wondered, knowing that deep within she hadn't trusted herself. Years of refusing to even think about feelings she wouldn't acknowledge didn't change the fact that Morgan measured all other men by Troy. By his looks, his strength of character, and his devotion to Beth. And no one, not even Kevin, could live up to that kind of scrutiny.

Enough of this! Morgan got to her feet, literally shaking her body, hoping to dislodge the feelings that were making her so uncomfortable. If it was guilt, what was she guilty of? Never once had she thought of acting on her feelings for Troy—she hadn't even allowed herself to acknowledge them in her own heart until this day.

I'm just feeling alone. Kevin had walked out on her. Beth was gone. And now, she and Troy had been thrown together by fate. *That's all it is. Pull yourself together.*

Noticing the bedside table on what used to be Beth's side, Morgan thought she'd better check it. Opening the drawer, her eyes fell upon the familiar, small white New Testament. Morgan picked it up and ran her finger across the almost obscure gold lettering. *Beth Ann Carruthers.* She would ask Troy if she could have this. It was the only personal thing belonging to Beth that Morgan felt she wanted to keep.

Unexpectedly, the small Bible fell open, revealing a three-and-a-half inch floppy computer disk. "What's this?" Morgan said aloud. On the disk was a white label, reading, *1 Peter 5:8—Heretics everywhere!*

Recognizing Beth's handwriting, Morgan immediately looked up the passage. What could her sister have meant by those strange words? *Heretics everywhere!* Locating the verse, she noted it was underlined, but the word *devil* was highlighted in yellow. She slowly read the words softly.

" 'Be vigilant; because your adversary the devil walks about like a roaring lion, seeking whom he may devour.' "

Her hands trembled as she again read the Bible passage. *Beth, what were you trying to tell us?* With these words her sister's murder began to take on a new and much more sinister significance.

Morgan was about to close the drawer when she noticed a stack of newspaper clippings pushed into the back. She took them out. Each appeared to be from a series on the dangers of the Internet. Morgan was surprised that her sister had any interest in computers beyond sending email. The "In the Know" columns were from the local *North Dallas Daily* and were all written by a woman named Dedra Koehler.

Morgan's eyes moved down the opening paragraphs of the first column:

PREDATORS IN CYBERSPACE

Beware: Cyberspace is more than just kid space. It's a mixture of educational, entertaining, and exciting Websites. Allowing your child or teen to surf the Web unsupervised is risky at best.

In most cases, going online can be an exhilarating experience. But in chat rooms, where role-playing and fantasy are often half the fun, new acquaintances aren't always who or how they seem.

With each word, Morgan felt a mounting awareness of foreboding in the room. She scrambled to her feet and moved about, hoping to break the strange awareness of evil she had never experienced before. A chill wrapped itself about her, and she shivered as she remembered the words she had written in her last email to Carl: *Whatever was frightening my sister is here, in this house. I have to find it.*

She was sure she had.

Thirty-five

$\mathcal{M}$ organ took the Bible, the clippings, and the disk and ran down the hallway to her room. Opening her laptop computer, she slipped Beth's disk into the floppy drive. In moments, she opened the directory, finding only one file, labeled *Heretics*. Her heart surged as she double-clicked on the file to open it.

There was no title, and it appeared to be a journal or diary of some kind. The two sisters had always kept diaries, but it looked like Beth had turned to this when she felt she had no one to talk with. *Why hadn't she come to me?* The answer to her own question broke her heart. Morgan had let her down. "I won't let you down again! I won't!" she said aloud as she started reading her sister's words. The first entry, made several weeks before her death, simply said:

> *Feb. 18—I've suspected they were contacting the children. Now I know. I have the proof. It all seems so farfetched, no one's going to believe me. God, help me, I know the evil is real. It's alive. He must be stopped.*

He . . . Who in the world was Beth afraid of—who was frightening her so? Morgan continued reading, devouring her sister's tortured words.

> *Feb. 20—Troy will think I've lost my mind. But the evil is out there, watching me. He knows what I'm doing every minute. My dear Troy is so very worried about me. God bless him. He has no idea what I've let into our home. I only meant to help. Please forgive me, Troy.*

Feb. 23—Spoke to Morgan. She insisted I see the doctor. How could I tell her, or anyone, what is going on? She wouldn't believe me. I told the doctor I spend long hours at night wide awake, unable to sleep. He gave me sleeping pills. But I can't take them. How can I when I must be vigilant?

"Who was doing this to you?" Morgan asked, trying to make some sense of what she was reading. Her sister's final days were filled with fear and panic. *Why didn't I come?* Morgan began crying, her thoughts racing on, *I was so self-centered. I knew something was wrong. I knew it.*

Morgan was convinced that the "he" Beth spoke about was the one responsible for her death. The murderer. She moved farther down the page.

March 3—I have found someone who will understand. She knows the truth. I can tell she does when I read her words. And she has the power to spread the word. To stop this infectious evil. I'll contact her. Meet with her.

I know my life's in danger. I'm very frightened, but I can't tell Troy. I must keep him and the children safe from this evil. I pray for protection. I can't stop. He is the devourer of so many. He's threatened me. Ordered me to stop. I have found out too much. He won't stop tormenting me. I know he's in my house, near my children. Sometimes I feel his presence, other times I'm certain I hear him moving about.

"She was being stalked!" Morgan was sure of it. Why hadn't Beth gone to Troy or the police? There was more on the disk, and she wanted to read every word. But suddenly, Morgan was startled by the sound of footsteps running up the stairs. She felt a scream forming in her throat. Jumping to her feet, she lunged at the door, slamming it shut!

Morgan leaned all her weight against it. She held her breath, afraid to move. Was this the same fear that tortured Beth all those weeks? The sound of Morgan's own heart beating blended with the frantic pounding on the other side of the door, making it almost impossible for her to hear the words of the hysterical child, terrified and alone.

"Aunt Morgie! Aunt Morgie! Let me in! Please, let me in!"

His cries finally reached her ears. "Michael!" Her breath came out in one giant release of emotion. Pulling open the door, she flung her arms around the frightened young boy. "Sweetheart, I'm so sorry. I didn't know it was you."

She held him tightly, waiting for them both to feel safe. When she finally let go, they both started to laugh. It was the hysterical laughter that so often accompanies fear.

"You scared me, kiddo," Morgan said. "Isn't that the silliest thing?" She gave him another hug.

"I was sorta scared, too," the youngster said, his voice still quivering. Wiping his sleeve across his eyes, he pointed to the floor. "What happened to your computer?"

Morgan hadn't noticed the shambles she had made of her laptop. When she'd jumped up to slam the door, it had fallen to the floor and was clearly broken, the dark, blank screen torn away from the keyboard on one side. She bent to pick it up. "I can't believe this. Looks like it's a goner."

"You can use Jenny's. It's really for all of us. It's not just hers."

Morgan smiled. "Thanks. I'll do that." Removing the disk from the drive, she laid it on the top of the dresser. Managing a reassuring smile, she turned to Michael. "Let's go downstairs and have some ice cream. What do you say?"

It made her happy to see a smile break through. "Great! How about a chocolate sundae?" he asked, sending her a knock-out crooked smile, so much like Troy's.

"Chocolate sundaes, it is! I even think there are a couple of cherries to go on top!" As he ran out the door, Morgan noticed he was carrying a large piece of art paper rolled into a tube and held with a rubber band. "Hey, what've you got there?" she called, following him into the hall.

Michael didn't hear her as he sped happily down the hallway. Morgan followed. Then Michael stopped at the door to his mother's bedroom, glancing inside.

"Oh no," Morgan sighed, realizing she had forgotten to close the door when she was in such a hurry to see the contents of the computer disk.

His happy, carefree smile melted. "What're you doing, Aunt Morgie?"

Knowing Michael had seen the packing boxes and the half-empty closet, Morgan took his hand and they walked into the room. She sat on the side of the bed and patted the bedspread next to her. "Here, sit down with me for a while. Please."

Her young nephew, still gripping the rolled-up art paper, did as she asked. He was visibly uneasy about even being in the room. "I don't like to come in here anymore."

With true understanding, she said, "It's hard for everyone. Especially your dad."

Michael bit the corner of his bottom lip, his eyes cast downward. "I wish we could move away from here."

"Your mother loved this house and all of you so much. She left that love right here for you. Just because I'm packing her things won't change the wonderful memories you have of her. I'm not taking away anything important."

He looked up at her defiantly. "Everyone wants to make it look like she never lived here. But she did! She did live here!"

Morgan put her arm around his shoulder and kissed the top of his head. "Yes, honey, she lived here. And she'll always live here as long as we keep remembering her." Morgan tried to ease the moment by motioning toward the art paper. She asked, "Did you draw a picture?"

He looked at it for a long moment. Then he said, "The teacher asked us to draw a picture of the most beautiful thing we could think of." Painstakingly the young boy removed the rubber band, and his small hands unrolled a chalk drawing. It was a child's drawing of an angel, with long blond hair, flying above a two-story red-brick house. "It's Mom."

"I know. And she's so beautiful." She was so moved by what she saw that she could barely get her breath.

"Mamaw said now Mom's living in heaven with God. But I like to think she's here with us, too."

"She is here, Michael. I know it." He looked more peaceful, and Morgan asked, "Do you want to hang this up in your room?"

He nodded his head. Then with pure childlike honesty, he asked, "Aunt Morgie, do you believe in heaven?"

Morgan got on her knees in front of Michael and put both

hands on his shoulders. She looked into his eyes and replied, "Oh yes. I believe in heaven with all my heart. And it's a beautiful, beautiful place."

Morgan watched in total amazement as the young boy slid off the bed and onto his knees beside her. Facing the bed, he put his hands together. "I've been thinking I should tell God some special things about Mom. Stuff He needs to know. Is that all right?"

Without a word, Morgan knelt next to her nephew, putting her clasped hands on the bed beside his. As she bowed her head, tears of sorrow mingled with joy filled her eyes.

Michael began, "Dear God, it's Michael. I hope you and Mom are okay. We miss her." He paused, swallowed hard, and continued. "I thought you'd like to know she likes that vanilla ice cream, the kind with the little black specks in it. She doesn't like spinach much, but if it's all mixed up with other stuff, she'll eat it. I was thinking that I'm pretty sure you've got lots and lots of flowers in heaven. Maybe you could let her help you take care of 'em. She's really good with flowers and I know she'd like that."

The little boy stopped for a moment to sniffle and wipe his nose on his shirt sleeve, then he continued. "I'm still mad at you for what happened. But I don't think you're bad or anything. My mom loved you a lot. Tell her I love her. And please don't let anything bad happen to my dad or my aunt Morgie. Oh yeah, or Jenny. Amen."

With the memory of the chill of evil she had felt in that room that afternoon, Morgan prayed, "Father, I ask for your loving protection for this family. . . ."

Thirty-six

"W elcome to the Catacomb," purred the soothing and hypnotic computerized female voice. "Enter your password."

Mystica. Letter by letter the word took shape in the box marked *password.* The visitor was given entrance to the Website, as the ominous, jiggling sewer cover dissolved into the fiery smoke that twisted and curled about the screen. Mystica was drawn into the swirling red vortex and into the animated main cave of the Catacomb.

As usual, frightening words crawled across the screen, giving a dire warning of what the visitor might encounter on this site:

> *Warning: This site and the chamber chat areas are not monitored or censored in any way. Here, I am the only authority. I am the only censor. So if you do not want to be violated by what you may see or experience on this site, leave now and do not return!!!*

Mystica was as thrilled at the experience of visiting this forbidding Website as she had been the first time she stumbled upon it months ago. Now she was a frequent visitor and had been embraced by this cyberspace community.

Her acceptance into this clandestine society gave her a feeling of belonging, as well as a power beyond her fifteen years. Here she was treated as an equal. Her life had changed since she experienced this strange unity with the Webmaster, Ara.

Mystica, tapping her pink fingernails on her computer keyboard, waited with delighted anticipation for the mysterious contact from the underbelly of the Catacomb.

It came quickly as a chat window labeled *Private Chamber Chat* popped open. Words, entered by unseen hands, took charge.

```
ARA:  WB, my friend...
MYSTICA:  Ara, I have something really exciting
to tell you.
ARA:  good ... but we have others here ... let
me bring us together.
```

It took only a moment until Ara had included Andromeda and Serpentine in the treacherous chat.

```
ARA:  it is so nice to have so many of my
spiderlings together :)
SERPENTINE:  It has been a while since we have
all spoken together openly.
ANDROMEDA:  I am glad it is time for another
Gathering. It always gives me strength. The
battle is going well.
ARA:  so i hear ... mystica, you said you have
news...
MYSTICA:  Yes! Cyclosa is moving on the new
prey. He told me she'll be with us soon. I'm
going to help. I've made contact.
ARA:  i knew there would be little trouble with
her once we were rid of beth ... be very
cautious, my little one ... you don't have the
experience of some of the others...
MYSTICA:  But you give me strength, Ara.
ARA:  serpentine, i'm not pleased that our
little plan failed to rid us of yet another
enemy ... i don't like being disappointed...
ANDROMEDA:  I sent Cyclosa to take care of that
reporter. He had done so well with the last one.
ARA:  how could you be so stupid :-( he's been
nervous and undependable since the last
```

assignment ... crying like a baby with fear.

ANDROMEDA: I did what I thought best.

ARA: FYI ... ridding us of this enemy is not child's play ... she is strong and more informed than the others ... but fear not ... soon she, too, will be vanquished.

SERPENTINE: And as for Morgan Carruthers, I'm watching her. She is stronger than her sister. Ara, should we be discussing this with Mystica?

MYSTICA: Hey, Serpentine. I can be trusted. I know all about how you got rid of Jenny's mom.

ARA: you are young and inexperienced, precious mystica ... a new spiderling ... perhaps you have been trusted with too much knowledge too soon. i fear you will become foolish ... it is my observation that you talk when you should not...

MYSTICA: I am a blood member of the Gathering. Why don't you trust me? I'm not too young. I don't like being put down.

ARA: you don't like it? you dare tell me what you like and what you don't like? ... as i feared you are indeed foolish my dear. i instruct you to remain silent ... do nothing to bring attention to yourself ... if you disobey me, you will surely regret it :-(

Ara eliminated Mystica from the chat, leaving Serpentine and Andromeda.

ARA: mystica has been released ... she is no longer in the chat and we can speak openly ... AISI we have made a mistake in including her in plans so soon.

ANDROMEDA: I agree, Ara.

ARA: keep an eye on her...

SERPENTINE: She is young, and perhaps the dedication you demand is beyond her capabilities.

ARA: perhaps...
ANDROMEDA: Decisions about her usefulness can
be made at the Gathering. For now, you can
rejoice in the victories we are having
throughout our area. Our number is growing. You
continue to gain control of many.
ARA: when·they are young and innocent the
victory is sweet :) you both are faithful
servants and it is energizing to have contact
with you...
ANDROMEDA: I will continue to spread news of
the Gathering.
ARA: the new convert must attend the next
meeting ... see to it, precious serpentine ...
we'll use her innocence to our purposes <grin>
SERPENTINE: She will be there, and you can claim
another victory, Ara.
ARA: for now, remain aware of the movements of
our friend morgan carruthers ... we cannot risk
exposure ... the woman has been warned ...
perhaps she needs a stronger warning ... SICS.
SERPENTINE: I will speak with Cyclosa. He
crawls easily within her walls. But the sooner
we are rid of her, the better for us all.

Thirty-seven

*T*roy was up before five every day, and rarely did Morgan
know when he left. But this morning, while both Michael
and Jenny were still asleep, she wanted to have the opportunity
to finish filling him in about her conversation with the 76 Station manager and the appointment she suspected Beth must
have had. She didn't want Troy thinking she hadn't told him
the whole story.

Now, however, there were the newspaper articles about the
Internet and the computer disk diary. She debated whether to
bring those up now, or wait until she had finished going through
all of it. *How can I tell him anything until I know what it's all
about?* She would wait on that information—for at least a few
hours.

Now that Troy had moved back into his upstairs bedroom,
she would be able to hear him moving about—if she could stay
awake. But this morning, there was little doubt she could. How
could she go back to sleep with her anxiety level in high gear
about getting back to the disk? She had no idea how much more
information Beth might have put onto it, but maybe she'd even
discover the name of the murderer. Then she would turn it all
over to Detective Hancock. It made perfect sense to her.

The house still dark and quiet, Morgan turned on the small
bedside lamp and padded barefooted across the thick carpet to
the dressing table. Removing the Bible, newspaper articles, and
disk from the drawer where she'd put them, she scurried back
to the warmth of her bed, pulling the sheet and quilt up over

her knees. Propping pillows behind her, Morgan held up the mysterious disk, turning it over and over thoughtfully. Seeing the strange label in Beth's handwriting gave her a sudden chill.

Oh, I pray you've told me who you were afraid of, Beth. Who are the "heretics"? Morgan glanced regretfully toward her broken laptop computer. She could barely contain her curiosity, wanting to open this disk and devour every single word her sister had written. But she had to wait, for the only computer, besides Troy's portable, was in Jenny's room.

Instead, Morgan used the time to begin reading Dedra Koehler's "In the Know" newspaper columns. Maybe there would be a clue as to why they had captured Beth's interest. From the picture of the columnist printed on the banner, Morgan thought it was likely that Ms. Koehler was a straightforward, straight-talking pundit.

Dedra's words instantly intrigued her, and she found herself regarding the Internet with new trepidation. "I had no idea," Morgan said aloud as she eagerly went to the next article.

> *Parents often find out too late the emotional effect Web-sites meant for adults can have on the minds of their children. This information and explicit material can traumatize them, causing fear, nightmares, and phobias that may plague them the rest of their lives.*
>
> *Often children are enticed by cartoon characters who invite them to leave personal information about themselves or their family on a site. This information often is misused by a twisted mind to gain entrance into the psyche and the life of your child.*

One by one, Dedra Koehler's columns began to shed light on an entirely different Web than Morgan had ever envisioned. But why had this been of such interest to her sister? What possible connection could all of this have had to her murder?

Morgan wasn't naive and realized x-rated material was out there—somewhere in cyberspace. But it never occurred to her that there were Websites poised like hungry predators waiting to pounce on unsuspecting, innocent minds that might stumble into their traps. Teens looking for a thrill could easily find them—and get much more than they bargained for in the transaction.

She had almost finished reading the last article when she heard the shower go on in Troy's bathroom. Shoving the disk and the clippings under the sheets, she quickly crawled out of bed. Her long, thick terry cloth bathrobe was comforting as she tied it around her waist and hurried downstairs.

When Troy came down a short time later, his hair was combed straight back, still damp from his shower. Instead of his usual suit, Troy was wearing jeans, snakeskin cowboy boots, and a blue collarless dress shirt. "Mmm!" He seemed pleasantly surprised to smell coffee and to find Morgan in the kitchen.

"Mornin', ma'am. Spoiling me isn't going to make me any less concerned about how you're putting yourself in danger, Morgan."

"I know. I just thought you might enjoy this." She set a mug of coffee and a large cinnamon roll before him.

"I'm not as dumb as I look. I know you're up to something or you'd still be snuggled down in that warm bed." He put his overflowing briefcase on the floor near the laundry room door and tossed his brown suede jacket on top of it.

Morgan cupped her hands around her warm cup of coffee and smiled. Troy sat across from her, and she simply replied, "I'm going to try harder with Jenny. There's got to be a way to break through to her."

"So that's it. Well, I'm planning to take her to dinner tonight. Just the two of us. I left a note under her door."

"How great! She'll love it, Troy. Maybe that's what Jenny's been wanting—more attention from her daddy."

He looked uneasy. "I don't have any idea how to talk to her. To have a real conversation with her. What am I going to say? I can just picture us sitting at Charlie's Steak House, staring at each other." He paused, looking a bit alarmed. "Gee, I hope she isn't going through any sort of vegetarian stage or something."

Morgan smiled at his nervousness. "You'll do just fine. I bet you'll find lots to talk about."

"Like you, for one."

"I wouldn't recommend that if you want to keep her in a good mood."

Troy took a big bite of the warm cinnamon roll, his eyes widening with delight. Incredulously he asked, "You make this?"

"No, I believe her name is Sara Lee. But we're great friends." They both laughed. She was glad he and Jenny were going to spend some time together alone. He was trying so hard.

"You still okay with my staying around for a while?" she asked, already pretty sure of his answer.

He looked at her over the rim of his coffee cup. "I wasn't throwing you out the other night. I'm just concerned. You've got to stay out of the investigation."

"But, Troy—"

"I mean it." Troy sat the cup down, resting his arms on either side of it. "You're going to get in over your head."

She looked down at her cup, hoping he couldn't read her expression, knowing she was again keeping something very big from him and from the police.

"There's a murderer out there." Troy put his hand out and touched hers. "I've already lost Beth. Please don't do something stupid, Morgan."

The touch of his hand brought back the unsettling feelings she'd experienced yesterday, and she quickly pulled back her hand and got to her feet. Walking to the counter, she leaned against it, rubbing both shoulders nervously.

"What's wrong? Did I say something wrong?" he asked, picking up on her sudden withdrawal.

"Of course not. Don't be silly. It's just all this talk about murderers . . ." She turned, grabbed the coffeepot, and filled her cup. "Want more coffee?"

"No. What I want is to know you're going to stop nosing around. It's dangerous."

What he really wanted was her word. Her promise. And she wasn't prepared to give that to him. Anyway, she planned to tell him and the police all about the disk and the articles—probably later that day.

"You'd better get going, Troy. I've kept you long enough.

Look, Detective Hancock has the notebook. We know where Beth bought gas and what time she was there." She held up his jacket for him as he put his arms into the sleeves.

"Morgan—"

"From what the detectives told me, they've narrowed down the area where Beth was that day." She wasn't going to give him any opportunity to get a word in edgewise. "They think, and I agree, that she was on her way to meet someone. They just don't know who." She kept talking as she moved him closer and closer to the door. "It must've been important. They figure that when Beth realized what time it was, she ran out of the station without completing the entry. She dropped the notebook on her way out." Morgan handed Troy his briefcase. "There, you have the whole story."

She continued to steer him through the laundry room and to the back door. Before Troy knew it, he was out the door and in the garage. He laughed as he shook his head in disbelief. "Anyone ever tell you that you're nuts? It's true, you know."

Morgan gave his shoulder a nudge. "And don't worry about Jenny. That'll work out . . . really, it will." She could tell Troy was about to speak again so she quickly closed the door. "Bye." Amused by the startled look on his face at her rapid departure, she laughed aloud. She hurried upstairs, anxious to get back to Dedra Koehler's columns.

Thirty-eight

*T*he spring morning had suddenly turned ugly. Lightning flashed, and the force of the ensuing thunder rattled the windowpanes in the homicide department. Detective Hancock looked up and could barely see out through the drenching rain.

Both he and Ballantine were absorbed in the Woodsen case. Chuck glared at his computer screen. After adding the 76 Station and the time 1:30 P.M. to the map, they had constructed Beth Woodsen's whereabouts as closely as they could on the day she was murdered. "That appointment had to be in this vicinity," Chuck said, moving his finger in a circle around the locations.

"How're we doing, Dell?" Sergeant Lasser approached his desk and sat down on the edge of it.

"Not so good, Hannah. We need a break. We thought the gas book might be it, but it gave us more questions than answers. Where was she going in such a hurry? Was she meeting someone? If so, who and why?" He looked very disturbed. "It's like this guy just dropped outta nowhere, like a phantom full of poisonous venom. Nobody saw him coming, and nobody saw him going." He twirled a yellow pencil nervously through the fingers of his right hand.

Lasser added, "Don't forget the tornado warnings and touchdowns that same afternoon. There weren't too many people on the roads, and if they were, they were running for cover. Everything played out in this guy's favor."

"Then why was Beth Woodsen out in that weather? What

could've been that important?" Using his right thumb, Dell unconsciously pressed on the pencil until it snapped.

"It'll come together, Dell. You're the best. Don't forget it."

"Yeah, sure," he mumbled as Lasser slid off his desk and returned to her office. Dell's eyes wandered to the large victim whiteboard. The one name that drew his attention was Beth Woodsen. "Where were you going, lady? Help us out here."

"Detective Hancock?"

Dell swung around in his chair to find himself facing a friendly, familiar face. The man was creating a puddle as water dripped from the wet raincoat he held out away from his gray suit.

"Could I hang this somewhere?" he inquired.

"Here, let me take that!" Dell quickly got to his feet and took the wet coat from the well dressed, forty-something man with a likeable, chiseled face and short, dark brown hair. *I always remember faces. What's wrong here?*

The detective had been caught unaware, and he was using the time it took to hang up the coat to search his usually sharp memory for a name to match the face. Luckily, when he turned back he had retrieved at least a portion of the man's identity. "Good morning, Pastor . . ."

"Shelby." The pastor smiled as he helped the struggling detective through this awkward moment. "Tom Shelby. Beth Woodsen's pastor."

Hancock felt embarrassed. "Of course. Pastor Shelby." He motioned for the man to have a seat.

"What brings you out in this lousy weather?"

Ballantine noticed the pastor and came over to join them. "Hello, Pastor Shelby. Nice to see you again." The two men shook hands.

"Detective Ballantine. I was just about to tell your partner here that I ran across some computer files you might be interested in." He removed several folded pieces of white paper. "I took the liberty of printing them out." Hancock took them and began looking through each one.

"I thought I'd told you everything when you came to see me right after the murder. But it looks like something new has turned up. The new youth director was updating attendance records and other department documents when she found a file called 'Beth Personal.' She didn't open it but contacted me."

Dell was looking through the pages. "Looks like some of that email stuff and an unfinished letter." He handed them to Ballantine.

Chuck glanced at the printouts. "Did Mrs. Woodsen have access to a computer at the church?"

"Yes. We have several."

Ballantine continued. "And do they have Internet access?"

"One does. The others are just used for church business."

Hancock leaned in toward Pastor Shelby with great interest. "Let's get back to that file. You opened it?"

"Yes. I felt I had to, under the circumstances. I told you Beth was working with our youth department on a part-time basis. The new director was sure I'd want to see this."

Chuck Ballantine pulled up a chair and sat down as the pastor continued. "Beth had a heart for teenagers. They often need a friendly ear, for it's tough on a lot of them at home. Parents and teens can be a volatile combination, but then I'm sure you know that. The church tries to offer some stability and counseling."

"And Beth Woodsen provided a friendly ear?"

"Yes. She was easy to talk to and well liked. But there were times when I thought she was there for another reason." He paused.

"You need to tell us everything you know, Pastor. Please." Hancock could tell he was weighing whether to go on.

"Well, I thought it was as much for her as it was for the kids. Beth was feeling a little lonely, what with Troy's career taking him away from the family so much. And there were problems with Jenny."

Hancock put him at ease. "We're aware of the family tensions. Please go on."

"Beth had voiced concern, on more than one occasion, about losing touch with Jenny. She was afraid the girl might get caught up in things she shouldn't. You know, dangerous things."

Hancock motioned to Hannah to join them. She came out of her office and over to his desk. "Pastor Shelby, this is Sergeant Lasser. She's the head of this homicide department. I thought she'd be interested in this."

"These emails are pretty disturbing. Talking about drugs and pornography and a worldwide mission," Ballantine said. "Do you know if Beth Woodsen had reason to believe any of them were written to her daughter?"

"No. I mean, I don't really know. I just knew you'd want to see them. I'm no Pollyanna, but I'm appalled to know that kind of filth was going to our teens right there at the church."

"It's going to kids through libraries, schools, and at home on their own PCs," Ballantine added. "It's everywhere in cyberspace."

"Let me see that letter, Chuck." Ballantine handed it back to Hancock, who held it up for the pastor to see.

"I can only assume Beth was the author, since it was in her private file. It looks like something she might've taken upon herself to send out—probably to our list of parents," Pastor Shelby stated.

Detective Hancock began to read it out loud. " 'Dear Parents, As a parent myself, I know I must get this information to you quickly so you will be aware of the evil that lies in wait for our children in a deceptively safe environment—your own home. Every home with a computer connected to the Internet is in great danger.' "

Sergeant Lasser, as well as several other detectives, moved closer to listen as Detective Hancock unknowingly drew a crowd as he read the impassioned letter. It was impossible not to be drawn in.

" 'The Web is not safe! Something out there is so horrible and so powerful it defies explanation. It has made itself known to me, and it tortures me day and night. I believe my own life is in danger because of what I know.

" 'If we don't stand between our children and this evil force, he will take them away from us, one by one.

" '1 Peter 5:8. "Be vigilant; because your adversary the devil walks about like a roaring lion, seeking whom he may devour." ' "

Hancock looked up at the pastor. "From the Bible?"

"Yes."

Dell said, "Guess it's been a while since I've read it." His eyes returned to the riveting words, and he continued to read.

" 'If I expose him, he has promised to take my own children. But I cannot remain silent.' "

Pastor Shelby added, "I believe someone made sure they silenced her for good. The letter is terrifying, but the emails . . ."

Ballantine showed them to Lasser and the others. "No real names are used here. Everyone goes by a screen name."

"They're all from someone named Serpentine. Can't we trace these by this tracking information at the bottom of each one of them?" Lasser asked Ballantine.

"Probably not. Whatever this thing is, it's organized. And I'll be willing to bet if we trace that information, we'll come up empty-handed. I'm sure they were sent via an anonymous email site that erases any viable tracks. People who know how to use the Net can email anything they want, to anyone they want, without being traced."

Lasser shook her head in disbelief. "Everything I find out about cyberspace makes me feel like I'm living out a science fiction movie."

"It's no movie, it's real." Chuck turned to Tom Shelby. "It sounds like kids who hang out at your youth center are using the church computer to access the Web. They're sending and receiving email they wouldn't take the chance of getting at home."

Pastor Shelby said, "I don't know how Beth got her hands on these. Maybe the kids made a mistake and saved them to the hard disk."

"That's possible," Ballantine asserted. "Maybe she stumbled onto them and printed them out."

"I don't think any of these kids realized the danger they were in. It was like a game to them. But when Beth found the email, she took it very seriously, as we all would. It wouldn't have mattered to her whether it was to Jenny or not. Beth knew she had to do something."

Hancock was puzzled. "But how could she have gotten so

involved? Did she find out who was sending this trash to the kids?"

"She could have, Dell." Ballantine looked serious, as it all began to fall together. "But she didn't have to find him, he probably found her. One of the kids might've discovered she knew something. Who knows what Beth might've said to one of them. An email from one kid to this Serpentine character could've started the whole thing crashing in on her."

Everyone listened as Detective Ballantine's computer knowledge paid off. "I know there are ways of finding out who's on a particular server and just where they're surfing. I'd say they started sending Beth email messages, all but inviting her to find them—they had to know who was trying to expose them. Once she entered their Website . . ." Ballantine brought his hand down hard on Hancock's desk. "Gotcha!"

Everyone jumped, including Hancock. "Okay, Mayberry, it's sounding plausible. You've earned your buck and a quarter."

"It's that easy?" The pastor asked the question on everyone's mind.

"It's that easy," Ballantine answered. "If they want to send kids pornographic pictures, get them to try drugs, or entice them to run away, they literally reach into our homes and lead them into the Web."

"Now, hold it a minute." Hancock looked dubious. "I think you're getting carried away."

"Listen to this." Incredulously, Lasser began reading from one of the emails.

"TO: Sweetiepie
"FROM: Serpentine
"SUBJECT: Strength in numbers

"Ara is pleased that you are being so strong. It is not easy to go against family and others who are not followers. You will be rewarded. Your involvement in calling other possible newcomers into the chat chambers shows your desire to be made part of this worldwide mission.

"You will be contacted. Remain careful. Speak only to others of a like mind. We are growing in number.

"Destroy this message, as you have the others.

"In the power, Serpentine"

"There it is. We teach our kids not to talk to strangers, then we put them on the Internet and walk away." Hannah held up several other emails. "These are all similar in nature. Some of them probably had pornographic images attached, while others give blatantly false information about drugs."

The older detective's voice was steady and thoughtful. "A cyberspace gang?" Hancock was thinking out loud as his mind tried to wrap around all the bizarre revelations this day had brought.

Ballantine almost leaped from his chair. "Are we saying there's a conspiracy of children out there, being lead by some nut on the Web?"

"Sounds like you may have nailed it, Mayberry."

One of the other detective's called across the room, "Hancock, it's the lab. They've got something for you."

Thirty-nine

*L*ater that morning, Morgan fed both of the children and made sure Michael had lunch money. The youngster gave her a big bear hug before he ran to his bus stop.

Jenny had little to say, not even a "good morning." Morgan tried to make conversation with her niece, to no avail. Monosyllabic answers were all she could elicit. "Yes." "No." "Sure." For someone who spent hours on the phone chatting, Jenny certainly could curtail her conversation when she wanted to.

"Are you taking the bus?" Morgan asked, as she passed the door to Jenny's room.

"Rebecca's mom is dropping us off."

Morgan then instructed Jenny to come home right after school. Jenny offered no reply. Not surprised, Morgan leaned into the room and said, "Have a nice day, honey. I'm going to take my shower. Be sure to arm the security alarm when you leave."

Morgan stood under the warm shower, placing the palms of her hands on the white tiles of the shower wall in front of her. She took her time, and rolling steam filled the guest bathroom. Morgan slowly turned her body under the warm water. She adored hot showers—they had a renewing effect on her being.

Her wet brown hair squeaked as she tilted her head under the stream of water and slid her palms through it, slicking it straight back from her face. She faced the showerhead and allowed the luxurious, warm droplets of water to run in swirling streams down the length of her tall, lean body.

Morgan loved long showers, but this morning she was languishing there only long enough to give Jenny time to leave for school. Then Morgan could venture into the young girl's room and slip the enticing disk into the computer.

Downstairs, a key turned in the lock of the back door. The security alarm began beeping slowly, giving a thirty-second warning before a full alarm would sound. A gloved hand deftly punched in the appropriate code. The system was silenced.

Footsteps fell softly on the carpeted stairway leading to the upstairs bedrooms. The intruder could hear the sound of the running shower. Disappearing into the guest bedroom, it took only moments and his task was completed.

Morgan turned off the shower, slid open the glass door, and reached for the thick pink towel she had left on the towel bar. With the water turned off, the house was very quiet. As she stepped from the shower stall, Morgan cocked her head and listened. She thought she heard the alarm system beeping as it does when the code has been entered and it is about to arm.

If it was Jenny, she was late for school. *But if it isn't Jenny . . .* Morgan quickly wrapped her wet body in her terry cloth robe. Had she allowed her nerves to get the best of her? Morgan tried to convince herself that she had not heard anything.

But without thinking, she called out "Troy! Jenny!" She listened, but there was no reply. Everything was very quiet.

Her feet were still wet as she ran to the alarm system keypad in the upstairs hallway. Everything looked fine. Jenny had armed it.

Back in her bedroom, Morgan leaned forward, rubbing her hair vigorously with the towel. With her head still down, she sat at the small dressing table. Tossing her head back, Morgan reached for her brush. A shiver of terror left her frozen as her eyes focused on the oval mirror. There, marring her reflection, was a crude lipstick drawing of a large spider.

Jumping to her feet, Morgan knocked over the chair, her body shaking. "What's going on?"

Her mind raced. Spiders! The black widow venom found in her sister's body and the large spider she killed in the laundry room—and now this grotesque drawing. It was the murderer! He had been in this very room while she was in the shower. *Is he out to kill me?* The shrill ringing of the phone shattered the horrifying thought.

She whirled around, her heart pounding and her breath coming in short gasps. Morgan stared at the phone as it continued to ring. She edged slowly toward the bedside table, her hand poised to answer it but momentarily frozen by fear.

One more ring and the answering machine would pick it up. Morgan grabbed the receiver. Pausing for a long moment she put the receiver to her ear. She could hear someone breathing. "Who is this?" she asked, unable to hide her terror.

"Oh dear, my little drawing frightened you, didn't it?"

"Who is this?" she screamed into the phone.

"There's no safe place, Morgan. Beth found that out. We're watching you." The sinister voice seemed muffled as though something was being held over the mouthpiece of the other phone.

"How did you get in here?" Morgan shouted indignantly.

"Your sister was foolish. If you want to live, Morgan, leave now!"

"Murderer!" she screamed into the phone. "You killed her!" Her voice shaking with anger and fear. "I'll find you! I promise!"

The phone went dead. The mysterious caller had vanished, leaving only the dial tone incessantly droning in her ear.

In shock, Morgan slowly hung up the receiver. Her knees gave out and she sunk to the edge of the bed. *Who could possibly have gotten into the house without setting off the alarm?* Someone had been here. They were watching her, stalking her, just as they had Beth.

Suddenly the phone rang again. She grabbed it. "Who are you?" she demanded in a quivering, angry voice.

"Morgan? Is that you? It's Detective Hancock. Are you all right?" He sounded terribly worried.

Morgan did her best to respond normally. "Yes, I'm fine. Just got me out of the shower! Some kids called earlier for Jenny

. . . they wouldn't tell me who they were. You know kids."

"Morgan, we've had a break. The lab just called in a report on that white powder you found on the keys. It was putty, the kind builders use around windows. It's soft, but it hardens."

"What was it doing on the keys?" she asked, turning away from the drawing on the mirror and trying to sound more in control.

"Someone made imprints of those keys in soft putty. It was probably done in a big hurry, and he didn't have time to clean it off." The detective paused. "Morgan, we're looking for someone who has access to that house."

Morgan shuddered. "Oh no. It *was* in the house."

"What? What'd you say?" Hancock asked.

Morgan's voice was slow and distant. "The terror that was closing in on Beth was right here . . . in her own house."

Hancock almost barked at her. "Looks that way. Listen, Morgan, I want you out of there—now! I'm going to call Troy. And I'm sending over a couple of detectives. They're going to go over that place with a fine-tooth comb. We're about to get this guy! I told you he had made a mistake! They always do!"

Morgan hung up the phone and grabbed the computer disk from the dressing table. She ran to Jenny's room. She knew she had to hurry if she was going to see everything on the disk before Hancock's men arrived. And Troy would most certainly send her back to Minneapolis.

Her hands shook as she slipped it into the drive. "Beth told me who you are! I know she did!" Using the mouse, she moved to the disk directory. But the Heretics file was not there.

"Tell me, Beth. Please, tell me who did this to you."

As she searched the disk, she found only one file: byebye.exe. "What's this?" Beth wondered out loud. She opened the strange file and to her horror, the words she longed to read were no longer on the disk. Instead, the screen became blazing red and was overrun with hundreds of repulsive, crawling spiders intermingled with the words *Leave Or Die.*

"No!" she screamed, hitting the keyboard and pushing herself away from the chilling menagerie on the screen. "Stupid! Stupid!" Morgan screamed at herself. Overcome by fear and despair, she put her head in her hands and wept.

Whoever had been in her room was not only a crude and sadistic artist, but a thief as well. Beth's disk had been switched for this one.

Pulling the disk from the drive, Morgan's worst fears were confirmed. It had no label. Beth's words, which might have lead Morgan to the killer, were lost to her forever. Why hadn't she protected the disk? Kept it hidden? Given it to the detectives? *I have to remember what she said!*

"I might as well have handed it to him!" she shouted out loud, feeling foolish and passionately angry with herself.

Obviously the murderer was not only cold-blooded but fiendishly clever as well. He had proven his point. Slipping in and out of the Woodsen house at will was no problem for him. Her body felt limp as it became clear to Morgan precisely what the caller meant when he said she could find no safe place.

I've got to talk to someone. Not Troy. Hancock was probably on the phone with him already. And she'd withheld this from Hancock because she wanted to face this murdering animal. He was close; he could smell her fear.

She hadn't been able to keep her sister from being killed, but Morgan was determined to finish whatever it was that drove Beth to her death.

Time was short and she had to hurry. Returning to the computer, she opened Jenny's Internet server. The modem dialed, then connected. Remembering Beth's screen name, she typed in *Gdword*. It then asked for her password. *What is it?* Morgan questioned, attempting to recall what Beth might possibly have used. She tried several words, but none of them worked. She then typed *Roses*. Gaining access, Morgan sighed with relief.

Clicking the Mail icon, Morgan began typing quickly:

```
TO: cmercer@heritage.com
FROM: Gdword@aol.com
SUBJECT: Urgent!

    It's Morgan! I'm using Beth's screen name. I broke my
computer and am using theirs. Contact me on my cell phone.
I have to leave the house. I'll be waiting! It's urgent.
Beth's murderer is back and he's after me.
```

Before she could send the frantic message, an Immediate Message window popped open.

```
ARA:  since we all know this can't be beth, it
must be Morgan ... we meet at last ... you see,
there is no safe place ...
```

Morgan's fingers froze. The murderer was monitoring the Internet. He obviously had known whenever Beth signed on. She had no privacy at all.

```
ARA:  my patience has run out, morgan.
```

Her fingers began almost automatically to type in her rage.

```
GDWORD:  Leave me alone! I know who you are!
ARA:  no, i don't think you do ... or you would
be much more afraid :-(
GDWORD:  You killed my sister! You're not
getting away with it!!! And your spiders aren't
going to scare me away!
ARA:  remember, they strike without a sound ...
you won't know until it is too late ... just like
precious beth. oh, by the way, i'd keep a close
eye on that pretty little jenny if i were you :)
```

The window disappeared as suddenly as it had appeared. So this was Beth's Internet stalker! The fear her nightmares were made of had a name: Ara.

Morgan's voice was filled with rage. "I'm not going to run away! And whoever you are, I'll find you! I promise!"

She still had enough presence of mind to use the mouse to click the Send icon. "Call me, Carl! Please!" she murmured, quickly signing off the server.

Returning to her room, Morgan pulled on a pair of jeans and a cream-colored pullover sweater. Her cowboy boots were broken in, and she slipped them on with very little effort.

The doorbell rang indicating that the police were finally here. She slipped the spidery disk into her shoulder bag, along with the newspaper clippings, then brushed her damp hair straight back into a ponytail and twisted a tan, suede scrunchie to hold it in place.

Moments later she was downstairs opening the front door. Two policemen introduced themselves, and she let them in.

"Detective Hancock wants you to come down to the station," one of them told her.

"Sure, ah . . . right away." Morgan stumbled over her words, knowing they weren't true.

"We're going to check out the house, look for forced entry, that sort of thing," added his partner.

She knew that when they went upstairs, they would discover the scrawled lipstick spider. That and Hancock's call to Troy would insure that Morgan would never have the opportunity to finish what her sister had started. She knew she had to hurry.

"Sure. You go ahead. Look around. I'm going to turn off the coffee and get going. The children are at school, but someone will be here to meet them later." She was pretty sure it wouldn't be her, because she couldn't let Troy or Hancock stop her now. She was so close.

While the two policemen began a systematic search of the windows and doors throughout the Woodsen house, Morgan hurried to the garage. There was no time to lose. She could feel her Internet stalker closing in.

As she pulled out of the driveway, her Infinity almost broadsided Justin's pickup truck, which was filled with building materials. She swerved, her tires skidding on the wet pavement. Justin slammed on his brakes, and a bag of caulking fell out of the truck bed and into the street. It burst in front of Morgan's car, sending a white, powdery cloud into the air.

"Justin?" she said in total horror.

The handsome young man angrily leaped out of his truck and stood in the road, waving his muscular arms in the air and shouting, "Hey, woman, what're you trying to do, kill us both?"

No. She was trying to save one of their lives . . . hers.

Forty

*T*he hallways of Roosevelt Junior High were quiet and mostly empty. A few students dashed up and down the center stairway. Suddenly a loud bell rang, echoing throughout the structure. Classroom doors opened and exuberant students flooded into the halls. The loud din of their laughter and talking became a roar.

"Jen! Hey, wait up!" Rebecca was hurrying through the crowd trying to catch up with her best friend. Jenny was obviously in a rush. She had already entered her locker combination and was tossing her books inside.

"I'm not eating in the cafeteria," Jenny said, as she slammed the locker door closed. "I've got something to do."

Rebecca looked disappointed. "During lunch?" They only had an hour and they always sat together. "Where're you going?"

"It's just important, okay? I've gotta go. See you later."

Jenny rushed off, disappearing into the crowd, leaving Rebecca feeling snubbed. Her friend had changed in the last few weeks. She no longer returned her phone calls, and when they did talk, Rebecca could tell that Jenny wasn't interested in their usual long conversations.

Rebecca shrugged and was about to head off for the cafeteria when she noticed that Jenny's locker hadn't quite shut. A thick piece of notebook paper, folded several times, had become lodged in the bottom of the door. Rebecca stooped down and pulled it out. It was a note to Jenny.

Her curiosity got the best of her. Looking to be sure Jenny was nowhere in sight, she unfolded the paper and read it.

Jenny,
I need to see you today. It's important. Don't bring Rebecca, come alone. I'll wait for you by the football stadium hot dog stand at lunch.
Pam

"How could you?" Rebecca said loud enough for several passing students to hear. They gave her a queer look, then moved on.

She was hurt to think that her best friend would go behind her back and meet Pam. Jenny knew how Rebecca felt about her. Angrily Rebecca crumpled up the paper and tossed it inside the locker, slamming the door closed with her foot. Could she be losing her best friend to Pam Ruston? Rebecca ran for the restroom as angry tears burned her eyes.

Thoughts of how she had treated Rebecca were far from Jenny's mind. Her own excitement and anticipation about this clandestine meeting with such a popular girl was all she could think about. Waiting for the lunch bell had been torture, and Jenny stopped only long enough to grab two cans of Dr Pepper from a dispenser before heading across the school lawn toward the stadium.

Most of the girls in the ninth grade, including Jenny, thought Pam was so cool and mature. From her long, pink porcelain fingernails to her high school friends, Pam exemplified the word *in*. Something exciting was always going on around her.

Pam had never shown much interest in having a friendship with Jenny. But the fact that she had suddenly sent her a secret note was intriguing beyond words to the fourteen-year-old.

"Hi, Jen," Pam called. Jenny ran to meet her. The stadium area was empty, except for a few members of the track team doing laps.

"Hi. I got your note. What's so important?" Jenny asked, trying not to sound overly impressed or anxious.

Pam led the way into the stadium, and the two girls sat about halfway up in the empty bleachers. "Here, I got you something to drink." Jenny handed her companion one of the sodas.

"I wanted to talk to you alone. That's hard to do, since Rebecca follows you around like a puppy."

"Yeah, I know. She's pretty clingy and immature." Jenny realized this was her best friend she was putting down, but at the moment it didn't matter.

"Someone I know wants to meet you."

"Me?" Jenny was not only surprised, but also flattered. "Who?"

Pam took a drink of her soda and looked around to be sure no one was watching them. "It's really terrible about what happened to your mom. We're all real sorry."

Jenny wasn't prepared for Pam to bring up the murder. It made her a little angry. "Guess that makes me sort of a freak. It happened—so what?" She bit her bottom lip and looked down through the bleachers to the red dirt below.

"But do the police know anything . . . like have they got any suspects?"

"Not yet. At least I don't think so. But then nobody tells me anything." She paused and looked up at Pam. "I don't want to talk about that, okay?"

"Guess so," Pam answered, disappointed.

Jenny looked intrigued. "So who wants to meet me? Is it some guy?"

"I guess. It's someone I met on the Internet. Someone who's got a Website and everything." Pam lowered her voice, "Have you had any interesting email or chats lately? Maybe from someone you didn't know?"

Jenny thought for a moment, then remembered the bizarre chat she'd had with the stranger calling himself Ara. "Yeah. A couple of times."

"From Ara?" Pam asked.

Jenny nodded her head, surprised that Pam knew. "He said we had some friends in common. I guess he meant you."

"You see, there's this sort of a group . . . and we get together and do really far out stuff." She paused for a moment, then looked excited. "If Ara asks you to come to this group, do it, Jen. He's incredible, and I know he's already interested in you."

"Really? Why me?"

Pam looked around nervously. "Don't ask any more questions. It's a secret group, Jen. And it's really out there. You get to do stuff you've never dreamed of."

Not totally understanding, Jenny said, "You're asking me to join?"

"No, I can't do that. But Ara wants you to come to the next meeting. It's a little scary at first. But don't get all freaked out or anything. It's something you've never experienced before. And the feeling you get just being part of the Gathering, well— it's amazing."

"Anyone else I know in this club?" Jenny asked with aroused interest.

An elusive smile crossed Pam's face. "You'd be surprised who the members are. That's all I can say right now."

Jenny could feel the titillating excitement all the way to the tips of her fingers. "Sure. When's the meeting?"

"You'll know. The Web, that's how we all stay in touch. It's the last place your parents would ever think about. And Ara and the others, they're always there for you. But swear you'll keep this a secret, Jenny. Swear."

"I swear."

"This means you can't tell Rebecca or anyone. That includes your dad and your aunt." The young girl's face became somber and very serious. "If you do, Jen, you'll be really sorry. I'm not kidding."

Pam abruptly got to her feet. "Now, sit here until lunch break is over. Don't follow me and keep your mouth shut." The girl ran down the stadium stairs and disappeared into the exit.

Jenny's mind was filled with the wondrous thrill of her possible acceptance into a secret club. A slight chill ran up her spine as she recalled the mysterious chats with Ara. It was creepy. Following Pam's instructions, Jenny didn't move until she heard the bell.

As she ran back to the building, she didn't notice that Rebecca was standing just under the bleachers.

Her next class was English Literature. Jenny was almost late and had barely slid into her seat when the bell rang. Rebecca was only seconds behind her.

Rebecca took her seat, which was almost directly across from Jenny. She looked troubled. "Jenny," she whispered.

"Shh. You're going to get us in trouble," Jenny replied, opening her book.

Rebecca tore a sheet of paper from her notebook and quickly scribbled a note. She folded the paper once and passed it to Jenny.

Jenny sighed in irritation, as she opened it and read. Angrily she turned and stared at Rebecca. "You were spying on me!"

"Don't get messed up with Pam."

"You're just jealous!"

"Jenny Woodsen! Please carry on that conversation in the hall . . . after class." Miss Galvin had heard them.

"Yes, ma'am." Jenny turned and glared at Rebecca, mouthing, "Thanks a lot."

Hurt, Rebecca slumped down in her chair. But as Jenny glanced at her again, a look of determination was set in her eyes.

Forty-one

After parking her car, Morgan hurried into the lobby of the *North Dallas Daily News* building. The rain had once again begun to fall, and there was a chill in the air.

Once inside, Morgan pulled the stack of "In the Know" newspaper articles from her bag, then scanned the directory. Dedra Koehler was on the second floor.

The receptionist invited her to sit, but Morgan declined. Pacing suited her mood. She had only been in the lobby for a few minutes when a female voice said, "You looking for Dedra Koehler?"

Morgan turned, recognizing the round face from the photo on the columns. "Yes. I'm Morgan Carruthers. And you're Dedra Koehler?"

"That's me. What can I do for you?" She seemed in a rush. "I don't mean to be rude, but I'm in kind of a hurry. We live by deadlines around here, you know."

"I'm sorry I didn't make an appointment. But this couldn't wait." There was no way to hide her heightened anxiety. "Could you please give me a few minutes? I really must talk to you."

Dedra cocked her head, listening carefully to the woman's voice. "Hey, did you call me up several weeks back? Needing to see me?"

"No."

The woman looked disappointed. "Oh. I thought for a minute there your voice sounded familiar." Dedra motioned for Morgan to follow her. "Come on back, Ms. Carruthers."

Morgan followed the heavy-set woman through the maze of office dividers and into a short hallway. "This is it," she said, disappearing inside a small, cluttered room. Morgan entered.

"Wooeee! Looks like a big one rolling in." Dedra noticed the storm clouds darkening through her single window. "I bet this one's gonna hang on for a spell. Those clouds are moving like tumbleweeds in the west Texas wind. Funny thing, but I love it."

"Storms unnerve me," Morgan added off-handedly, her mind on much more serious and frightening matters than the weather. She looked around for a place to sit.

"I'm pretty sure there's a chair under all these magazines." Dedra shoved a teetering stack of periodicals to the floor and motioned for Morgan to sit down. "I'd ask you to excuse the mess, but if you ever come back, it'll be just the same, maybe worse."

"Thanks for seeing me."

Dedra let her full weight fall into her chair, then took a deep breath. "That's about as much exercise as I've had in a spell." She wiggled her fingers in the air. "But these babies can do over one hundred words a minute."

Morgan began speaking, trying to show she hadn't come for chitchat. "I'm not really familiar with your column, Ms. Koehler. You see, I'm from Minneapolis." Reaching into her bag, she pulled out the collection of Dedra's columns.

"Well, looks to me like somebody's been clipping more than coupons." Dedra smiled. "One of these days a syndicate's gonna pick up on how terrific I am, and then you'll be seeing my column in a whole bunch of papers—maybe even in Minneapolis." She chuckled. "I'm a dreamer."

"I'd never read them until yesterday. They're very good. You've done a lot of research about the Internet."

"It's quite a place. Not all of it friendly, though," the reporter replied.

Morgan added, "I've been on the Internet, mostly for research, and I thought I knew a lot about it. But after reading your columns, well, you've made me pretty scared to even log on."

"And you should be scared . . . if you have kids. Makes me feel like I've done my job if you're concerned." Dedra sat forward and leaned her arms on her desk. "Other than the fact that you're a budding fan, there must be more to this visit. You look like a woman with a mission."

"I hope you can help me." Morgan took a deep breath, praying that the reporter in front of her would prove to be a vital piece of the puzzle. "Almost two months ago, my sister was murdered in North Dallas. At first, the police thought it was a car accident, but—"

Dedra interrupted her. "Hold on there. The Woodsen woman? Was she your sister?"

"Yes. I still can't believe Beth's gone."

Dedra suddenly looked curious. "Beth? Her name *was* Beth. That's right."

"Did you know her?" Morgan asked hopefully.

"No." Dedra quickly responded. She seemed to be trying to recall something important. She shook her head, returning her focus to Morgan. "I'm sure sorry, Ms. Carruthers. What a tragedy. That case certainly turned into a real conundrum. Off the record, have the police got anything yet?"

Morgan's disappointment was evident. "Detective Hancock's been working on it. I can't believe someone could just kill her in broad daylight, set up the car accident, and walk away—without anyone seeing something."

"It happens all the time. It shouldn't, but it does." Dedra paused, then began again. "Word's out that they found spider venom in her blood. I know they've asked the press not to print that, but it's pretty hard to keep something that bizarre totally quiet."

"It was black widow venom and a drug called fentanyl."

"Twisted. That's what's happened to this world. It's becoming full of twisted minds. I'm not surprised at anything anymore." Dedra lightly touched the back of her neck.

"I'm going to trust you, Ms. Koehler, because I think my sister trusted you." Morgan laid the newspaper clippings on Dedra's desk. "I found these in a drawer in my sister's bedroom, along with a computer disk containing a diary of sorts. She wrote in it during the last few weeks of her life."

"Well, that'll be helpful to the police."

Morgan looked uneasy. "It might've been. However, before I could finish reading it myself, the disk was stolen."

She nervously got to her feet and paced the width of the small office. Dedra waited, enthralled by her story. Morgan stopped and looked directly at Dedra. "It sounds crazy, but I know my sister was stalked and murdered because of something she knew about the Internet."

Dedra thumbed through the columns. "Could be. The only columns she seemed interested in were the ones I've written on the Web. Did she mention me in this diary?"

Morgan continued, "No, not by name. But she did say something about finding a woman who would understand. Someone who could spread the word—and she had these columns. Ms. Koehler, I believe the woman she was talking about is you. But before she could talk to you, she was murdered."

A glimmer of recognition appeared in Dedra's eyes. "Sit down, Ms. Carruthers. I want you to hear something."

Curious, Morgan sat back down in the chair as the reporter hit the Message button on her phone. It was on "speaker," and they could both hear the dial tone, then the four tones that opened her voice mailbox. The computerized voice said, "You have one saved message. To listen to that message, dial seven." Dedra punched the 7. She then sat back, putting her elbows on the arms of her chair and holding her fingers together, steeple fashion, in front of her mouth. Morgan, not sure what to expect, waited.

"March 5, 12:14 P.M." With the first words of the message, Morgan knew it was Beth. "Ms. Koehler, you don't know me, but . . . I've jut got to talk to you, immediately! There's no time to lose. It's very, very important. It's urgent!"

Morgan had not heard her sister's voice since their last telephone conversation. Tears began to roll down her cheeks. Dedra, seeing her distress, reached to stop the message. But Morgan waved her off. She had to hear every word.

"You can help. I know you can. I can't leave a number. But . . . tomorrow at two P.M., please meet me . . . on the first level of the Galleria Mall . . . the circular marble bench outside Saks Fifth Avenue. I'll recognize you. Oh, please come! I'll be waiting.''

Dedra saved the message once more. "I didn't mean to shock you. But I had to know if that call was from your sister. Because, you see, I didn't hear it until March seventeenth. I was on vacation the day she called.''

Morgan took a moment to steady herself. "Then *you* were the appointment Beth was hurrying to make. She was on her way to meet you at the Galleria.''

"And I never got there.''

"I know she must've waited. Beth would've waited until she was sure you weren't coming.''

"There was no way for her to check, either. If she'd called here, the voice mail was all she would've gotten again. Stupid vacation! I didn't want to take it anyway.'' Dedra thought for a moment. "You know, I remember March sixth real well. It was kinda like today.'' She nodded toward the window. "Started out sunny and *bam*—it turned on us. If your sister waited for me, and we're both sure she did, she would've been at the Galleria when they issued that tornado warning.''

"And the killer was watching her. Stalking her. He followed her all day. He knew she was at the mall.'' Morgan paused, trying to hold back her rage, but she couldn't. She screamed out, "He was watching her! Waiting for her to come out . . . so he could kill her! Somehow he knew she would leave that mall without having talked with you. How would he know that?''

Dedra tried to calm Morgan. "Ms. Carruthers, are you all right?''

Morgan continued the gruesome reconstruction, "He could've known you were on vacation, too. Ms. Koehler, trust me. This maniac knows everything.''

"You don't have to convince me, honey. I do believe I've had the displeasure of meeting up with this psychopath.''

"Thank goodness you believe me! Today while I was in the shower, he broke into my sister's house. He drew a spider on a mirror with lipstick and switched the disks. That's why I don't have Beth's diary any longer! All I have is this!'' Morgan handed her the floppy disk.

Dedra slipped it into her floppy drive. Soon she had the same screen full of crawling spiders and the words *Leave Or Die*. The reporter went to Morgan. She took her hands and looked her straight in the eye. "Yes, I believe you, Ms. Carruthers. I believe every word you're saying."

"Then you believe this Internet stalker killed my sister?" Morgan asked.

Dedra turned and walked to the window, looking out onto the parking lot. Her voice took on a mysterious tone as she said, "If my old truck hadn't played out the other night . . ." Without finishing her sentence, the reporter turned to find Morgan's chair empty. The intense young woman had vanished. Dedra grabbed her phone and dialed a familiar number.

Forty-two

The din in the Cybersurf Café was louder than usual. A young man had gone behind the bar and cranked up the volume of the music until the bass beat could literally be felt pounding away.

"It's a good thing Les isn't here. He'd make you turn that down," called one of the young waitresses, having to scream to be heard.

All of the cyberbooths were filled and so were most of the tables. Pam was cuddled up with a guy several years older than she at a corner table. He kissed her neck and she giggled.

Pam ran her spider fingernail down his cheek. "I'm having a ball. I didn't think you'd ever ask me out."

"I've had my eye on you, Pam. I was just waiting for the right time." He called a waitress over and ordered two cups of cappuccino.

"It'll give me a caffeine buzz," Pam said. "I'll be up all night."

The boy smiled mischievously, pulling her closer to him.

A lone figure sat in a cyberbooth in the back of the café. His hands flew over the keyboard as he accessed the Web and swiftly surfed to a familiar address.

"Welcome to the Catacomb," purred the slithery computerized female voice. "Enter your password."

The visitor typed in *Cyclosa* and immediately accessed the corrupt depths of this site. Within a moment, a Private Chamber Chat window popped open. The unseen hands of Ara began spewing his poisonous message.

ARA: what have you to report, cyclosa?

CYCLOSA: I destroyed the disk. Andromeda has
been following Morgan Carruthers. She went to
see Dedra Koehler.

ARA: no!!! i have lost my patience!

CYCLOSA: There was nothing I could do to stop
her.

ARA: she is clever ... if you had not failed me—
they would never have met ... my wrath is to be
feared, cyclosa! you can no longer be trusted :-(

CYCLOSA: No ... please, I'll bring the innocent
prey. When is the meeting? I can bring her, I
promise. Whatever it takes. When is it, Ara?

ARA: TONIGHT!!! there is no time to waste ...
little miss carruthers must be silenced ... we
cannot have all of our work ruined ... I WON'T
HAVE IT!!! pass the word to all my spiderlings
... tonight at the Gathering we will meet our
enemies and the final victory will be mine.

❧ ❧ ❧ ❧

Dedra had been waiting only a short time in her favorite booth at Nettie's Diner. Her face lit up when she saw her old friend enter. He hardly had time to hang up his wet raincoat before she threw her arms around him.

Detective Hancock smiled and gave her a big friendly hug. "Why, how you all doin', darlin'?" he asked, giving her his best phony Texas accent. Ballantine watched in amazement at the unfamiliar display of public affection being offered by his robust partner.

"I'm fine, you big handsome hunk. Sit down, I've ordered up some of Nettie's hot peach cobbler." She slid back into the red plastic booth, and Hancock took the seat across from her.

"Now, don't squeeze me in here, Mayberry. Pull up a chair." Chuck had already decided not to attempt the booth, and he pulled a chair over from a nearby table. Turning it around, he straddled it, leaning his arms on the back.

"Dedra, this is my partner, Chuck 'Mayberry' Ballantine. Chuck, this is one of my dearest friends, Dedra Koehler—a big reporter over at the *North Dallas Daily*."

She gave a jolly laugh. "Yeah, one of the 'biggest.' "

Chuck nodded politely. "Nice to meet you, ma'am. I'm familiar with your column. Really enjoy it."

"Well, it's a pleasure to meet ya." She stuck out her hand. The two shook hands, and Chuck was surprised at the strength of her grip.

"Sorry I couldn't take your call, Dedra, but we were involved in some new information on that Woodsen murder case."

"Yeah, terrible thing. That's why I wanted to talk to you, Dell. I just spent a little time with the victim's sister."

"You what?" Before Hancock could voice his full response, the tall, thin waitress brought three bowls of peach cobbler with vanilla ice cream.

"Nettie sends her greetin's," she said, setting a large serving in front of each of them.

Dedra poised her spoon over the top of the steaming cobbler just long enough to say, "I understand you're wondering who Beth Woodsen was going to meet that afternoon." Her spoon dug into the ice cream, and she rolled her eyes and sighed as the first spoonful disappeared into her mouth.

"We sure are. Got any ideas?"

With her mouth full of ice cream, Dedra managed to say, "Yeah . . . me."

Ballantine's eyes grew large, and Hancock stopped midspoonful. Stunned, Chuck leaned forward. "Beth Woodsen was going to meet *you*?"

"At the Galleria Mall, at two P.M. But I didn't show 'cause I didn't know anything about it until I got back to my office on the seventeenth." She reached in her pocket and took out a small tape recorder. "Listen."

The two detectives listened closely as Dedra played the heartwrenching tape of Beth Woodsen's phone call. "I know it's Woodsen. Her sister identified it in my office. Seems the victim had collected a batch of my columns on the dangers of the Internet."

"I saw 'em. They were terrific." Ballantine leaned in, becoming more interested.

"Dedra, I'm a little confused here. How did Morgan Carruthers find you?" Hancock looked down in surprise, realizing he had almost inhaled the entire cobbler. "Mayberry, now why'd you let me eat this? You're supposed to be my conscience."

"I saw that look in your eyes, and I wasn't about to get in between you and that cobbler."

"Getting back to the murder," Dedra commented with determination, "the victim had collected my columns. Her sister found them hidden away with a disk. Seems the victim kept a computer diary during the last weeks of her life."

The large detective looked like he was about to explode. "Are you telling us Morgan has a diary and she didn't give it to us?"

"Watch your blood pressure, honey. What I'm tellin' you is that she *had*—not has—that disk. Someone broke into the Woodsen house this morning while she was in the shower. Creepy, isn't it? Right out of Alfred Hitchcock. Anyway, that someone left a spooky lipstick drawing of a spider on the mirror."

"I know. My men found it."

"And while he was there, he switched the disks. Left her a disk full of spiders and a death threat. Nice guy."

Hancock's face was beet red as his temper boiled over. "A diary? Newspaper clippings? And tell me, why am I hearing about all this from you and not from Morgan Carruthers? Huh? Tell me!"

Ballantine remarked much less emotionally, "For the same reason we found her talking to the service station manager. She's determined to find this killer herself. Something about owing it to her sister."

"And if she finds the guy, what's she gonna do with him? That gal's gonna get herself killed! She was supposed to meet me down at the station earlier today, but she never showed." Dell shook his head and ran his fingers through his hair. "Women! Present company excluded, of course."

"Dell, Beth Woodsen got involved in something bad on the Web. I know 'cause I've run into this psycho myself. Now, we don't have time to go into all that right now, but just let me tell you—this guy's really out there. Calls himself Ara. Pops right up on your computer screen and starts threatening and throwing his cyber-weight around. I don't know what the Woodsen woman found out about him, but whatever it was . . . it got her killed."

"I'm gonna tell you something, Dedra, off the record. It just came out of nowhere. I had a visit from Beth Woodsen's pastor. He brought in some email sent to kids at the church and a letter the Woodsen woman was planning to send out to parents. But she never had the chance." He leaned in close and lowered his voice. "Are you religious? I mean do you believe in God and . . . you know, the other guy?"

"You betcha. They're both as real as this table." She knocked her hand on the old, peeling red table. "And don't you forget it. How can you lead the life you do, Dell, and question that? You've seen the face of the devil more than most of us."

Ballantine felt like he was at a tennis match. His head was going first to Dedra, then to Hancock. He didn't want to miss a thing.

Dedra continued, "The name Ara got me to thinking. I remembered a bit of Greek mythology—a story about a foolish woman who challenged the goddess Athena to a weaving competition. Athena changed her into a spider. Her name was Arachne, the mother of all spiders."

"Arachnophobia!" Ballantine shouted, leaping up off his chair. "That's the message! The spider venom, the black widow spiders. He was telling us to go to the Web all the time. He was saying 'Come get me, I'm on the Web'!"

Dedra put her hand on her neck, feeling the bandage. "Spider bites, Dell! They're a serious bunch. And if there's one spider, there's a nest nearby. That's how he's drawing in our kids. He's got a nest of spiderlings, Dell, I'm sure of it."

"He's building a cult right under our noses." Dell was pushing his way out of the booth before she could finish. "Listen, you go home, lock your doors, and stay there until I call you."

She started shaking her head and waving her arms. "Oh no you don't. I'm not taking any more forced vacations, spiders or no spiders. Don't worry about me. But you'd better find Morgan Carruthers before Ara and his nest of spiderlings do, or you may be looking at another victim."

Forty-three

Morgan refused to answer the ringing phone. She knew it was probably Troy or Detective Hancock, and she wasn't ready to talk to either one of them. Afraid to drive back to the house where the car could be seen, she had parked on the street just on the other side of the wooded clearing in the Woodsen backyard and made her way through the mud. She entered the house through a back entrance, which couldn't be seen from the cul-de-sac.

After this morning and what she had seen in Justin's truck, she was certain that the danger was close at hand.

Before coming here, she had been sure Marge King would take Michael. But she had no idea where to find Jenny.

It was immediately clear that Troy had already been home looking for her, for his briefcase and jacket were dropped in the middle of the kitchen floor. However, now the house was empty. She knew Hancock had called him and they would both be looking for her. And she knew she was worrying Troy sick, but she owed this to Beth. She couldn't stop until she carried out her sister's wish. She had to stop this Internet psychopath and then—only then—would it be over.

Maybe she could coax him out of the dark corners of cyberspace. Without bothering to wipe the mud from her boots, she ran up the white carpeted stairs and into Jenny's room.

After logging on with Beth's screen name and password, she waited. "Come on, you crazed maniac! Come on!"

But he wasn't playing her game. "Come on!" she screamed.

But nothing. Ara was silent. Terror filled her heart, knowing he was lurking there, laughing. Enticing his next innocent prey.

᭙   ᭙   ᭙   ᭙

The rain had stopped, but the cool spring breeze and the damp air made it a chilly walk for Rebecca and Jenny. The school bus dropped them off as usual about three blocks from the cul-de-sac. They were having a heated discussion.

"Grow up, Rebecca! We're going to be fifteen next year." Jenny sped up, obviously hoping her friend would take the next corner and head home. It was clear that she was tired of discussing her lunch meeting with Pam Ruston. But Rebecca wasn't giving up. She hurried to catch up with Jenny, passing her own corner.

"You've been acting so strange."

"Really. We'll my mother's been murdered! My whole life's been turned upside down. Do you think that might have something to do with it? Everyone's on my back about something. Morgie. Dad. Now you!"

"But you're my best friend. I worry about you."

Jenny snapped back. "Well, stop worrying."

Rebecca got in front of her friend and was walking backward so she could look into Jenny's eyes. "Pam's trouble. And I don't want to see you get mixed up with her."

Jenny stopped and glared at the other young girl. "You're still jealous that she dated Freddie. Give me a break. It's not like you were going steady with him or anything. And now you're jealous that I might want to make friends with her. What's your problem, Rebecca? You don't own me."

Jenny's words devastated Rebecca. "Fine. If you want that kind of scum in your life . . . well, then, go ahead. Be friends— see if I care!" She whirled around and ran back to her corner, tears burning her eyes.

Suddenly a black Chevy Camaro came roaring down the street with the radio blaring hard rock music. Rebecca glanced at it as it passed and saw two high school age guys in the front and some other kids in the back. But all she could think of was getting home where she could be alone.

She heard the Camaro screech to a stop further down the street. Something made her turn and look. It had stopped alongside Jenny. Someone in the car was talking to her, but Jenny was trying to ignore them. Then she started walking faster. As she did, the car moved along the curb following her.

Rebecca could see that Jenny was frightened. "Jenny!" she called as loudly as she could. But there was no chance her friend would hear her over the blaring music.

Something wasn't right. She started running toward Jenny. Suddenly the car door opened and Cade jumped out. Rebecca couldn't hear what Cade was saying to Jenny, but it was clear he was trying to get her into the car.

Rebecca watched in horror as Jenny got into the backseat of the car. It sped off, disappearing around a corner. There was only one thing Rebecca could think of—to get Jenny's aunt. The Woodsen house was closer than her own. She dropped her books and took off running as fast as she could. "Somebody be there. Please!" Her frantic words were mingled with fear and tears.

Morgan was still on the computer, waiting, when she heard the frantic pounding on the front door. "Help! Please! Help!" The voice wasn't familiar, but Morgan could tell it was a youngster. She ran downstairs and threw open the door. "Rebecca? What's wrong, honey?"

Rebecca was standing there with tears streaming down her face, her fists red from slamming them against the hard wooden door. The trembling young girl almost fell into the room as she muttered, "Jenny's in trouble!"

Her words were alarming. Morgan helped the girl to a chair. She knelt down in front of her. "Rebecca, tell me what's wrong. What's happened to Jenny?"

The violent sobbing made it difficult to understand her. "She's in the car. They made her get in the car."

Morgan's heart was filling with a growing horror. "What car?" She found herself putting her arms on the girl's shoulders and shaking her. "Rebecca, I can't do anything to help unless I know what happened."

Rebecca calmed herself a bit and then continued. "We had a fight, and so I wasn't walking with her. We always walk together. Then this black car filled with kids stopped, and Cade got out."

"Cade? But he's her friend," Morgan said incredulously.

"I guess . . . but this was different. Something was wrong. I couldn't hear what they were saying, the radio was so loud." She paused, to regain control. "Jenny didn't *want* to get in that car. I know it."

Morgan got to her feet. "You mean Cade forced Jenny into the car?"

"I think so."

"Who else was in the car, Rebecca? Think." Morgan's words were sharp as she felt fear take hold of her senses. "Think, Rebecca. Who else was in there?"

The young girl just shook her head. "I don't know. I think it was just some other high school guys. But nobody I know for sure."

"Did you recognize the car? Have you seen it before?"

The young girl shook her head again, and her words tumbled out. "But today at school . . . she and that Pam Ruston. It's something about a secret club. Pam's in it, I think, and they want Jenny to join. But she told her not to tell you or her dad."

"Do you think Cade is part of this club?"

"Maybe . . . when we're down at the Cybersurf, he's pretty chummy with Pam." Jenny stopped, remembering something. "I don't know if it means anything or not, but Pam's got these long fake fingernails and on this one"—she held up her right index finger—"there's a spider painted on it. She's weird."

"Spider!" A chill shot up Morgan's spine like a spike. The venom in Beth's blood, the spider in her kitchen, the drawing on the mirror . . . the disk! "They murdered Beth! This secret club!"

Her words frightened Rebecca, and she began crying again. "What do you mean? Is somebody going to kill Jenny, too?"

Morgan started up the stairs, calling back to the young girl.

"Rebecca, go home, honey. Go home now!"

Morgan's hands trembled as she logged back on the Internet. Her voice was full of rage as she mumbled, "Come on, Ara, you animal. You know I'm online. You're out there, I know you are."

Suddenly, just as Morgan had hoped, the Immediate Message window popped up.

```
ARA: well ... if it isn't beautiful little
morgan :)
GDWORD: Where is she, Ara??? I know you've got
Jenny!
ARA: SICS ... she's with friends ... there's
really no need to worry...
GDWORD: Where is she, you murderer!!!!
ARA: i warned you ... but you kept on ... it's
over now, and i've won.
GDWORD: Please tell me where she is. Don't hurt
her. I beg you.
ARA: hmmmm ... let's see ... you want precious
jenny and i've got her ... dear me, what are we
going to do. <grin>
GDWORD: But it's me you really want, isn't it?
```

As she typed, Morgan quickly grabbed a floppy disk and slipped it into the drive. She started logging the chat, saving it to the disk.

```
ARA: ah yes ... that would indeed be sweet.
would you be suggesting a trade? ... your life
for hers?
GDWORD: Yes.
ARA: and why should i believe you?
GDWORD: I'll come to you. But you must let me
see that Jenny is all right.
ARA: you've tempted me ... usually it's the
other way around, isn't it? ... we'll see if you
are sincere. drive to tioga ... if you call
```

anyone, i will know and you will never see jenny
alive again :-(

Morgan wished her written words could spew the rage she
felt in her soul. He was leaving her with little choice. *Is this what
they did to Beth?* No wonder she had almost lost her mind.

GDWORD: When I get there, where do I go?
ARA: i'll know when you've arrived ... you'll
be escorted to a small Gathering of my closest
friends ... there you will find sweet jenny.
GDWORD: How do I know you'll keep your word?
ARA: you don't ... and that, my dear, is the
delicious part :) remember, i told you not to
defy me or you would see a much more violent
side of me? ... well, how do you like it?
<laughing>

The window disappeared as suddenly as it had appeared.
Morgan was terrified and furious all at once. She quickly pulled
the disk from the drive. Grabbing a pen she scribbled on the
label *Ara killed Beth. He has Jenny. We need help! Read disk!*

Morgan was already speeding along Preston Road, heading
north, when she reached for her cell phone to call Troy. She
hadn't wanted to waste any time getting to Tioga. *Jenny must
be terrified.*

Her hand searched the seat next to her, and she glanced
down at the floor. Getting panicky, she dumped the contents of
her bag onto the passenger seat. No phone.

Then she remembered. "No!" She'd left it in the charger in
her room.

"Troy! I need you!" But she recalled Ara's threatening
words. And she was probably being followed. He had eyes
everywhere.

She spotted a small service station as she turned on to Highway 380. Without warning to the cars behind her, she swerved
across the lanes and exited. Morgan heard the screeching of
brakes and skidding tires. She had almost caused an accident.

It was a small station, only two pumps. A young man came

out to the car—a definite answer to prayer. "May I help you, ma'am?"

"Yes. Put some gas in my car."

"How much?"

"Anything, just do it. I'm in trouble and I need your help."

A look of alarm came over the young man's face as he nervously looked around. She opened the gas door; he unscrewed the cap and inserted the nozzle.

Morgan grabbed a receipt she'd gotten at the grocery store and rummaged through the things on the seat, finding a pen. She scribbled Troy's number on the paper.

"That's enough," she called out the window.

The young man quickly pulled the pump nozzle, replaced the cap, and shut the door. It was clearly evident he thought she was nuts. He eased over to the door. "That'll be $5.87."

"Here." She shoved a twenty dollar bill into his hand, receipt folded inside. "Keep it. Do me a big favor. Call that number. Tell Troy Morgan's on the way to Tioga. Jenny's in trouble. There's a disk on the kitchen table. Tell him to call the police."

All of this information was overwhelming to the young man, but he nodded. "Okay. Troy. Morgan going to Tioga. Jenny in trouble."

"The disk—don't forget about the disk!"

"Yeah, on the kitchen table. And call the police. I've got it."

"Thanks, you may have saved my life."

Morgan drove off, leaving the attendant standing in the drive looking completely bewildered. She watched him apprehensively through the rearview mirror. "Go on, make the call! Make the call!" After a moment, she gave a sigh of relief as she saw him look down at the note and run toward the station.

"Please, God, let Troy be there." Morgan knew she was on the way to meet her sister's murderer and now he wanted to kill her. She was walking right into the nest of spiders where Ara would be waiting.

Forty-four

*T*he black Camaro sped along the almost deserted county road outside Tioga. Jenny and Cade were in the backseat with the man who had been with Pam earlier at the Cybersurf.

A sinister blend of punk and gothic music was turned up, and it vibrated the speakers in the back window.

"This is gonna be really rad, Jen. I promise." Cade smiled at her. But it wasn't a comforting, friendly smile. It only added to her anxiety. She had asked Cade several times who the other three guys were but had only been told, "You'll find out later."

She bit the corner of her lip, trying to hold back her tears. "I need to call home, Cade. They're going to be worried about me. Aunt Morgie made me promise not to be late."

"Forget them. This night's for you. And it's going to be unforgettable."

Jenny kept telling herself that Cade was her friend. He wouldn't let anything bad happen to her. The thought didn't calm her as she remembered he had almost forced her into the car.

"I want to go home, Cade. Please. Take me home."

"Jen, don't worry." Then, as he raised his right arm to put it around her, she saw the spider tattoo on the inside of his upper arm. She gasped. It was just like the one on Pam's fingernail. *This must be the sign of the secret club.* Now she knew that whatever this club was, Cade was a part of it. Everyone in the car but Jenny had the mark of the spider.

"It's not far now," the driver yelled, trying to be heard over the music.

The somber-looking teen in the passenger seat was dressed all in black. He turned and smiled playfully at Jenny. Pulling a red bandana off his head, his long, stringy bleached-white hair fell into his face. "It's time," he said, handing the scarf back to Cade.

Jenny was terrified. She couldn't comprehend her friend's actions. Tears began to flood her eyes. "Cade, what's going on? I've changed my mind. I don't want to be part of this club. Please, take me home," she pleaded.

"Sorry, Jen, but it's too late for that now. You've already seen too much." Cade folded the bandana and held it up to her face. "But we can't let you see exactly where the Gathering is held. This won't hurt. I'm just going to cover your eyes."

"No!" she screamed, grabbing the bandana. "Don't! I don't know how I got involved in all this. I thought we were just playing games on the computer. That Ara was just a made up thing."

The driver looked back at her. "Ara wouldn't like that. He's real. Very real. But then, you'll find out. Won't she, guys?"

Cade overpowered Jenny, and with the help of the other young man in the backseat with them, he blindfolded her.

"Now, Jen, don't pull it off. If you do, we'll have to do something to restrain you. And I don't want to do that."

Cade sounded strange—so sinister. Why hadn't she seen this side of him before? He had made her mother nervous. She'd tried to get Jenny to stop running around with him. Why hadn't she listened?

"Pam said it was going to be fun! But it's not! It's scary." Jenny began flailing her arms about, trying to fight her way to the door. "Let me go! Please!"

The driver looked into his rearview mirror at Cade. "I told you, man. Pam's a big problem."

"Not after tonight," replied the other teen sitting next to Jenny. "She thought I was taking her on a date. Can you dig it? I put a little something in her cappuccino." Then he laughed. "And she thought it was going to keep her up all night. Surprise, Pam."

They all laughed. Then the driver spoke again. "Hey, Jenny! Ara's gonna be real happy to see you. He's been watching you for a long time. He knew your mom, too."

Trembling, Jenny cried softly as she felt the car turn off the pavement and onto a rutted dirt road.

᪥   ᪥   ᪥   ᪥

"Morgan's somewhere on the road heading for Tioga." Troy's fear for her life gripped his heart. He held his cell phone with one hand while he drove his Ford Explorer toward home through late afternoon traffic. "When that station attendant called, I was out the door. He said she was scared and in trouble."

Hancock sounded mad—the kind of mad a caring parent feels when his child is late and he's worried to death. "I knew it! Now she's gone and done it! I thought you were with her. After I talked with your office, they said they'd tell you to get home right away."

"I called home. One of your officers answered and told me Morgan had gone to the station to meet you."

"Well, she didn't. So now we've got our hands full. I've got a lot of news to tell you, Woodsen. We're getting close, but I'm afraid Morgan's gotten a lot closer. Look, Troy, I'm at home. But I can be on the road in five minutes."

Troy could hear Hancock grabbing his shoulder holster and police revolver as he continued talking. "I'll head on out to Tioga. Listen, I've got some information that makes it pretty clear that we're dealing with a cult or some kind of strange gang."

"A cult?"

"I'll give you all the details when we meet at Tioga. All I can tell you is that we'd better find her fast." Hancock's voice was full of concern. "Look, if that disk is where the guy told you it is, access it on your computer and call my office. They'll patch you through to my cell phone. Ballantine sure picked a dandy weekend to go hunting. Looks like it's me and you."

"But Tioga's out of your territory!"

"You think that's gonna stop me? I'll be waiting for your call." He paused a moment. "Troy, we *are* going to get there in time. I promise."

"Sure," Troy said, his voice lacking the confidence he wished he felt. Pulling into the cul-de-sac, he said, "I'm home. Bye."

Troy ran into the house, leaving the back door ajar. There

was the disk! *Thank you, Morgan.* He grabbed it and read the label as he took the stairs two at a time. Ara killed Beth. He has Jenny. We need help! Read disk!

"Hope you left us some clues, Morgan." He quickly moved the mouse to the disk drive directory, clicking on it. He found one file labeled Help! He double-clicked on it, and the file opened.

It was clearly an Internet chat between Gdword and Ara. Troy had so many questions. "Ara has Jenny! Who is he? And who is Gdword?"

His eyes scanned down, reading the bitter words between the two unknown screen names.

```
ARA:  ah yes ... that would indeed be sweet.
would you be suggesting a trade? ... your life
for hers?
GDWORD: Yes.
ARA:  and why should I believe you?
GDWORD:  i'll come to you. But you must let me
see that Jenny is all right.
```

There was no more. Troy couldn't believe his eyes. "This Ara is actually threatening to kill Jenny! And Gdword—that must be Morgan!" She obviously had wanted to be sure he knew who was behind Jenny's disappearance.

Troy wasted no time. Running into his den, he threw books off the bookshelf. There in the wall was a safe. Sweat began to collect on his brow as he raced with time, entering the safe combination. Opening it, he reached inside and took out a nine-millimeter automatic pistol and two spring clips, pressing one into the pistol and putting the other in his jacket pocket.

In seconds he was back in the four-by-four and racing out of the cul-de-sac heading north. As he drove, Troy put the pistol into the center compartment, then grabbed his phone and called Hancock's office.

His call was patched through immediately. "Hancock here."

"Okay, I'm back on the road. Look, the disk only told me that Ara has Jenny and he's planning to kill her. Sounded like Morgan's supposed to be the trade-off. Her life for Jenny's."

Hancock knew better. "Trust me, from what I've found out

about Ara, he doesn't make trade-offs. It's all or nothing with this guy. A deal with the devil never pays off. Look, Woodsen, I'm on the 377 heading toward Pilot Point."

Troy raced down Highway 380. "I'm about ten or eleven miles behind you. What're we supposed to do when we get to Tioga? We don't know where they've taken them. If he gave Morgan any directions, it didn't get saved to the disk."

Hancock replied, "We'll figure it out when we get there. Look, I'm hopping off—need to contact the Cooke County Sheriff. Gonna need some backup out there. My badge is no good in those woods. See ya in Tioga, buddy. By the way, it's pouring out here!"

Troy was already into the rain. He flipped on the wipers and the rhythmic *swish, swish* sound reminded him of a clock ticking away. *Swish, swish.* Would he find them in time? *Swish, swish.* Would time run out for Jenny and Morgan?

As he drove, Troy found himself talking to God. "I don't know what to do, God. I'm asking you to help us find them. Don't let this Ara guy hurt my Jenny . . . or Morgan. I love them both . . . so much." He paused and then heard words he'd never said, not out loud. "I'm scared, God. I'm real scared."

His prayer was cut short as Troy suddenly spotted the 377 turnoff. He'd gotten there quicker than he thought. The rain was coming down in sheets, and it was hard to see anything, especially the road. He was going much too fast, and the combination of the wet road and the sharp turn sent him sliding onto the rain-soaked shoulder. It was deep mud. With lightning speed he switched to four-wheel drive.

The Explorer roared with power as it grabbed the boggy, rim-deep shoulder. Troy fought with it but regained control and drove back up onto the highway. "Good boy!" He patted the dashboard like a faithful old dog.

He was still a good twenty miles from Tioga. *And after Tioga, what?* he wondered. How would they ever find them out in this wooded countryside? Despite his questions, Troy made a promise. *I'm coming, Jenny. Dad's coming!*

Forty-five

Jenny shivered as she huddled like a frightened animal in the backseat of the empty, locked car. Heavy rain pounded the roof, and the windows had fogged over, leaving her more alone than she had ever felt in her life.

When Cade removed her blindfold, he had warned her not to try escaping. He wasn't the Cade she had known for so many years. Why hadn't she seen this dark side of him? The question carried the horror of admitting she had known he was a bit dangerous, and she had found that intriguing.

Jenny was sure that outside the fogged windows they were watching the car. Hoping she was wrong, she cleared a small area with her cold fingers. Peering out, see could only see darkness. There was no moon. Thunder rolled in the distance. Jenny pulled up her knees, wrapping her arms around them, and cried softly. "Daddy, please come get me. Please."

Suddenly Jenny heard a sound coming from the trunk. It startled her, and she listened closely and again heard the sound. *Thud! Thud!* Someone was in the trunk.

Jenny leaned close against the backseat and said, "I can hear you. Are you all right?" She listened. There was no response. Jenny was about to try once again to make contact with the other captive in the trunk when she heard approaching footsteps. The car door was pulled open, causing the interior light to come on.

"Cade?" Jenny asked expectantly. But it wasn't Cade or any of the other boys who had kidnapped her. Instead, it was two large, unidentifiable hooded figures in long black robes with a spider crudely drawn on the front with iridescent white paint.

Jenny moved as far back into the corner of the seat as she could. "Who are you? Please don't hurt me."

One of them reached out to her. "We're ready, Jenny." The voice sounded somewhat familiar, but she couldn't place it.

She knew there was no need to fight. Shivering from the cold, Jenny crawled from the backseat. She stumbled through the mud as the hooded figures made their way past a clump of trees to a small cabin.

Jenny could see many candles licking at the darkness inside the cabin. She could hear the sound of sinister chanting, "Ara, Ara, come to us. Ara, Ara, come to us."

Ara? The stranger on the computer! What's happening?

One of the figures opened the door. Jenny pulled back in horror as her eyes focused on the scene before her. There, lying on the floor in the center of a large drawing of a black widow spider, was her aunt Morgan. Surrounding her was a ring of hooded figures all wearing robes. Their macabre chanting continued.

Jenny screamed, "Aunt Morgie!" Then, turning to one of the hooded men, she appealed, "What's wrong with her? What've you done to her?"

They offered no answer.

"Aunt Morgie!" Jenny screamed once again. But Morgan didn't move. Jenny jerked violently, trying to free her arms, but the two hooded figures easily restrained the young girl. She was helpless.

"Jen, she came here hoping she could save you."

Recognizing the voice, Jenny turned to a hooded figure and found herself looking into Cade's eyes. "Cade! I know it's you! How could you bring me here? What've you done to my aunt?"

"I'm not Cade. I'm Cyclosa." The familiar voice had an evil edge to it that chilled her to the bone. "I only use Cade's body to do Ara's bidding."

Jenny screamed at him. "No. It's you, Cade. I know it's you! Have you lost your mind?" She began sobbing in fear and terror. "Please . . . don't let her be dead! Morgan! Wake up, please!"

One of the hooded figures stepped away from the ring and approached Jenny. "Don't fight us, Jenny. Don't fight Ara. You can't win." The closer the figure came, the more intensely his emerald green eyes seemed to blaze. "Ara tried to warn your mother, but she wouldn't listen. She wanted to expose him, expose the Gathering. She paid for that mistake."

Jenny was horrified by his words. "You all murdered my mother!" She went limp in the arms of her captors.

Cyclosa stepped forward and looked deep into the horrified eyes of the tormented teen. Slowly he said, "No, Jen, I did it. Cyclosa murdered her—for Ara!"

"Cade . . . no!" Jenny's words were almost unintelligible as she wept violently. "But why? How could you do that, Cade. Mom was your friend."

"Ara's spiderlings do whatever he asks. He offers us power. We give him total allegiance." Any semblance of Cade disappeared. "You made it so easy, Jen. Giving Cade your alarm code—" He broke off laughing. "That's why we love innocence. You made it so easy for us to torment your mother. To make her life hell."

Anger and retaliation surged through Jenny, giving her strength beyond her size. She pulled her arms free and ran toward Cyclosa. Before they could stop her, Jenny ripped off his hood and began slapping at his face. Cade was exposed.

"Murderer! Killer! I hate you!"

The two hooded figures grabbed the girl's arms and dragged her away from Cade. She kept screaming through her tears. "You won't get away with this! Aunt Morgie! Please wake up!"

Morgan did not move, but Jenny could see that she was breathing. "Did she see you, Cade? Did Mom know it was you?"

Cade's eyes became like steel—cold and hard. Then an evil smile came across his lips. "She never knew I was waiting in her car. Ara planned it all so perfectly."

When this frightening figure who once had been her friend began to speak, Jenny stopped struggling. Her crying became soft, uncontrolled weeping as she listened in horror to Cade's gruesome words.

"It was so easy. I made copies of the car keys you always left hanging beside the door. When she got into the car, it only took a moment. And then I took her for a little drive." He drew in an excited breath. "It made me feel so powerful!"

"No!" Jenny felt as if she was going to faint. "Have you done the same thing to Aunt Morgie? Is she dying? Oh, God, . . . please. No!"

Cade, now Cyclosa, grabbed his hood from the floor and pulled it on. He then rejoined the circle of followers, and they began the supernatural chant again, softly at first:

"Ara, Ara, we wait for you."

"You're going to kill me, too, aren't you? Aren't you?" Jenny screamed.

The green-eyed, hooded figure spoke. "If Ara chooses. Ara sits at the center of his web with each of his eight legs poised on a different thread. When prey wanders in and is caught, Ara feels the vibrations. It's his sounding board to the world."

Even in Jenny's heightened state of panic, her mind seized the words and began putting it all together. "Ara's Web! The Internet?"

The man continued, ignoring her question. "Ara instructed us to bring you and Morgan here. You're caught in his web. . . ." Reverently, he raised his fist into the air. "Ara is all powerful."

Morgan moaned and moved slightly. Whatever they had given her was wearing off—consciousness was slowly returning.

"Aunt Morgie!" Jenny screamed, struggling to get loose.

"Release her," said another figure.

Jenny ran to Morgan and kneeled down beside her. With their prey in the center of the black widow spider, the circle of followers began chanting louder and more intensely.

"Ara, Ara, come to us. Ara, Ara, come to us."

The circle of hooded figures moved slowly, closing in on Jenny and the semi-conscious Morgan.

"Aunt Morgie! Wake up! Please, wake up!" The young girl shook her aunt, pleading with her. "Aunt Morgie, please . . ." Her ability to speak fled as she watched the green-eyed figure step forward, pulling a spider-handled hunting knife from his robe.

"Ara! The Gathering offers these lives to you!" He raised the knife above Jenny.

She screamed. Her eyes darted about, searching for any way of escape. There was none. Jenny covered her ears, attempting to shut out the sinister chant—certain she was about to die.

Suddenly the cabin became flooded with light from an unknown source outside. The hooded figures scattered like spiders seeking to crawl into the cover of darkness. Voices from outside yelled. "Sheriff's department!" Warning shots rang out. "We're coming in!"

Detective Hancock burst through the open door, followed by Troy. They spotted the two captives on the floor.

"Jenny!" Troy shouted.

She leaped to her feet and ran to her father. "Dad! Oh, Dad, they were going to kill us! They killed Mom! I know who killed Mom!"

Troy held Jenny tightly, stroking her hair and kissing the top of her head. "I was so afraid I'd lost you, too. But you're okay, sweetheart."

The detective lifted Morgan's head off the floor and cradled it in his huge hands. "Morgan! Morgan, it's over. You're safe." He turned and called out, "Somebody get an ambulance!"

Morgan's eyes opened slowly. The first thing she saw through her fog was the smiling face of Detective Hancock leaning over her. "Welcome back," he said, his familiar gruffness gone.

She rubbed her forehead and sighed. In a groggy voice she murmured, "If this is heaven, you're one beautiful angel, Hancock."

"You sure look like one to me, lady," he said, helping her sit up.

"Morgan." Troy looked as though he was going to cry. Hancock moved aside, and Troy took Morgan into his arms, holding her gently. "You're safe."

"Jenny? What about Jenny?" Morgan struggled to get to her feet.

"I'm right here, Aunt Morgie." The young girl stepped closer.

When Morgan saw her, she started crying with joy. Stretching out her hand, Jenny came to her and they hugged tightly. "I thought . . ." Morgan couldn't finish her sentence.

Jenny, looking for the first time like the little girl Morgan remembered, asked, "Can you ever forgive me? I was terrible. I'm so sorry."

Morgan put her hands on Jenny's tear-stained face. "Sweetie, there's nothing to forgive."

Then Morgan's gaze returned to Troy's handsome face. Speaking softly and slowly, as if she were just waking from an anesthetic, Morgan said, "What're you doing way out here in the middle of nowhere, cowboy?"

Troy smiled broadly. "Why, rescuing damsels in distress, ma'am."

Forty-six

Morgan leaned on Troy as they emerged from the cabin, followed by Detective Hancock and Jenny. There was a flurry of police activity. It was the first time she realized that the lights flooding the cabin were from the headlights of five sheriff's department vehicles.

"How'd you find us?" Morgan asked.

"I got the message from the station attendant. Very smart move," Troy said.

"You did it, Morgan. You nabbed the killer. Glad you were on our team." Hancock gave her a gruff smile.

Morgan had kept her promise to Beth. She gave him a weak but very sincere smile. "Thanks."

Hancock added, "And these guys didn't count on the rain. When Troy spotted your empty car just outside Tioga, he put that four-by-four in gear, and we ate up their muddy tracks. They lead us right to the cabin." Dell couldn't help but laugh at the thought. "But then, nobody said these guys were smart."

Morgan stopped short and leaned closer to Troy when she saw some of the unhooded figures—young teenaged girls and boys in handcuffs. She looked up at her rescuer, relieved. "It's over, isn't it?"

"It's over." He tightened his arm around her shivering shoulder.

Jenny looked up at the detective with fear still in her eyes. "But what about that Ara guy on the Web? Was he here? Did you get him?"

Morgan and Troy overheard Hancock's disturbing reply. "No, Jenny. A guy like that lets others do his dirty work. Ara and others just like him are still out there, preying on innocent minds."

It wasn't what Morgan or the others wanted to hear. The battle was far from over.

The Cooke County Sheriff walked over to speak with Hancock. "We got 'em all. Most of 'em were just kids. You know—sixteen, seventeen. We'll take 'em in, book 'em, and call their parents. I'll get you the list tomorrow."

Hancock nodded his okay. "Thanks for your help."

Morgan spoke up. "Yes, thank you, Sheriff."

He touched the tip of his Stetson with two fingers and smiled. "Our pleasure, ma'am. We've been keeping an eye on this cabin. Had a feelin' something mighty strange was going on out here. The place belongs to a fella named Justin Mc-Guire."

At that moment, deputies unhooded three remaining hand-cuffed cult members, exposing the faces of Les, Justin, and Cade.

Jenny noticed a deputy helping a trembling Pam out of the trunk of the Camaro. She watched as he removed tape from the young girl's wrists and ankles. She was sobbing. "They were going to kill me," she murmured. "I want to go home. Please." Jenny looked away, thanking God both she and Pam had not been added to Ara's victim list.

The sight of both Justin and Cade made Morgan's blood run cold. Jenny had told them the unbelievable truth that Cade had killed her mother. All this time, Beth's murderer had been only two houses away.

Cade stood handcuffed, staring right at Morgan. She could not break the mesmerizing stare and shuddered as a devilish smirk crept across his lips. Her knees felt weak, and Troy helped to steady her. *What could have turned this teenager into a murderer?* Morgan wondered. Gathering her strength she asked, "Why, Cade? Why?"

Completely devoid of any remorse, the boy answered, "It was her or us. I'd do it again if Ara asked me to."

Troy looked as though he was going to tear Cade apart, but Hancock rushed up and put his hand on Troy's arm, holding him back. "It won't help, Troy," he said, understanding the man's rage.

Morgan kept her arm around Jenny as they stood watching Cade while the sheriff's car drove him away. Before he was out of sight, the boy turned to look back at them all through the dripping, foggy window . . . and laughed.

Now she knew why Beth had to go on, why she couldn't let evil have her silence. Morgan's eyes filled with tears as she watched the red taillights disappear into the night.

Then she whispered, needing only Beth to hear. "We will be vigilant . . . for the devil walks about like a roaring lion, seeking whom he may devour."

Epilogue

J enny and Michael anxiously waited at the gate to the Weatherford ranch. "Do you see them yet?" Michael called, leaning out over the white wooden fence and looking down the twisting road.

Jenny started jumping up and down, "Yes! There they are!"

The two ran to the gate just as the white Explorer turned off the road into the drive. The car had barely stopped when the passenger door opened and Morgan jumped out. Smiles and tears mingled as she scooped them both up into her arms. "I've missed you so much!" They were taller, and a bit more maturity had been added to the faces she loved so much.

Pleased and amused by the joyous greetings, Troy joined them. "Well, Morgan, what do you think?" he asked, looking very happy and proud.

The soft breeze blowing through her hair, Morgan lifted her sunglasses and turned slowly, taking in the extraordinary beauty of what she saw. "It's incredible, Troy. Just like you described it."

She could see the rambling ranch house in the distance. The once rutted dirt road was now a paved, winding drive edged with pecan and magnolia trees. "What a difference a year can make. The last time I saw this land it was just a piece of empty real estate, but now, Troy . . . you've turned it into a real home."

"I'm so glad you're back, Aunt Morgie." Jenny gave her another big hug.

Morgan suddenly remembered something. "Hey, wait until

you see this." They all exchanged questioning looks as Morgan ran to the car and pulled a postcard from her shoulder bag.

With a big grin, she handed it to Troy. He glanced at it and began to laugh. "Well, good for him."

Jenny and Michael were craning their necks trying to see it. They both giggled when they saw the cartoon sketch of a big, fat man wearing a loud Hawaiian shirt and plaid Bermuda shorts. He was standing on a pier proudly holding up a very tiny fish. The caption read: *I've still got big dreams!*

Flipping it over, Troy read: " 'Having a great time. Named my boat the Texas Lady. Wonder who I was thinking about? Bring the whole bunch and come on down. I'm loving it. Hancock.' "

Michael shouted, "Oh, let's go! I wanna go!"

"We'll have to do that one of these days," Troy added. "Hey, kids, Morgan's moving back home. She's bought a place in Fort Worth."

"You mean you're coming back to Texas to stay?" Jenny asked excitedly.

Morgan kicked at the red dirt with her boot. "A real Texan can't ever stay away from—"

Jenny interrupted her. "Yeah, it's something God put into this red dirt." They all laughed. The kids ran excitedly toward the house.

As Troy looked into Morgan's beautiful and peaceful brown eyes, his growing love for her was as clear as the blue Texas sky. Time was healing the wounds of tragedy and returning the joy of life. With a very charming wink he said, "Well, ma'am, in a state the size of Texas, you just might find yourself that perfect man."

She gazed into his strong, handsome face and replied, "Why, sir, I think you're absolutely right."